# The Native
# Play Festival: A Four Year
# Celebration

By

Ranell Collins, Diane Glancy, Bret Jones
and Russ Tall Chief

With an introduction by Sarah dAngelo

Edited by
Sarah dAngelo and
Regina McManigell Grijalva

**NoPassport Press**

*The Native American New Play Festival: A Four Year Celebration* by Ranell Collins, Diane Glancy, Bret Jones and Russ Tall Chief

Introduction 2016 by Sarah dAngelo
Edited by Sarah dAngelo and Regina McManigell Grijalva

Copyright 2016 by Sarah dAngelo and Regina McManigell Grijalva

Cover design: Wanbli Tall Chief

**NoPassport Press**
PO Box 1786, South Gate, CA 90280 USA
NoPassportPress@aol.com, www.nopassport.org

**Second Edition**
**ISBN: 978-1-365-89991-1**

NoPassport

**NoPassport** is a theatre alliance & press devoted to live, virtual and print action, advocacy and change toward the fostering of cross-cultural and aesthetic diversity in the arts.

**NoPassport Press'** Dreaming the Americas Series and Theatre & Performance PlayTexts Series promotes new writing for the stage, texts on theory and practice and theatrical translations.

**NoPassport** is a sponsored project of Fractured Atlas. Tax-deductible donations to NoPassport to fund future publications, conferences and performance events may be made directly to http://www.fracturedatlas.org/donate/2623

## A CREATION STORY:

Launched in 2010, the Oklahoma City Theatre Company's annual Native American New Play Festival is a one-of-a-kind event in the region, and has since become a major national showcase for new Native American plays. April, 2017 marked the festival's eighth year. This anthology is a representative sampling of the first four years of its success.

Rick Nelson, Oklahoma City Theatre Company's founding artistic director initiated the festival to expand the company's artistic mission by bringing voice to the ethnic and cultural landscape of the Native American community in Oklahoma. This expanded mission envisioned creating an artistic home for Native artists who are frequently overlooked by mainstream venues. The festival has substantially grown into an annual event for the performance of new Native American plays with Native artists. No other mainstream theatre in the region devotes a portion of their regular season to this theatrical spectrum.

Oklahoma City Theatre Company's Native American New Play Festival is groundbreaking both to the general theatre and to the field of Native Theatre performance. Despite the deep resonance from this hemisphere, Native authored plays featuring Native artists do not receive the level of production or movement given to other American works in professional mainstream theatres. Shockingly instead, the use of "redface" prevails on the American stage. The Wooster Groups' 2014 production of *Cry Trojans* directed and conceived by the company's founder, Elizabeth LeCompte gave rise to public protests and fervent opposition on social media from Native artists over its use of "redface" in the production. Based on Shakespeare's Troilus and Cressida, the production merged the Greek extermination of the Trojans with the United States' genocidal efforts of the American Indians. *Cry Trojans* depicted the Trojans played by non-Native actors as 19th century Plains Indians reminiscent of spaghetti western caricatures replete with appropriated cultural imagery, sacred items, regalia and 'injun-speak.'

The 2010 premier of the musical farce *Bloody, Bloody Andrew Jackson* developed at the Public Theatre in New York also sparked controversy within the Native Theatre community. Native audiences and performers alike viewed the play's cultural misrepresentations, racial epithets and the fictionalized success of the U.S. Indian genocide as dehumanizing and an offensive distortion of history. Furthering the debacle, *Bloody, Bloody Andrew Jackson* coincided with the Public's Native Theater Initiative, a resident program aimed to support the creative development of Native plays and performance. This well-funded initiative was staffed and advised by Indian Country's top luminaries in film, theatre and literature and featured an annual Native Theater Festival event from 2007 to 2009. Protesters claimed the Public was remiss for not consulting with its Native Theater Initiative advisers during the play's development and subsequent premier at the Public believing this may have averted so offensive a production.

Stanford University cancelled a planned production of the show in November, 2014 amid protests from their Native student population as did Raleigh Little Theatre in North Carolina following discussions with the Native Community. Minneapolis Musical Theatre's production in June, 2014 went forward despite a staged protest opening night at the theatre, national press and an open letter from New Native Theatre Artistic Director, Rhiana Yazzie.

Playwright Mary Kathryn Nagle, a recent voice in Native Theatre whose play *Manahatta* was the featured production of the Oklahoma City Theatre Company's Native American New Play Festival in 2014 states in her Native Voices Series, a collection of essays found online at Howlround.com, "Our identity has been appropriated and used on the American stage for hundreds of years—we've just never had any say in it." She maintains the prevalence of "redface" is "a colonial creation aimed to silence authentic Native voices." She and many other Native Playwrights who have challenged this practice continue to face exclusion more often than not in the production of their plays from mainstream theatres who cite mythological and groundless rationales for not producing Native plays. It is a well-known narrative to Native playwrights who are told by literary agents and mainstream theatres alike "no one is interested in seeing these plays" or "we don't know how or where to find Native artists." In this same essay series, Randy Reinholz also confronts "redface" in his essay, "The Current State of Native Theatre." Reinholz is the founding artistic director of Native Voices at the Autry in Los Angeles. The theatre is the only Equity Theatre Company in the U.S. dedicated solely to developing and producing new works by and with Native artists and has been in operation since 1993. Reinholz calls for further accountability stating:

Professionals who claim not to be able to find Indians in theatre or in their cities are displaying grand ignorance, not proclaiming 'the state of affairs' within the American Theatre. Today there are more experienced, informed Native American theatre artists working in the U.S. and Canada than ever before. They are writing and acting and informing scripts written by others. We are creative, passionate, and dedicated to our craft and stories, yet agile enough to tell any story. Google "Native American Theatre" and you'll get more than 32,000 results. People who portray Indians on stage as stereotypes of savage American Indians should first consult with professionals, scholars, and culture bearers who work in the field for advice and guidance. We are in plain sight and just a click away. It is a great time to make a play by and with Native Americans. All of us could do more to make art that tells the whole story.

Reinholz makes the point that native artists are multi-talented, trained professionals who are in plain sight and accessible to mainstream venues. The exclusion of Native stories and artists indicates a disconnect to this vibrant field of performance and tells only part of the story of the American Theatre.

The Oklahoma Theatre Company's Native American New Play Festival has been telling that story. Since 2010, 21 Native plays have been presented to Oklahoma audiences, representing the work of 13 Native playwrights. The festival has featured an impressive roster of playwrights including Arigon Starr, Lori Favela, Vicky Lynn Mooney, Jason Grasl, Mary Kathryn Nagle, Larissa Fast Horse, Jaisey Bates and Laura Shamas. The festival has grown rapidly since its launch attracting a new generation of renowned and cutting edge Native playwrights whose work has been developed in theatres in New York, Los Angeles, Minneapolis and beyond. The plays performed each year during the festival are selected through a competitive submission process with a majority of Native artists at the creative helm. The plays are presented as staged readings open to the public and followed by audience talk back sessions with the playwrights and directors. The talk back sessions educate audiences unfamiliar with the style and themes found in

Native theatre and provide great value to both the playwright and the theatre in terms of nurturing new work, measuring audience appeal and determining production feasibility. Each year, a play is selected from the readings and receives a fully-staged production at the theatre as the featured event the following festival year. *The Native American New Play Festival: A Four Year Celebration* features world and regional premiers from the new generation of award-winning, notable and rising Native playwrights.

Many of the plays in the anthology are set in present-day and address the complexities found in urban, rural and reservation experiences. In these plays, we see enactments of what Anishinaabe cultural theorist, Gerald Vizenor, refers to as Survivance: the act of resisting the Native stereotype of a "vanishing race" with a sense of Native presence over absence, nihility and victimry. Survivance actively occurs and stories transform when colonial mindsets are deconstructed. In *Dirty Laundry* by Ranell Collins, we bear witness to the characters navigating narrative paths of presence with the challenges of mixed-blood, multi-generational households, career ambitions and duty to family. Survivance occurs as resiliency when the tensions between Christianity and traditional practices underscore revenge and an intergenerational family feud on the reservation, as in *Salvage* by Diane Glancy. In *Chalk in the Rain* by Bret Jones, a young woman failed by the foster care system and subjected to sexual trauma overcomes victimry by confronting the past to begin a healing future.

Time and place are fluid and central entities to the Native American aesthetic. Jacobson and the Kiowa Five by Russ Tall Chief chronicles the lives and careers of five Kiowa visual artists recruited from their rural native communities by Professor Oscar Jacobson to attend the University of Oklahoma's Fine Arts program in 1927. Set in time just three years after the federal government recognized Native Americans as U.S. "citizens," this docu-style play based on historic events expands individual and tribal identities. The play re-presents history in the Kiowa voice as the characters engage in song, dance, painting and dialogue at times directly addressing the audience. Tall Chief's play is a living intersection of time and cultures creating a collective and individual Kiowa narrative while transforming the audience into a community bearing witness to this historical event. Choctaw writer and literary theorist, LeAnne Howe's notion of Tribalography resonates in the interwoven construction of this historical story of cross-cultural exchange. According to Howe, "Tribalography is a story that links Indians and non-Indians" which gives a fuller version of individual and tribal identities.

The plays in the anthology are interwoven in the way Native epistemology emerges in the aesthetic of all expressive arts: each play touching on the core values of home, family, community, connection to culture and identity. Refreshingly, the style of storytelling found in each play is as vastly diverse as the Nations themselves. We see structures influenced by practices of performative memory, ritual, convergences with time and place, exchanges with the unseen, and Native language.

This anthology also embodies a creation story of Native Theatre performance taking place annually in Oklahoma City. The growth, the range of styles in festival productions and the rising voices of this generation's Native playwrights has brought sustainability and vitality each year to the festival. The plays appear chronologically, and are authored by writers of an Oklahoma Native Nation. Many of the plays are set in Oklahoma. This thread of interconnectedness emerged on its own and continues to persist in each festival year. An Oklahoma theme or author is not a festival submission requirement. Yet the plays in this anthology have themselves become interwoven and rooted in the very landscape from which they speak. This interconnectedness harkens again to the need for increased Native play production and the vast numbers of Native playwrights seeking an artistic space. The festival has also become an annual gathering place for actors, designers, directors, panel experts, cultural teachers, fluent language speakers, traditional storytellers, singers, dancers and visual artists who come each year with diverse expressions of the history, culture and lifeways reflected in their individual and tribal knowledge and aesthetic.

There is a great need to bring to the general public notice, not only the written works of this generation's Native American Playwrights, but also the performance of them. Native writers and artists must continue to challenge the majority of U.S. Theatres who proclaim in their artistic mission statements, "diverse plays of ideas, views and cultures," yet avoid authentic Native narratives on their stages.

Native plays reflect both an urban and a rural American narrative and directly contribute to the American literary cannon. As theatre makers of the American theatre, we determine the plays to be considered influential works to us as storytellers and as human beings. The plays in this anthology are not static in nature, nor do they represent a singular identity of "Native American." The plays are influential works rich in theatricality with the ability to broaden performance practices across geopolitical boundaries. These plays invite further productions in other mainstream theatres in other cities. The plays in this anthology carry a living story that Native Theatre can be and *is* being successfully produced.

REFERENCES

Gioia, Michael. "Native American Artists Will Protest Minneapolis Production of Bloody Bloody Andrew Jackson." *Playbill.* 6 June 2014. http://www.playbill.com/article/native-american-artists-will-protest-minneapolis-production-of-bloody-bloody-andrew-jackson-com-322147

Howe, LeAnne. "The Story of America: A Tribalography"*Clearing a Path: Theorizing the Past in Native American Studies,* edited by Nancy Shoemaker, Routledge, 2002, p. 46.

Levine, D.M. "Native Americans Protest 'Bloody Bloody Andrew Jackson" *Politico New York.* Politico, 24 June 2010. http://www.politico.com/states/new-york/city-hall/story/2010/06/native-americans-protest-bloody-bloody-andrew-jackson-067223

Nagle, Mary Kathryn. "Native Voices On the American Stage: A Constitutional Crisis." *HowlRound.* Emerson College, 22 Feb. 2015. http://howlround.com/native-voices-on-the-american-stage-a-constitutional-crisis

New, Jake. "Too Controversial for Stanford." *Inside Higher Ed.* 24 Nov. 2014. https://www.insidehighered.com/news/2014/11/24/stude nts-cancel-musical-stanford-amid-concerns-raised-native-american group?utm_ source=slate&utm_ medium=referral&utmterm=partner

Reinholz, Randy. "The Current State of Native Theatre." Howlround. Emerson College, 25 Feb. 2015. http://howlround.com/the-current-state-of-native-theatre

Vizenor, Gerald Robert, ed. *Survivance: Narratives of Native Presence.* University of Nebraska Press, 2008, p. 1.

# Dirty Laundry

A Play

By


Ranell Collins

CHARACTER LIST:

JENNY NEUGIN - 89, in remission from cancer and suffering the first stages of dementia. She is sharp and plain-spoken one minute and confused the next.

RUTH BAKER - 55, Jenny's daughter, 1/2 Cherokee from her father's side. She is a caregiver who gives too much. She is physically exhausted most of the time and has become resentful.

JOHN NEUGIN - 57, Jenny's son, 1/2 Cherokee from his father's side. He is the favorite child, who only comes to see his mother when he wants something. Manipulation is his M.O.

STEW BAKER - 31, Ruth's son, 1/4 Cherokee. An intelligent sloth, who cannot seem to operate in the real world. His mother's home is his safe house that he returns to again and again. He needs her yet he resents her.

WES CHAMBERS - 48, an attractive and compassionate hospice nurse, who, over the years, has allowed his career to prevent him from having a personal life.

*Dirty Laundry* was performed as a staged reading during the inaugural Oklahoma City Theatre Company's Native American New Play Festival in June, 2010. It was selected as the featured production for the second annual festival and performed March 25-April 3, 2011. It was a world premier directed by Rachel Irick with the following cast:

| | |
|---|---|
| RUTH: | Sarah dAngelo* |
| JENNY: | Angie Duke |
| WES: | Josh Irick |
| JOHN: | D.G. Smalling |
| STEW: | Randall Guild |

*Appeared courtesy of Actors Equity Association

Other parts played by the company

Lighting, Set Design by Paul Huebner
Costume Design by Brenda Nelson
Sound Design by Megan Skinner Shrock
Makeup/Hair by Suzette C. Donelson
Properties by Suzette C. Donelson
Set Construction by Paul Huebner
Stage Manager Kelsie Morris
Assistant Stage Manager Emily Germany
Festival House Manager Misty Red Elk
Medical Consultant Carolyn Woolems, R.N.

**Ranell Collins** (Playwright)

Collins is a citizen of the Cherokee Nation and a member of the Dramatists Guild. Her plays draw upon the theme of family social conflict. *Dirty Laundry* was performed as the featured production in the second annual Oklahoma City Theatre Company Native American New Play Festival in 2011. In the fall of 2015, the University of Central Oklahoma Theatre Department performed *Dirty Laundry* as part of the University of Central Oklahoma's Passport to Native America program. Her plays have won Oklahoma City's Carpenter Square Theatre's "Best in Ten" and the University of Central Oklahoma's ten minute play competitions. Her most recent full-length play, *Happily Only After*, won third place in Oklahoma City's Jewel Box Theatre's annual playwriting competition and finished in the top ten in the Robert J Pickering for Playwriting Excellence competition. Before her experience as a playwright, Collins wrote lyrics and fronted the Oklahoma-based alt rock band Crush Molly Sunshine, winner of the Best New Album award by the RMS Music Society. She graduated Summa Cum Laude with a B.A. in English Education and an M.A. with honors in English/Creative Writing from the University of Central Oklahoma. Collins has taught at Oklahoma City Community College since 2012. Ranell Collins can be contacted at the following email address: ranellgivens2000@yahoo.com.

## NOTES ON THE PLAY:

Of *Dirty Laundry*, Collins says, "The inspiration for this play came from having observed family and friends dealing with issues involving the sandwich generation. This made me reflect on the complexities of family dynamics, the circumstances of life that lead people to become dependent upon one another, and all of the frustration and bitterness that can evolve--on both sides--from this dependence. By placing this story within the context of this blended family, I hoped to highlight those experiences in life that cross ethnic boundaries, rather than those that divide us. The caregiver issue, in particular, is such a relevant and universal one-- one that involves both the reality of loneliness and the potential for growth, one that I wanted to bring to audiences so that people will contemplate and decide for themselves."

### TIME:
Present

### SETTING:
Ruth's home in Oklahoma City. There are three doors on the back wall: the one on the right leads to the kitchen; the one in the middle leads outside, and the one on the left, to the hallway. On the back wall, between the hallway and the front door, is a hospital bed. To the right of it is a night stand; to the left is a laundry hamper and a chest of drawers. Between the front door and the kitchen is a console table with a manual

typewriter case underneath and a small trash can nearby. Downstage is a couch, rocking chair, end table, coffee table, and TV. A walker sits next to the rocking chair and a remote control is on the coffee table. To the right of this area, closer to the kitchen door, is a dining table. The furniture is drab and there are no decorations of any kind.

*Script Note: The IPA pronunciation for the Cherokee word "princess" is: *u ga wa ya he u way a či a te.*

## ACT I

### SCENE ONE

(Jenny rocks in her chair, staring blankly across the room. She is wearing a faded purple housecoat and red slippers. There is a barely-touched plate of toast and bacon on the coffee table. Ruth enters… wearing a pair of old sweats and loaded down with grocery sacks…)

RUTH: (TIRED) Did you eat your breakfast?
JENNY: The burnt toast and bacon?
RUTH: It wasn't burnt.
JENNY: It was burnt. And the bacon was so sharp it could slit your throat.
RUTH: You wanted it crispy.

JENNY: I could have choked.

>     (Ruth sets the bags down on the bed,
>     pulls out a box of tissue, and sets it on
>     the night stand.)

JENNY: Is that the lotion kind? You know I like
the lotion kind.
RUTH: That's the only kind I ever buy you.

>     (Ruth pulls a hair pick out of the bag...)

RUTH: I bought you a new pick. This one's
plastic. Maybe you won't bloody your scalp
with it.

>     (Ruth picks up the bags and walks
>     toward the kitchen...)

JENNY: My scalp itches. I can't help it.
RUTH: There's nothing wrong with your scalp.
JENNY: I have dandruff.
RUTH: I've checked your scalp. There's nothing
there except skin.

>     (Ruth exits through the kitchen door...)

JENNY: I have dandruff!

>     (After a moment Ruth reenters. She
>     walks over and lifts up the lid to the
>     hamper...)

RUTH: Where are all your dirty clothes?
JENNY: What?
RUTH: Your dirty clothes. Where are they?
JENNY: They're in the hamper.
RUTH: There's one blouse in here.

>(Ruth begins rifling through the chest of
>drawers. She pulls out a couple of
>blouses, sniffs them, then tosses them in
>the hamper...)

JENNY: Where's that son of yours?
RUTH: You know he never gets up before noon.

>(Ruth feels up under the mattress and
>pulls out several pairs of panties.)

RUTH: (HOLDING UP THE PANTIES) Mom,
why do you do this?
JENNY: Do what?
RUTH: There's a hamper right here for your
laundry.
JENNY: I know that.
RUTH: Then why don't you use it?

>(There is a knock at the door.)

JENNY: Someone's knocking.

>(Ruth tosses the panties into the hamper
>and walks toward the door. She stops
>halfway there and turns back toward her
>mother.)

RUTH: I called and asked them to send Karen back out.

JENNY: What for? I'm in remission, right? You said so yourself.

RUTH: I know, but you've been losing weight again and--

> (Another knock... Ruth walks toward the door...)

JENNY: Well, they should just let me die. Then you'd all be happy.

> (Ruth ignores this and opens the door. On the other side is an attractive middle-aged man, Wes. HE is wearing hospital scrubs and has a photo I.D. clipped to his shirt.)

RUTH: Oh...hello. We were expecting Karen.

WES: Yes, ma'am. Karen's on vacation.

> (Extending his hand...)

I'm Wes. I'm picking up a couple of her patients while she's gone.

RUTH: (ACCEPTING HIS HAND) Well, it's nice to meet you. I'm Ruth, Jenny's daughter. Come on in.

> (Wes steps inside, pulling a small case behind him. He smiles at Jenny...)

WES: This must be our patient.

JENNY: Who are you?

RUTH: This is Wes, mother. He's a nurse.

JENNY: (TO WES) You're a man.

WES: Well...yes Mrs. Neugin, I am. Karen's on vacation and--

JENNY: It doesn't matter. I don't need either of you. I'm in remission...or don't you read the charts?

WES: It's very unusual for someone your age to be able to fight this cancer the way you have. You must be a pretty tough lady.

JENNY: (SARCASTICALLY) And you must be a really tough man, being a nurse and all.

RUTH: Mother, this nice man is an RN just like Karen. There's nothing to be concerned about. It's just a check up.

JENNY: Nice man? How do you know he's nice. You just met him two seconds ago. He could be Dr. Kevorkian for all we know.

> (Wes pulls his bag around and sits down on the couch, next to Jenny's chair.)

WES: That would be Nurse Kevorkian...or...you can just call me Wes.

> (Jenny stares at him for a moment, not knowing how to respond...)

RUTH: See, Mom, he's even got a sense of humor.

JENNY: (SARCASTICALLY) Yes. Very funny...a regular Jack Benny.

> (Wes opens his bag and pulls out a folder, a blood pressure cuff, and a stethoscope.)

WES: Jack Benny, huh...? My dad used to watch that show.

> (Wes walks around to the side of Jenny's chair with the cuff and the stethoscope...)

Okay, Mrs. Neugin, I'm just going to slip this cuff around your arm.

> (Ruth walks over and sits down on the couch…)

RUTH: Did you watch it with him?
WES: Pardon?
RUTH: Jack Benny...with your dad?
WES: (FASTENING THE CUFF) Oh...no, I was too young. But, I caught some of the re-runs when I was older.

> (As Wes is airing up the cuff, he stands straight up and attempts his best "Benny" impersonation.)

WES: "Oh, Rochester..."

(Ruth laughs…)

JENNY: (SARCASTICALLY) I'm glad you two are finding humor in this.

(Wes bends down, places the stethoscope in his ears and the chest piece against the crease of her elbow. He begins to listen to her pulse…)

RUTH: Come on, Mom. You used to love Jack Benny.
JENNY: Yes. (POINTING TO WES) But, he's no "Benny."
RUTH: Be nice.
WES: Okay, Mrs. Neugin, I need you to be really still…
RUTH: He means be quiet.

(Jenny cuts her eyes at her daughter.) Wes listens for a few seconds, then releases the cuff. He puts his fingers to her wrist and stares down at his watch.)

JENNY: (TO WES) Can you find it?

(He smiles…)

I'm not dead yet, am I?
WES: (RELEASING HER WRIST) No, ma'am. Your vital signs are excellent.
JENNY: I told you that when you walked in.

(Wes sits down on the couch and begins
to write in the chart...)

WES: So, I hear you're not eating much.
JENNY: I eat.
RUTH: She picks at her food, actually.
JENNY: (TO WES) If you had to eat her cooking,
you'd "pick" too.
WES: It's really important that you get those
three square meals a day...to keep your strength
up.
JENNY: What for? I've never heard of a
marathon for old ladies on walkers...
(CONTEMPLATES THIS) Although, if they had
one, I'd smoke all those old biddies. You can be
sure of that.
WES: (LAUGHING) Yes, I've no doubt.

(Wes flips a page in the chart...)

WES: Okay, I need to ask you a couple of
questions...Have you noticed any weakening of
your muscles?
JENNY: No.
RUTH: She's a little slower on her walker than
she used to be.
JENNY: I'm a little older than I used to be.
WES: Have you had any sudden onset of pain
recently?
JENNY: No.
RUTH: You told me your legs were hurting the
other day.

JENNY: That's because you wanted me to go walk with you.

WES: Exercise is good. You don't want those muscles to atrophy. Even if you just walk a little ways down the sidewalk and back a couple of times a day...

RUTH: That's what I've been telling her.

WES: (WRITING IN THE CHART) How are your bowel movements?

JENNY: They're brown.

RUTH: Mom, stop being difficult.

WES: It's okay. She has a sense of humor. I like it.

(There is a knock at the door...)

JENNY: Someone's knocking.

RUTH: Excuse me.

(Ruth gets up and walks toward the door. Wes gets up, carrying his stethoscope and walks around to the side of Jenny's chair...)

WES: Okay, Mrs. Neugin. I'm just going to listen to your lungs now. (PUTS THE SCOPE TO HER BACK) Take a deep breath in for me and slowly release it.

(Jenny does this...Ruth opens the door. John is standing on the other side in a rumpled suit and an open collared shirt.

He is holding a bouquet of lavender
lilies...)

JOHN: Hey, Sis.

(He walks right past Ruth and into the
house...)

JOHN: Knock, knock.
JENNY: (THRILLED) Johnny!

(He walks over and kisses Jenny on the
cheek.)

JOHN: Hey, pretty lady. I brought you some
flowers.
JENNY: They're lovely. My favorite color.

(Ruth rolls her eyes and walks over
toward him.)

RUTH: Here, I'll take them.
JOHN: Thanks, Sis.

(Ruth takes the flowers and walks
toward the kitchen.)

JENNY: (TO WES) This is my son, Johnny. (TO
JOHN) And this is Jes.
RUTH: (AS SHE IS EXITING) Wes.

(The two men shake hands...)

WES: Nice to meet you, Johnny.
JOHN: Call me "John."

    (WES places the scope against JENNY'S chest.)

WES: (TO JENNY) Okay, now breathe normally.

    (Jenny takes a deep breath and releases it.)

JOHN: You been causing trouble again, Momma?
JENNY: No, no. You know your sister. She's as paranoid as a prisoner who just dropped the soap.

    (John laughs...)

JOHN: Now, Momma. I'm sure she just wants to make sure you're okay. She cares about you.
JENNY: Yeah, I know, I know.
JOHN: (TO WES) So, how is this ornery little lady?
WES: She's great. Her vital signs are all within normal range and her lungs sound clear...She just needs to eat a little more and get some exercise.
JENNY: (TO JOHN) He wants me to go out and walk up and down the driveway like some senile old kook.
JOHN: Now, now...you should listen to the doctor.

JENNY: He's a nurse.
JOHN: Really?

>(Wes smiles and holds up his I.D. badge…)

JOHN: (READING IT TO HIMSELF) Wes Chambers, R.N. (ALOUD, CONDESCENING) Well, I'll be...hmm.
WES: She needs to stay active so those muscles don't give out on her.
JOHN: Don't worry. I'll take her out for a few laps later.

>(Ruth reenters with the vase of lilies and puts them down on the console table...)

WES: (PACKING UP HIS BAG) Well, it was very nice meeting you all.
RUTH: Leaving so soon? Would you like something to drink before you go? Iced tea or soda?
WES: No, thanks. I have a full schedule today.
RUTH: Well...um...if...if you're back this way and you get thirsty or something...feel free to stop by.

>(Wes holds her gaze for a moment…)

WES: Thank you. That's very kind of you.
RUTH: (BLUSHING)...It's just that I know it's really hot out there today and—
JENNY: It's a little hot in here if you ask me.

31

WES: (IGNORING JENNY) Yeah, it's supposed to get up into the 90s.

(An uncomfortable moment of silence…)

…Oh, and remember to keep on her about the food and exercise.

RUTH: Easier said than done.
WES: (SMILING) Yes. She's a live one, isn't she?

(HE walks toward the door.)

WES: Bye, Mrs. Neugin.
JENNY: Uh, huh.
JOHN: So long, Doc.

(Ruth walks behind Wes…)

RUTH: Have a nice day.
WES: You too.

(Ruth closes the door behind him…)

JENNY: (TO RUTH) Maybe you could get that excited about getting your brother some iced tea.
JOHN: Oh…no, thank you. I'm fine.
JENNY: (TO JOHN) So, sit down over here. What have you been up to? How is everyone?
RUTH: Yeah. To what do we owe this honor?
JOHN: (IGNORING RUTH AND SITTING) Oh, fine. They're fine. We're all really…good.

JENNY: How's your job? You still liking it?

JOHN: Lord, Momma, how long have you had that housecoat?

JENNY: (LAUGHING) About a hundred years.

RUTH: At least.

JENNY: Ruth, did you buy me some tissue?

RUTH: Yes, they're right over here.

(Ruth walks over and retrieves the box of tissue from the night stand...)

JENNY: Are they the lotion kind?

RUTH: (HANDING HER THE BOX) Yes, Mother.

(Jenny pulls a tissue out and blows her nose...a moment of uncomfortable silence)

JENNY: (LEANING OVER AND PATTING JOHN'S LEG) So.... my boy.

JOHN: Life treating you okay, Momma?

JENNY: Life? Yes. People?...They all hate me. And that's fine...I'll be dead soon enough.

JOHN: Hate you? How could anyone hate such a pretty lady?

JENNY: (SMILING) They're jealous, I suppose.

JOHN: Damn right, they are.

RUTH: (TO JOHN) So what exactly is it that you're doing now?

JOHN: What?

RUTH: For work?

JOHN: On second thought, I will take that glass of iced tea.

(Ruth studies him with suspicion...)

JOHN: ...If it's not too much trouble.
JENNY: Of course not. (TO RUTH) Ruth, get your brother some iced tea.

(Ruth gets up and exits through the kitchen door. John waits until Ruth is completely out of earshot...)

JOHN: Listen, Mom, I wanted to talk to you about something.
JENNY: What is it?
JOHN: Do you remember my friend Bill that I told you about?
JENNY: Bill...? Oh, yes, the one who owns the Laundromat.
JOHN: Actually, he's an entrepreneur.
JENNY: Ooh, sounds like a nice young man.
JOHN: Yes, he is...and very smart, too.
JENNY: (PATS HIS LEG) Not as smart as my boy.
JOHN: There's this opportunity, Mom.
JENNY: Really? Well, I'm very happy for you.
JOHN: For us.
JENNY: What?

(John gets up and walks over toward the kitchen door and listens for a moment...)

JOHN: Listen, Mom, we don't have much time.
JENNY: You have plenty of time, Dear. I'm the one staring down the Grim Reaper.

(John walks over and sits back down next to Jenny...)

JOHN: It's magnetism.
JENNY: For goodness sake, Johnny. What are you talking about?
JOHN: It's our future...

(The kitchen door opens a crack. John does not notice it.)

JOHN: A new source of energy...for our cars, our heaters and air conditioners...even our washers and dryers.
JENNY: Sounds complicated.
JOHN: It's revolutionary. And you and I have a chance to get in on the ground floor.
JENNY: How's that?
JOHN: Through Bill.
JENNY: Who's Bill?
JOHN: (FRUSTRATED) My friend, the—

(He stops, composes himself, then takes her hand...)

JOHN: Mom, you know I love you.
JENNY: And I love you. You're my boy...my only son.

JOHN: Dad asked me to take care of you, and that's what I'm trying to do.
JENNY: I know. It's so sweet of you to stop by.
JOHN: So, you know I wouldn't steer you wrong.
JENNY: In what way?

(Moment of silence...)

JOHN: I need money, Momma.
JENNY: I don't have much.
JOHN: You have enough...Listen, we could double Dad's pension, triple it...in no time. You would have--

(Ruth reenters, carrying a glass of iced tea and a soda can.)

JENNY: Ruth, look who's here. Johnny stopped by.
RUTH: Yeah. I can see that.

(Ruth sets the glass of tea down in front of John...)

JENNY: He was just telling me about his nice friend... (TO JOHN) What was his name again?
JOHN: (GETTING UP) Listen, Mom. I better go.
JENNY: So soon? I thought we were going for a walk?

(He bends over and kisses her cheek...)

JOHN: Next time.
JENNY: Okay, Dear. Say hello to your friend
with the Laundromat.
JOHN: Yeah.

(He walks toward the door. Ruth steps in
front of him and stares him down for a
full three count, then she speaks...)

RUTH: Next time.

(He steps around her and walks out the
door.)

JENNY: Oh...my boy...Isn't he a jewel?
RUTH: Yes...a genuine diamonelle.
JENNY: Are you drinking that nasty soda again?
I told you, it's poison. You're going to drop dead
someday.
RUTH: (UNDER HER BREATH) If I'm lucky.
JENNY: What?

(Ruth picks up the used tissue, then
walks over and throws it in the garbage
can.)

RUTH: (WALKING BACK TOWARDS JENNY)
Let's go, Mom.
JENNY: Where are we going?
RUTH: To walk. You need your exercise.
JENNY: (PUSHING HERSELF UP ON HER
WALKER) Oh, yes...up and down the

driveway...the neighbors will all be talking about the senile old lady.

(Ruth holds Jenny's arm as they make their way toward the door.)

RUTH: Probably so.

(The lights fade...)

## ACT I

### SCENE TWO

(Jenny is lying in her bed asleep. Ruth is folding laundry on the dining table. Stew enters from the hallway, wearing only his boxers. He has just woken up, and his hair has yet to see a comb.)

RUTH: Good Afternoon
STEW: You get my M&M's?
RUTH: Yes.
STEW: The peanut kind?
RUTH: That's the only kind I ever buy you.

(She gets up and walks into the kitchen. Stew falls down onto the couch, grabs the remote and turns the TV on... Ruth reenters with the bag of candy, tosses it to him, then sits back down at the table and continues folding...)

RUTH: There's a newspaper in the kitchen.
STEW: (FOCUSED ON THE TV) Uh-huh.

      (He rips open the M&Ms with his teeth
      and pours a few pieces into his mouth...)

RUTH: Just thought you might want to check
out the classifieds.
STEW: (FLIPPING THROUGH THE
CHANNELS) Man, there's nothing but a bunch
of shit on daytime TV.
RUTH: (FOLDING) Probably because most
people work during the day.

      (Stew ignores this and turns the TV
      volume up louder.)

RUTH: (LOUD WHISPER) Stewart! Your
grandmother's trying to sleep.
STEW: (MUTING THE TV) Huh?
JENNY: She said I'm "trying to sleep."

      (Jenny pushes herself up, yawns, pulls
      her walker over, and begins to slowly
      shuffle her way over to her chair...Stew
      turns the TV back up, but to a lower
      volume...)

JENNY: What are you watching, Stewie?
STEW: Nothing. Like every other day, it's all
crap.

JENNY: (SEATING HERSELF AND REACHING) Well, hand over the remote. My program's coming on.

STEW: (HANDS HER THE REMOTE) Which one?..."The Young and the Sexless" or "As the World Squirms."

RUTH: There's nothing "sexless" about any of them.

JENNY: General Hospital.

STEW: Ah, yes...General Hospital...I'll save you the trouble, Grams: (IN A MOCKING TONE) a man's in a coma, waiting for some altruistic soul to die so that he can finally get that brain transplant he's been needing for so long, and his wife's weeping at his side, begging, "Please forgive me. I never meant to sleep with your best friend, and if you could just find it in your heart to give me a second chance, I swear I'll spend the rest of my life making it up to you."... (DEADPAN) Meanwhile, the doctor and nurse are screwing in the janitor's closet.

RUTH: How do you know the nurse is a woman?

STEW: I never said the doctor was a man.

JENNY: No one ever screws in the janitor's closet.

STEW: Really? Then, why are we watching it?

JENNY: Keep it down, I'm trying to listen.

STEW: Sorry, Grams.

> (Stew lies down for a few seconds,
> staring at the TV, then sits back up.)

STEW: ...But, you could at least get me current.
JENNY: On what?
STEW: (POINTING) Well, like, who's that sitting in the waiting room, filing her nails.
JENNY: (IN DISGUEST) Ugh...That's Carly...slut.
STEW: What does she do?
JENNY: I don't know...first she was a physical therapist, then she owned something...uh, a makeup company or something...now I think she owns a hotel.
STEW: (SARCASTICALLY) That seems like a natural progression.
JENNY: She's sure been "progressing" through a lot of men. I can tell you that.
STEW: Oh, yeah?

> (Ruth carries one stack of the folded clothes out through the hallway door...)

JENNY: Well, she got pregnant with A.J.'s baby, then she drugged him...
STEW: The baby?
JENNY: No, A.J....then she met Sonny and they did the deed—
STEW: The "deed"?
JENNY: Yes, in a limo...and then she was with Jax because he needed someone to help him take care of his baby--although I don't know why he'd ever choose that tramp--but then she couldn't forget about Sonny and--
STEW: Hold on, hold on. Let's go back to the limo part.

RUTH: (REENTERING THE ROOM) Mom, you
need to put something on your stomach before I
give you your meds.
JENNY: I'm not hungry.
RUTH: I'll bring you some saltines.

(Ruth exits through the kitchen door...)

STEW: So, who's in the hospital...Sonny?
JENNY: No...I guess...I don't remember.
Probably another one of her victims.
STEW: This woman is wicked evil.
JENNY: Venomous.
STEW: And she sleeps around a lot?
JENNY: Her knees have two different zip codes.

(Ruth reenters with a package of saltines.
She opens it and sets it down next to her
mother...)

RUTH: Here. I just need you to eat a couple of
these, okay?
JENNY: What happened to the Zestas?
RUTH: They were out of Zestas at the store. This
is all they had...just a couple, okay?

(Jenny takes one of the crackers and
begins chewing on it... Stew reaches,
grabs a couple and stuffs them into his
mouth...)

RUTH: (TO STEW) The trash is full.
STEW: (CHEWING) I'll get to it.

(Ruth exits into the kitchen...)

STEW: (FOCUSED ON THE TV) Why is she crying?

JENNY: She's faking it.

STEW: How do you know?

JENNY: She's got a heart made of playdough. That's how I know.

STEW: Ah, Grams. I bet you had your share of men in your day.

JENNY: I most certainly did not.

STEW: Come on. Be honest.

JENNY: Your dear Grandfather was my first love...my only love.

STEW: That's pretty boring.

JENNY: Oh, he was far from boring.

STEW: Really? Any "limos" in your past?

JENNY: (TRYING NOT TO SMILE) No...but there was a grassy field or two.

STEW: (TEASING) Tsk, tsk, Grams...sex in a public place. That wouldn't set well with the local Neighborhood Watch Association.

JENNY: No one was watching. That's the whole idea...Christ, I have to teach you everything.

(Ruth reenters with a glass of water and some pills...)

RUTH: (HANDING THEM TO JENNY) Alright, get these all down...And swallow them one at a time. I don't want you choking like you did yesterday.

STEW: I think maybe you could teach Ruth a thing or two.

JENNY: (POPPING ONE OF THE PILLS) No, that's a hopeless cause.

RUTH: What are you talking about?

JENNY: Your love life...or lack thereof.

RUTH: Yeah, well, I would hope the two of you could find something more productive to do with your day.

STEW: You're right, Grams. It's pretty hopeless.

> (Ruth ignores this, picks up the other stack of clothes off the table, carries them over to Jenny's chest of drawers, and begins putting them away...)

JENNY: Although...I did see her get a little flustered over that nurse earlier.

STEW: What nurse?

JENNY: Isn't that right, Ruth?

> (Still ignoring them, Ruth finishes putting the clothes away...)

STEW: What are you talking about? What nurse?

> (Ruth walks across the room, pulls the typewriter out from under the console table and sets it up on the dining table... She pulls some paper out of the console table drawer and sits down in front of the typewriter...)

JENNY: (SARCASTICALLY) Ah, here she goes again. She's going to be a real writer someday. Someone's going to read her novel and the next thing you know it, Bam! She'll be a best-selling author on...What's that list called?

STEW: The New York Times.

JENNY: Yes. The New York Times.

STEW: Grams...are you going to tell me about the nurse or what?

JENNY: What nurse? On the show?

STEW: No, the one that Ruth got "flustered" about.

JENNY: Oh, yes...Well, your mother thinks I'm dying again, so she sent out for reinforcements and they sent this guy...um...Jes, I think...

RUTH: (TYPING) Wes.

JENNY: ...and your mother turned school-girl pink.

STEW: What kind of nurse flirts with a client?

JENNY: Oh, he wasn't the one doing the flirting. It was Ruth who was stammering and offering to serve him up a little of her nectar.

> (Ruth pulls the page out of the typewriter, wads it up, and throws it in the trash. Then, she puts a clean sheet in and begins typing with bitter determination...)

STEW: Okay, that's disgusting. I don't want to know anymore.

JENNY: I didn't really understand the attraction myself. He looked like a bit of a fluffer to me.
STEW: (LAUGHING) Fluffer...? (REALIZING HER MALAPROPISM) Oh, you mean he's gay? How could you tell?
JENNY: His walk, the way he combs his hair...You know, the usual stuff.

(Ruth continues to type without looking up.)

JENNY: But, that didn't seem to bother your mom. I guess after you've suffered such a dry spell, you're determined to find that water...even in the Sahara.
STEW: (WALKING TO THE KITCHEN) Now I need something on my stomach.

(As he exits, he does a full-body shiver...)

RUTH: (TO STEW) Get the trash!

(Ruth stops typing...)

RUTH: (TO JENNY) Why do you have to go on like that?
JENNY: What?
RUTH: You know what I mean.
JENNY: I enjoy amusing the boy.
RUTH: Yes, at my expense...and he's hardly a boy.
JENNY: Really? What is it about him that makes him a man...besides his age?

(Ruth ignores this and begins typing again.)

That's what I thought.

(Jenny focuses her attention back on the TV…)

JENNY: Oh, these people will never learn.

(Ruth gets up and exits through the hallway.)

JENNY: (TO THE TV) What you're doing will never bring her back…(TOWARD THE HALLWAY)…you know that don't you?

(Blackout…)


## ACT I

### SCENE THREE

(Ruth is sitting back at the dining table, typing away. Jenny is sitting in her rocking chair with her head down, asleep. There is a knock at the door…Ruth gets up and answers it, still lost in her train of thought…Wes stands on the other side...)

RUTH: Oh...Hi...You're back.

WES: (HANDING HER A BUSINESS CARD) Yeah, I...wanted to give you my card. In case there are any changes or anything, you can call me directly...on my cell.

RUTH: Thank you. That's very nice. (AWKWARD MOMENT OF SILENCE) I'm sorry. Would you like to come in?

WES: (STEPPING INSIDE) Sure. I just finished up with my last patient, so I think I'll take you up on that offer you made earlier.

RUTH: Offer?

WES: Something to drink.

RUTH: Oh, right....um...I have tea, soda, and water.

WES: Iced tea would be great.

RUTH: Coming right up.

> (Ruth exits through the kitchen door... Wes notices the typewriter. He sees some pages with text sitting next to it... He glances down, then looks away for a few moments, then walks closer and begins reading...)

RUTH: (OFF STAGE) Do you like sugar in it?

WES: No, thanks.

> (He continues reading. Ruth pushes the door open and Wes averts his gaze, as if he is taking in the contents of the room. She hands him the tea and sets a can of soda down at the table for herself.)

WES: Thank you.
RUTH: Have a seat.

(Wes sits down at the table.)

WES: (POINTING TOWARD JENNY) Are we
going to wake her up?
RUTH: No. Only the television can do that.

(Ruth begins putting the typewriter into
the case...)

WES: Wow! An old Royal model?
RUTH: Yeah.
WES: 1950s, right?
RUTH: I believe so...It was my father's, actually.
WES: Was he a writer?

(She sticks the typewriter underneath the
console table and sets the pages on top of
the table.)

RUTH: He was...a little bit of everything.
WES: And how about you? Are you a writer?
RUTH: No...not really...I mean, it's just
something I do for relaxation...It's sort of
cathartic.
WES: Well, we all need that.

(A moment of silence...)

Mine's needlepoint.
RUTH: What?

WES: My cathartic thing.

RUTH: Needlepoint? Really?

WES: Yeah. My grandmother taught me when I was young. She said I was a natural. And I thought it was cool watching this work of art come to life under my fingertips...Anyway, I stopped when I got into high school because, you know...

RUTH: Mean boys?

(Wes smiles and shrugs his shoulders...)

RUTH: (TEASING) Oh, it was the girls you were worried about.

WES: Yeah, you know, a stud like myself couldn't be seen walking around carrying his needlepoint.

RUTH: (LAUGHING) So, when did you pick it back up?

WES: When I started working in the ER. Nothing's more stressful than the night shift in the Emergency Room.

RUTH: God, I can't even imagine.

WES: Some nights everything was just so erratic...people running back and forth, doctors shouting orders, patients screaming, family members crying...(BEAT)...then I'd go home and sit down in my recliner and I'd push that needle through...and suddenly all my focus was on that one thing...and my world was calm again.

RUTH: That sounds nice.

(A moment of silence...)

WES: So...what do you write about?

RUTH: Oh...just...stupid stuff...nothing I'd want anyone to see.

WES: Is it like fiction or...

RUTH: Yes, kind of...It's fiction, but it's based on some truth.

(The phone rings…)

RUTH: (GETTING UP) I'm sorry. I'm sure that's my aunt. She calls once a week like clockwork. I'll tell her I'll call her back.

> (Wes nods and smiles. Ruth exits through the kitchen door… After she is out of the room, he walks over toward the console table and peers down at the pages. After a few moments, he hears the door open… He quickly leans over as if to smell the flowers in the vase...)

WES: These are really nice flowers your brother brought over.

RUTH: Yes. He always knows how to make a grand entrance.

(They sit back down at the table...)

WES: Let me guess...you're the giver; he's the taker...but, somehow, he's always been the favorite. Am I right?

RUTH: Yeah...I guess that was kind of obvious from the show you saw this morning.

WES: Oh, it's not so uncommon really.

RUTH: He never comes to see her unless he wants something...and she always makes excuses for him..."My dear boy, Johnny, he works so hard. They never give him any time off."...It's just infuriating.

WES: Do you ever take any time off?

RUTH: Are you kidding? This place would crumble to the ground if I was gone more than an hour. Besides, Mom's dementia's getting worse...It's just so strange because she seems perfectly lucid one minute, and then she'll turn right around and forget where she is.

WES: I hate to say this, but that part's only going to get worse.

RUTH: So I've been told.

WES: Do you have anyone that can relieve you once in a while...a relative or a close friend?

RUTH: I used to...When my husband was around, we worked different shifts, so there was always someone here...But, he left several months ago...(thinking) I guess about 7 or 8 months...anyway, I didn't have anyone to help me take care of Mom anymore, so I just decided at that point to retire early.

WES: You're a good daughter.

RUTH: I'm a tired daughter.

WES: That's another reason I wanted you to have my number...Caregivers are always so busy worrying about other people that they neglect their own needs...

RUTH: (BLUSHING)...You mean...?

WES: ...You should have someone to vent to.

RUTH: (EMBARRASSED) Oh...oh, of course...

WES: So, you were telling me about your writing.

RUTH: I was?

WES: Fiction based on truth?

RUTH: Yes...um...It's kind of silly actually.

WES: So, it's a comedy?

RUTH: No...well, it's not supposed to be anyway. But, I'm afraid I've never had any formal training and--

WES: Training? Why do you need training? So you can end up sounding like everyone else?

RUTH: (SMILING) You have a point.

WES: Some people just have a natural gift for it.

RUTH: I think that's stretching it a bit for me.

WES: Can I be the judge of that?

RUTH: What?

WES: Do you mind if I read some of your work?

RUTH: You want to read my stuff?

WES: Yes.

RUTH: Why?

WES: You like to write; I like to read...let's just say I'm interested.

RUTH: I'm sure the books you're used to reading--

WES: Are commercially-driven swill...most of them anyway. It's hard to find real stories anymore.

RUTH: What makes you so sure mine isn't swill?

WES: I don't know. You just don't seem like the swill type, I guess.

(HE stares at her intensely.)

RUTH: (UNCOMFORTABLE)...Um...Would you like some more tea?
WES: (LOOKING DOWN AT HIS GLASS) I guess I was thirsty.
RUTH: There's plenty.

(She takes the glass and exits.)

RUTH: (OFF STAGE) Still no sugar?
WES: No. The caffeine will keep me going for a while.

(He hears a noise coming from the other side of the room and turns to look. With her eyes still closed, Jenny is waving her arms violently about, appearing to catch something in her hands, then stuffing it down her shirt... He watches her for a moment, amused. Ruth reenters and sees this...)

RUTH: I see Mom's won Publisher's Clearinghouse again.
WES: Publisher's Clearinghouse?
RUTH: Yeah, she has this recurring dream that she's won all this money. Ed McMahon used to bring it right up to her front door, piled up on this great big pallet.

WES: Ed was pulling the pallet?
RUTH: Uh-huh...right up until he died.
WES: Now what?
RUTH: Now they just shoot it at her from this huge cannon.
WES: And she stuffs it all down her shirt?
RUTH: Down her shirt, down her pants, whatever it takes.
WES: (LAUGHING) That's the funniest thing I've seen in a long time.

> (Ruth watches her mother for a moment and begins to laugh...)

RUTH: I really should videotape it sometime.
JENNY: (EYES STILL CLOSED) That's mine, you old biddy!

> (They laugh harder...)

WES: Wow...even in her sleep.
RUTH: (CONFIRMING) Even in her sleep.
WES: She's so funny.
RUTH: She's a handful.

> (Jenny goes back to her relaxed position again, head down, fast asleep.)

WES: I've had a lot of caregivers tell me how strange it feels when they realize they've switched roles with their parents.
RUTH: It's like I'm taking care of a small child, again.

WES: I bet that's hard.

RUTH: It feels about the same as it did the first time. He never listened to me; neither does she.

WES: You have a son?

RUTH: Yeah.

WES: Does he live around here?

RUTH: Pretty close by. How about you? Do you have any kids?

WES: No...I was married once. We tried for several years, but we couldn't have any...I couldn't have any...And she wanted someone who could.

RUTH: I'm sorry.

WES: Nah, that's life, I guess...Besides, that was about the time I was doing that night shift in the ER, and I don't think I was very easy to live with back then.

RUTH: So, tell me what that was like.

WES: The marriage or the ER?

RUTH: Same difference, right?

(Wes laughs...)

RUTH: No, I'm kidding...the ER.

WES: Hmm...Where do I start? ...Well, lots of patients and lots of sleep-deprived doctors and nurses.

RUTH: Anything like that TV show?...the one with George Clooney?

WES: I suppose there was some truth to that show, but there were no doctors and nurses kissing over the top of unconscious patients or getting it on in the janitor's closet.

RUTH: Really? Not ever?

WES: Not to my knowledge.

RUTH: That's a shame.

WES: It was either really dead--pardon the pun--or just so crazy that you couldn't stop to think about anything. And, more times than not, it was crazy.

RUTH: I don't see how you guys can do it.

WES: Well, you just switch over to automatic-pilot. You have to. And then, on the way home, you scream or cry or play some really loud music...whatever it takes to clear the slate so you can start over the next day.

RUTH: Needlepoint?

WES: Exactly.

(Moment of silence...)

WES: What really used to drive me crazy were those people that would come in with a cold and act like they were dying.

(Ruth chuckles...)

WES: No, seriously, they were almost always the ones demanding to be seen or whining because they had a runny nose...Meanwhile you have the other side of it...like this guy one night who came in with a knife stuck in the side of his head...

RUTH: Oh my God. And he was still alive?

WES: Yep. Alive, conscious, and completely calm. No whining.

RUTH: How is that possible?

WES: (GESTURING) The insertion point was through his left temporal lobe and the point of the knife came out into his mouth.

RUTH: And he lived?

WES: Not only did he live, but he left without any permanent damage...just some stitches.

RUTH: That's amazing...You should be the one writing the book.

WES: Oh, that's nothing...One night this lady—

(He stops himself in mid-sentence.)

RUTH: What? Keep going.

WES: I don't know...It's pretty sick.

RUTH: Sick as in bloody or sick as in twisted?

WES: Twisted.

RUTH: I love "twisted."

WES: Alright, but don't say I didn't warn you...Okay, so this lady came in one night complaining of pelvic pain. The doctor asked her the usual questions about her periods and if she might be pregnant...

RUTH: Was she?

WES: No, it wasn't anything like that. So, after he exhausted the normal possibilities of what was causing the pain, he decided to do a pelvic exam...Are you sure you want to hear this?

RUTH: Yes, yes, keep going.

WES: Okay, well, during the procedure, he found...something.

RUTH: What?

WES: He reached in and pulled out a roll of money (GESTURING) this big.
RUTH: (SUPPRESSING A LAUGH) She was keeping her money in her--
WES: Yes, but that's not the best part...The attending nurse had already come out and told us the story and we were laughing and cracking jokes...I know you're not supposed to do that...ethically, but--
RUTH: But, how could you not?
WES: Right, so then the doctor comes out, looks around at us and says: "Talk about payment at the time of service."

(Ruth bursts out laughing. After a moment, she catches her breath...)

RUTH: She didn't ask for change, did she?
WES: (LAUGHING WITH HER) Yeah, but the coins kept falling back out.
RUTH: (TRYING TO CATCH HER BREATH) So, that's why they say you should always wash your hands after touching money.
WES: With antibacterial soap.
JENNY: (WITH HER EYES STILL CLOSED) It's mine!!

(They laugh even harder...)

RUTH: (BENDING AND HOLDING HER SIDE) My side hurts.

(Ruth walks over, grabs a Kleenex, and begins wiping her eyes...Stew walks through the front door as Ruth and Wes are still laughing.)

RUTH: Stew...
STEW: What's...going on here?
RUTH: This is Wes. He's your grandmother's nurse. (TO WES) This is my son.
WES: (EXTENDING HIS HAND) Nice to meet you.

(Stew ignores this gesture and walks toward the couch.)

STEW: So, you're the fluffer.
WES: Fluffer? I'm sorry I don't know--
RUTH: Oh, it's nothing...just...it's nothing, really.
(A moment of silence...)

WES: (SMILING AT RUTH) Well, I better get going?
STEW: (SARCASTICALLY) So soon? But, we haven't had a chance to get to know each other yet.
WES: (TO RUTH) Thanks for the tea.
RUTH: Sure...anytime you get thirsty...
WES: Thanks.
RUTH: Thanks for stopping by...I haven't laughed that hard in a really long time.
WES: Me either.

(He glances over at Stew, then looks back at Ruth...)

WES: And think about what I said about your own needs.

(Stew cranks up the volume on the TV. Jenny begins to stir... Wes walks toward the door...Ruth follows behind him....)

RUTH: (OVER THE VOLUME OF THE TV) Have a nice evening.

(He smiles and exits... Ruth closes the door behind him...)

STEW: (TURNING THE TV DOWN) "Anytime you get thirsty?" Jesus, Ruth, why don't you just hang a red light in the window?
JENNY: What are you watching, Stewie?
STEW: Nothing.
JENNY: I'm hungry.
STEW: Yeah. Well, I doubt there's anything cooking in the oven.
JENNY: Ruth, what are we eating?

(Ruth ignores this...)

JENNY: (TO STEW) Give me that remote. I want to watch my shows.
STEW: It's 6 o'clock, Grandma. Your shows are over.

(Ruth walks over to the dining table, pick up Wes's card and smiles.)

(The lights fade…)

## ACT II

### SCENE ONE

(Jenny is rocking in her chair… staring blankly across the room...a room that has been, somewhat, brought back to life with splashes of color, such as the arrangement of flowers that sits on the console table, a decorative throw that hangs over the back of the couch, and a painting of a young Native American girl on the wall. Yet, Jenny seems unaffected. Ruth enters from the hallway, wearing a pair of slacks and a nice blouse. She is wearing makeup, and her freshly-washed hair is flowing down her back. She carries a fresh set of sheets over to the bed. A plate with a barely-touched sandwich sits on the coffee table…)

RUTH: You didn't eat your sandwich.

(During the following conversation, Ruth strips the old sheets off the bed and puts the fresh ones on...)

JENNY: I like ham.
RUTH: That is ham.

(Jenny looks puzzled, leans over to
examine the sandwich, then sits back...)

JENNY: I wanted tuna.
RUTH: Well, you got ham and you need to eat
it...remember what your nurse said about
keeping up your strength?
JENNY: You mean the nurse you've been
diddling?
RUTH: Behave yourself, Mother.
JENNY: I still think he's a fluffer...but, what
puzzles me is...what does that make you?
RUTH: A fluffer lover, I guess.
JENNY: I guess so.

(A moment of silence as Jenny rocks and
Ruth continues making the bed...)

JENNY: What do you really know about this
"man" anyway?
RUTH: Well, let's see...he's about 5'10"; he's into
threesomes, and he has a dick the size of a
torpedo.
JENNY: (AMUSED) Feeling a little feisty today,
are we?
RUTH: Just trying to keep up with you.
JENNY: No, I would have said "submarine."
RUTH: That doesn't surprise me.
JENNY: Just make sure that thing doesn't
"surface" while I'm around.

RUTH: Aren't your shows on?

JENNY: I'm tired of those people.

RUTH: Okay, then, let me see what I can find.

(Ruth picks up the remote and begins surfing through the channels. After a few seconds, Jenny reaches toward her.)

JENNY: Give me that thing.

RUTH: That's what I thought.

(She hands Jenny the remote and walks back toward the bed... After a moment, Ruth realizes that Jenny is struggling.)

RUTH: What's wrong?

JENNY: I don't understand...there's some kind of cowboy movie on my station.

RUTH: (REACHING FOR THE REMOTE) Here, Mom. Let me see...oh, you have it on channel 25. Your show's on 8, remember?

(Jenny snatches the remote back...)

JENNY: (DEFENSIVE) I know what channel it's on. Don't treat me like a child. I gave birth to you, remember?

RUTH: No, I'll have to say that I don't remember that. But, I've--

JENNY: Well, I most certainly do...You came out fat and screaming like a chimpanzee...

RUTH: Yes, I've heard this story.

JENNY: ...that piercing scream...You had everyone in the room rattled with that piercing scream...It was like a...uh...a...

RUTH: An alarm.

JENNY: Yes, like a high-pitched alarm that you can't shut off...the nurses were scrambling to find some way to pacify you, to shut off that alarm...

RUTH: But, they couldn't.

JENNY: And when I got you home, it wasn't any better. You cried constantly...finally, I just handed you over to your father. "Here," I said. "This one's yours. I can't handle her." And he took you--

RUTH: And I stopped crying.

JENNY: And I'll be damned if you didn't stop crying...Daddy's Cherokee princess, his little shadow...You never wanted anything to do with me.

RUTH: That's not true.

JENNY: From the time I squeezed out your fat little body, you've had an attitude toward me. I was good enough to cook your food and do your laundry, but I was never him.

RUTH: Doesn't it mean something that you're here? Now?

JENNY: Only because he made you promise to take care of me.

(Ruth looks away...)

JENNY: Yes, I overheard your conversation. And, as I remember, you weren't exactly sold on the idea. But, you never denied him anything...as he never did you...Once you came along, you were his one true love...and I became the maid...there was the occasional perfunctory sex, but mostly I was just there to feed you all and to make sure your dirty laundry was taken care of...I guess having a daughter changes everything, doesn't it?

(Ruth darts her eyes at her mother, then walks toward the kitchen...)

RUTH: I'm going to get your medicine.

(She exits...Jenny picks up the remote and turns the volume up a bit. Stew enters, wearing his boxers and messy hair... He plops down on the couch...)

STEW: What's up, Grams?
JENNY: I'm trying to watch my show.

(He picks up the sandwich and begins devouring it...)

STEW: How's our little slut Carly doing?
JENNY: She'll never learn.
STEW: Let's hope not. That's the only thing that makes this show interesting.

(Ruth returns, carrying a dish of pills and a glass of water. She sets them down

next to her mother and exits through the
hallway...)

STEW: Your drugs have arrived.
JENNY: I'm watching my show.

(With sandwich still in hand, Stew
begins rifling through the pills...)

STEW: What does this red one do?
JENNY: It wards off dirty old men.
STEW: You're funny, Grams. But, you're really
going to have to start sharing the drugs. What
does the white one do?

(Ruth reenters, carrying a pair of men's
jeans and a newspaper... She throws
them both over the back of the couch and
snatches the sandwich and the pill dish
out of Stew's hands...)

STEW: What the...?
RUTH: This is your grandmother's sandwich. If
you want something to eat, the kitchen is that
way.
RUTH: (TO JENNY) Mother, you're going to eat
part of this sandwich if I have to force-feed you.
Then, you will take these pills, one at a time so
that you don't choke. Now, are you going to
cooperate or are we going to fight some more?
JENNY: (SNATCHING THE SANDWICH) You
sure are bitchy today.

RUTH: (TO STEW) Put these jeans on. I'm tired of you sprawling out in my living room with your baloney pony on display. And here's the classifieds. I've already circled some jobs for you. After you take out the trash, you can go put in some applications.

(Ruth exits into the kitchen...)

STEW: (PUTTING ON THE JEANS) What the hell's wrong with her?
JENNY: It's that girly nurse boy. He's been putting ideas in her head.

(Stew shakes his head and exits through the hallway... Jenny begrudgingly takes a bite of the sandwich and begins chewing...)

JENNY: (YELLING TOWARD THE KITCHEN) I like tuna!

(Ruth re-enters, holding a can of soda. She pulls the typewriter out and sets it on the table.)

JENNY: So, what are we cooking up this time, Ms. Bronte?
RUTH: Oh, I had an idea for this story where a middle-aged woman is driven mad by her mooching sloth of a son and her evil, elderly mother.
JENNY: What happens?

RUTH: She poisons their food.

(Jenny stares down at her sandwich, then
sets it back on the plate. Ruth begins
typing. Stew returns, fully dressed and
heads toward the front door.)

STEW: I'm going to Taco Bell.
RUTH: (JUMPING UP) Don't forget to take this
with you.

(She holds the classifieds out...He stares
at her, then snatches the paper, and
slams the front door behind him...)

JENNY: Great. The last time that boy ate at Taco
Bell he farted for two days.
RUTH: (SITTING BACK DOWN AT THE
TYPEWRITER) Did you take your pills, yet?
JENNY: I'm taking them, I'm taking them,
alright?

(Ruth continues typing. Jenny stares
down at the water, sniffs it, looks toward
Ruth, then begins to take the pills,
dramatically pretends to pass out, holds
the position for a second, then opens one
eye to find that Ruth is ignoring her...
When Jenny finishes, she pushes herself
up on her walker and makes her way,
very slowly toward her bed. Ruth
watches her struggle with a look of
concern, but remains seated...)

JENNY: I'm taking my nap now. Don't smother me in my sleep.

> (She lies down... Ruth stops typing and stares out, as if contemplating something, then she continues typing. She repeats this sequence several times during which Jenny begins to snore, stirs slightly, then rolls over onto her side...)

RUTH: (TO HERSELF) Let's see...how is she going to tell him--

> (She is startled by a knock at the door... She smiles, gets up, and opens it...Wes stands on the other side, holding a take-out bag in his hand...)

WES: You still hungry?
RUTH: Starving.

> (He kisses her, then walks toward the table and sets the lunch down...)

RUTH: (MOVING THE TYPEWRITER) Let me get this out of the way.
WES: Sorry I'm a little late. One of my patients was having a tough time today.
RUTH: I'm sorry to hear that.

> (Wes distributes the lunch...They begin to eat...)

WES: How's your mom?

RUTH: I'm a little concerned...I mean, she's still as mean as ever, but she seems to be getting weaker.

WES: How's the eating and the exercise going?

RUTH: Ugh! She's so damned stubborn...I had to threaten to force-feed her today, and getting her outside to exercise is like trying to get a 5 year-old to take a bath.

WES: Have you thought anymore about getting someone in here to help you?

RUTH: No...no, I can do it.

WES: I'm just worried about what this is doing to you.

RUTH: I'm tough.

WES: Yeah, well I think that "stubbornness" you were talking about runs in the family.

RUTH: Oh yeah?

WES: Yeah.

(He leans over and kisses her...)

WES: I'll check her out when we finish eating.

RUTH: There's also some bruising...

WES: More than usual?

RUTH: Yes. It seems to be getting worse lately.

WES: The skin gets thinner at her age, so it could just be that, but I'll take some blood...just to be on the safe side.

(He notices her tension and changes the subject.)

WES: So, did I tell you that I've always had this thing for "lunch ladies."

RUTH: (SMILING) Yeah, right.

WES: No, I'm serious.

RUTH: Well, that wasn't exactly my dream job...I just sort of ended up there.

WES: What was your dream?

RUTH: I was going to school to be a teacher...

WES: Really? What happened to that?

RUTH: In my second semester I met my ex-husband...and, well, sometimes the dream dies along with the rabbit...I got a job at a middle school cafeteria and...I just stayed there.

(A moment of silence...)

RUTH: So, you had a thing, huh?

WES: Uh-huh.

RUTH: I'm listening...

WES: When I was in the eighth grade, there was this lady that worked in the cafeteria that was so...fine...

RUTH: Really? How could you tell with the hairnet and the frumpy smock?

WES: Oh, a growing young boy can tell, trust me...Anyway, everyday when I walked through the line my heart would start pounding and I could feel the sweat beading up on my forehead...

RUTH: And then what?

WES: And then, she would look over and wink at me...and I swear, there were a couple of times that I had to position that tray carefully in front of my pants to disguise my joy.

(Ruth begins to laugh hysterically...)

WES: What?
RUTH: (STILL LAUGHING) Nothing...It's just...
WES: What?
RUTH: It's just that no matter what we're talking about, you can always make me laugh.
WES: I'm just trying to point out how inspirational you might have been without knowing it.
RUTH: Well, thank you. But, I can honestly say that never crossed my mind.

(Moment of silence...)

WES: So, what about this teaching thing?
RUTH: I tried to go back at one point...to school, I mean. But, it was just too hard to work, go to school, and raise kids. I knew something was going to suffer, and I didn't want it to be my children.
WES: Children? As in more than one?

(Ruth stays silent for a moment...)

WES: I'm sorry, if you don't—
RUTH: I had a daughter...Beth...She died in a car wreck when she was three.
WES: ...I had no idea. I'm so--

RUTH: It's fine...(BEAT)...We were in the car--
the kids and I--on our way to Beth's doctor's
appointment...And they were both really
cranky. Beth wasn't feeling well, and Stew was
just a colicky baby. Anyway, Beth dropped her
juice bottle on the floor and started throwing
this huge fit...All I could think about was that I
needed her to stop crying. So, I leaned over-
-just for a second--to get the bottle, and I missed
the red light. I don't know how, but I
did...and...the car t-boned us.
WES: (PLACING HIS HAND OVER HERS) I'm
so sorry.
RUTH: It's okay. I...I don't know why I decided
to burden you with that...kind of brought down
the mood, didn't I?
WES: No. I'm glad you felt comfortable enough
to share it with me.
RUTH: I know I haven't been the world's
greatest mom to my son. I've never been as strict
with him as I should've been...My mother calls
me an "enabler."...And I'm sure she's right...but
when you only have one child left, you want to
give him the world and at the same time, you
don't want to let him too far out of your sight.
WES: Which is why he lives with you?
RUTH: Yeah. I actually had some hope for him
when he was younger. He was fascinated by
everything, and he loved to learn. We had this
old set of encyclopedias, and he used to spend
hours, lying on the floor, reading them from
cover to cover.
WES: Wow. You don't see many kids doing that.

RUTH: No. But, he would just lose himself in those books.

WES: How was he with other children?

RUTH: Pretty withdrawn most of the time... (RECALLING, AMUSED) Although, there was this one time when he was in the 5th grade. It was Oklahoma Land Run Day at school--

WES: I remember Land Run Day. Everyone lines up and dashes across the playground with their flags, trying to stake claim to the best piece of land.

RUTH: Right. Well, that's the way it's supposed to work. But, Stew would have no part of it. The students were all lined up, ready to go, and just before the teacher blew the whistle, he ran out in front of everyone and shouted, "Stop. The white man promised that as long as the sun rose on this land, it would belong to the Indians."

WES: (LAUGHING) He said that?

RUTH: Yep.

WES: That's great.

RUTH: I thought so, too. I was actually kind of proud of him when I heard about it later. But, needless to say, the teachers weren't amused, and they drug him back to the line with the others.

WES: So, what happened?

RUTH: When he got home, they'd already called, so I asked him about it. He said, "Mom, I ended up with a crappy piece of land just like the Indians always do."

(They both laugh...)

WES: That's pretty intelligent.

RUTH: Yes. And he still is. But, without ambition, intelligence won't even get you out the front door...(BEAT)...Sometimes I look at him lounging on that couch and I get so pissed. I think, how dare he take advantage of me this way...But, I'm the Frankenstein who created that monster, and now...I have to deal with him.

WES: Look...I'm the last person in the world to give parenting advice...But, I'm just concerned about what this is doing to you.

RUTH: I told you, I'm tough.

WES: "Tough" meaning "stubborn."

RUTH: I suppose.

(Moment of silence...)

WES: Why don't you go back to school?

RUTH: You do realize how old I am, don't you?

WES: There are plenty of people older than you in college.

RUTH: Yeah, that's great, then it's just three steps from graduation to the morgue.

WES: Well, just think about it this way--People will already be here for your graduation, so they won't have to make two trips.

RUTH: You're a smart ass, you know it?

WES: No, seriously, I can bring you the college application forms to fill out...since you don't believe in computers.

RUTH: I don't have the money for school. You know that.

WES: So, you could get a government grant, or you could apply for a scholarship through your tribe...

RUTH: You have an answer for everything, don't you?

WES: I just think that you should do something for yourself...for once.

> (Ruth gets up and starts walking toward the kitchen.)

RUTH: Would you like some tea?

WES: I'd love some.

> (After she exits, Wes walks over to the console table and begins reading her pages... He smiles and nods his head. When he hears her return, he pretends he is smelling the flower arrangement. She sees him and begins to laugh...)

RUTH: Those are fake, you know?

WES: They looked so real.

RUTH: Here's your tea.

WES: Thanks...I've been meaning to tell you that the house looks great.

RUTH: Oh, thanks.

WES: Is that a new painting?

RUTH: No, it's been in the attic forever. My Dad bought it for me years ago. It's called "Wind Whisperer." But, he called it, "u gv wi yu u we tsi a ti."

WES: You wanna repeat that?

RUTH: (LAUGHING) It means "princess."
WES: Ah. And you're the princess, right?
RUTH: Yeah. That's always been a source of
contention between Mom and I. So, when he
died, I decided to put the "princess" in the
attic...just as a peace offering, I guess.
WES: And now?
RUTH: And now I'm letting her breathe a little.
WES: (EMBRACING RUTH) Good. She
deserves to breathe a little, don't you think?

(RUTH smiles and kisses him...)

WES: I'll go out and get my bag. I hate to wake
her, but--
RUTH: No, that's fine. I'll wake her while you're
gone.

(Wes exits... Ruth walks over to the bed
to stir her mother...)

RUTH: (GENTLY SHAKING HER) Mom?
JENNY: (VERY GROGGY) Huh?
RUTH: Mom, wake up. Your nurse is here.
JENNY: Who?
RUTH: Your nurse.
JENNY: Karen?
RUTH: No, Wes...remember?
JENNY: (SLOWLY STIRRING) Where's Karen?

(Ruth grabs some pillows off the couch
to put behind Jenny's back.)

RUTH: Let's sit you up so he can examine you.
JENNY: What for?
RUTH: It's just a precaution.
JENNY: I'm fine.

> (Wes returns, pulling his bag behind him.)

WES: Hello, Mrs. Neugin.

> (Jenny stares at him for a moment, then she recalls.)

JENNY: Ah, Nurse Kevorkian.
WES: You remembered.

> (He opens his bag and pulls out a folder, a blood pressure cuff, and a stethoscope...)

JENNY: How could I forget. We've had such a lovely relationship.
WES: Okay, Mrs. Neugin, I'm just going to slip this cuff around your arm.

> (He pushes up her sleeve...)

WES: You've got a lot of bruising going on here.
JENNY: My daughter beats me.
WES: I seriously doubt that.

> (He slips the cuff over her arm...)

WES: I'm going to start pumping this cuff, but you let me know if it hurts, okay?

JENNY: Speaking of "pumping," what have you two been doing while I was asleep?

RUTH: You're not supposed to talk while he's doing this.

JENNY: It better not have been on my chair.

WES: Okay, Mrs. Neugin, I need you to be very still and quiet.

> (Wes bends down, places the stethoscope in his ears and the chestpiece against the crease of her elbow... He begins to listen to her pulse... After a few seconds, he releases the cuff, then puts his fingers to her wrist and stares down at his watch...)

JENNY: When's Karen coming back?

RUTH: You're being rude.

> (He releases her wrist and begins writing in her chart...)

WES: Okay, Mrs. Neugin. I'm just going to listen to your lungs now. (PUTS THE SCOPE TO HER BACK) Take a deep breath in for me and slowly release it.

> (She takes a deep breath...)

WES: Another.

> (She does...)

WES: Now, I'm moving the scope around to your chest.
JENNY: Sure you can find it, girly boy?
RUTH: Mother! (TO WES) I'm sorry.
WES: (TO JENNY) Deep breath in and slowly release.

(She does... He pulls the stethoscope away and writes in her chart. Then he pulls a vile and disposable needle from his bag.... He also pulls out a pair of latex gloves and begins to put them on…)

WES: Almost done, Mrs. Neugin. I just need to take some blood, okay?
JENNY: What's going on here? I'm in remission. (TO RUTH)You told me I was in remission. Why are you letting him do this?
RUTH: Mother, I told you, it's just a precaution.
WES: You'll just feel a little pinch. Are you ready?
JENNY: (GLARING AT THE BOTH OF THEM) Fine. Just get it done and leave me alone.

(He wraps a tourniquet around her arm, swabs it with alcohol, then takes the blood...)

WES: There, that wasn't so bad, was it?

(Jenny doesn't answer...Wes packs up his things.)

WES: (TO RUTH) I'll get this to the lab and let you know what I find out.
RUTH: Thanks.

(Wes begins walking toward the front door. Ruth follows him…)

RUTH: And thanks for lunch. I had a nice time.
WES: Me too…Think about what I said…about school.
RUTH: (SMILING) I'll think about it.

(He kisses her and exits…)

JENNY: What was he saying about "school"?
RUTH: Nothing important…That was a really short nap. You sure you're ready to get up?
JENNY: (SLOWLY PUSHING HERSELF UP) Yes. I don't want to miss my show.
RUTH: (LOOKING DOWN AT HER WATCH) I think your show's about over, Mom.
JENNY: (SLOWLY MAKING HER WAY TO THE CHAIR) He thinks you're just perfect, doesn't he?
RUTH: Who?
JENNY: The nurse.
RUTH: I doubt it. No one's perfect.
JENNY: Ah, but I think you have him fooled. Just like you did your father.
RUTH: I'm not trying to fool anyone.
JENNY: Really…? Have you told him everything?

RUTH: Don't start.

JENNY: Did you tell him about the teacher...the married teacher?

RUTH: That was a long time ago.

JENNY: Still, relationships are supposed to be built on trust, aren't they?

RUTH: We just met two weeks ago.

JENNY: Uh-huh...And how many times have you bedded-down in two weeks?

(Ruth ignores her, walks over and begins putting the leftovers from lunch back into the take-out bag...)

JENNY: At least three that I remember.

(Ruth looks at her, quizzically...)

JENNY: Just because I'm old, doesn't mean I'm deaf.

RUTH: I'm not having this conversation with you. This is my home, and I'm a grown woman-

JENNY: --who still screams like a chimpanzee.

(Ruth picks up the take-out bag and walks toward the kitchen. Just as she is exiting, Jenny does her best chimpanzee scream...)

JENNY: Whoo-Haaaaa!! Whoo-Haaaaa!!

(Ruth exits. Jenny points the remote toward the television...The lights fade...)

## ACT II

## SCENE TWO

(Jenny sits in her chair, rocking, and digging at her scalp with her new pick. There is a bowl of mostly-eaten oatmeal sitting next to her...Ruth enters from the hallway and walks toward the console table...She is wearing a nice, but somewhat outdated business suit and is carrying some papers in her hand...)

RUTH: Wow. You actually ate your breakfast this morning.
JENNY: I poured it in the plant.
RUTH: We don't have a plant.
JENNY: We don't?
RUTH: No.
JENNY: Well, you better check behind the couch then.

(Ruth's eyes widen...Slowly and with apprehension, she leans and peeks behind the couch. Then she shoots a look of disapproval toward her mother...)

RUTH: You're bluffing, old lady.
JENNY: "Old," huh? Who's going to be the "old lady" when she walks into that college today?
RUTH: (LAYING HER PAPERS ON THE CONSOLE TABLE) I'm just going up there to turn in my application.

JENNY: Yeah, well, when it's time to pay tuition, don't forget to ask for the Senior Discount.

(Ruth exits through the kitchen door... Jenny picks up the bowl and finishes the last of her oatmeal. Then, she sets it back down quickly and wipes her mouth with her hand. Ruth returns, carrying a glass of water and a pill dish...)

RUTH: Time for your meds.

(Jenny starts to raise the pill dish to her mouth...)

RUTH: (PUSHING THE DISH BACK DOWN) One at a time.

(Jenny begrudgingly obeys... Ruth exits through the kitchen door and returns, carrying a cordless phone and a piece of paper...)

RUTH: I shouldn't be gone long, Mom. But, if something happens...anything...you can call Ms. Spencer across the street. You remember her, don't you?
JENNY: Yeah, I remember Ms. Spinster.
RUTH: "Spencer."
JENNY: Isn't Stewie home?

RUTH: Trust me, Mom. It would be much faster to call Ms. Spencer. I've talked to her, and she already knows the situation.
JENNY: I don't like her.
RUTH: You don't like anyone. Now, finish taking your pills.

(Ruth exits through the hallway...)

JENNY: (BETWEEN PILLS IN A MOCKING VOICE) "One at a time...I can't take you to the morgue today, Mom, 'cause I'm going to college."

(Ruth returns, carrying her purse...)

RUTH: Do you need me to help you to the bathroom before I leave?

(Jenny ignores her...)

RUTH: Alright, then. I'll be back soon.
JENNY: (YELLING AFTER HER) Ruth.
RUTH: (TURNS BACK) Yes?
JENNY: Nothing.

(Ruth reaches for the door...)

JENNY: Ruth.
RUTH: (TURNS BACK AGAIN) Yes?

(Jenny swallows hard, then speaks, avoiding eye contact...)

JENNY: Don't leave.
RUTH: Mother, I'll only be gone for--
JENNY: No...(BEAT)...I mean...don't leave me.

(Ruth walks back over toward Jenny...)

RUTH: *Leave* you?

(A moment of uncomfortable
silence...Ruth picks up the piece of paper
and shows it to Jenny again...)

RUTH: (GENTLE TONE) Just call Ms. Spencer,
Mom. If you need anything, just pick up the
phone and dial this number, okay?

(Jenny takes the paper from her...)

RUTH: I'll be back soon.

(Ruth exits...Jenny picks up the remote,
turns the TV on and begins flipping
through the channels...After a few
moments, she is startled by a knock at
the front door...)

JENNY: Ruth?

(Another knock...)

JENNY: (TOWARD THE HALLWAY) Stewie?

(Another knock, louder this time...Jenny picks up the piece of paper, contemplates for a moment, then picks up the phone and begins to dial...)

JOHN: (OFF STAGE) Momma?
JENNY: Johnny? (INTO THE PHONE) Oh, sorry Ms. Spinster, never mind.

(She hangs up, pushes herself up with her walker, then moves slowly toward the front door...)

JOHN: (OFF STAGE) Momma? You in there?
JENNY: I'm here, Johnny. Give me just a minute...I'm coming...almost there.

(She makes it to the door, unlocks and opens it... John is standing on the other side, holding a bouquet of lavender lilies...)

JOHN: There's my girl.

(He walks in and hugs her...)

JENNY: They let you off work today.
JOHN: What...? Oh...yeah...I just told them I had an appointment with a lovely, young lady. (HOLDING THE FLOWERS OUT) These are for you.
JENNY: (SMELLING THEM) They're beautiful. You can just lay them on the dining table for

now. I'll have Ruth put them in some water
when she gets home.

> (Jenny begins to make her way back over
> to her chair.)

JOHN: Where'd she run off to, anyway?
JENNY: Who?
JOHN: Ruth.

> (Jenny struggles a bit, as if the walker
> has suddenly become heavier.)

JOHN: Momma, you okay?

> (He walks over to her...)

Here, take my arm.

> (She grabs hold of his arm... He pushes
> the walker out of the way and guides her
> back to her chair... Then, he sits down on
> the couch...)

So, you were about to tell me where Ruth was
going.
JENNY: Ugh...She's lost her mind. That girly
boy nurse...Did you meet him, by the way...?
JOHN: Yeah, the last time I was here. He
seemed nice enough.
JENNY: Well, he and your sister have been--
how shall I put it?--"co-mingling."
JOHN: (GENUINELY SHOCKED) No.

JENNY: Uh-huh.

JOHN: Ruth and the nurse?

JENNY: Uh-huh.

JOHN: Wow.

JENNY: So, now that all the blood has rushed out of her head to (gesturing) "other regions," he's managed to convince her that she's going to be a teacher when she grows up...Can you believe that?...At her age?

JOHN: How's she going to do that?

JENNY: She's going down to the college today to sign up...She'll be on Medicare by the time she gets her first job teaching.

JOHN: Do you think she'll be gone long?

JENNY: Who knows?

JOHN: Well, you're the one I came to see, anyway.

JENNY: I'm glad you're here. It's so nice when you come by. Your sister's always nagging me about something and that son of hers is never going to separate himself from her teat.

JOHN: That's what I was talking about, Momma...the last time I was here. Do you remember?

JENNY: About Stewie?

JOHN: No. About getting you away from here.

JENNY: Oh, I don't--

JOHN: Wouldn't you like that, Momma?

JENNY: I don't know. Would I be living with you?

JOHN: No, Momma...I didn't mean that...What I meant was that you'll have enough money to live on your own and hire a live-in nurse.

JENNY: (DISAPPOINTED) A nurse, huh?

JOHN: Sure. With the kind of money you'll have, you could do just about anything you wanted.

JENNY: Money? What money?

JOHN: Do you remember me telling you about Bill? My friend, Bill?

JENNY: Bill...? Oh, yes the smart one...with the laundromat.

JOHN: Do you remember how I told you about the investment opportunity we have?

JENNY: You did?

JOHN: Yes, Momma...magnetism, remember?

JENNY: Magnetism?

JOHN: Yes. It's going to make us both very rich.

JENNY: I don't understand, Johnny.

JOHN: (WITH HIS HAND ON HER LEG) All you need to know is that we have a wonderful opportunity, but we have to have the investment money to get started.

JENNY: Where are we going to get that?

JOHN: (TAKES HER HAND) Listen, Momma, I know you have some money.

JENNY: Not much, really.

JOHN: You have enough. And what good is it doing you if it's just sitting somewhere gathering dust?

JENNY: Oh, it's not gathering much dust under the mattress.

> (John's eyes widen... He gets up and begins to walk over toward her bed...)

JOHN: Let's just take a look and see how much you got, Momma, okay?
JENNY: Well...okay...I haven't counted it in some time.

(John bends down and feels under the mattress...He removes a pair of panties and quickly shoves them back where he found them...Then he reaches deeper and smiles as he pulls out a roll of cash...)

JOHN: (STANDING UP) You know, you really shouldn't hide your cash under the mattress. That's the first place thieves look.

(Suddenly, the front door swings open...)

RUTH: Mom, why's this door un—

(Ruth sees John next to the bed, holding the cash in his hand...She slams the front door...)

JENNY: Why are you back so soon?
RUTH: (GLARING AT JOHN) I forgot my application.
JENNY: Look who stopped by.
RUTH: My loving brother...It's funny...I didn't see your car parked out front.
JOHN: Oh, I...parked in the alley...to leave the driveway open for you.

RUTH: Really? How very kind of you. Now, you want to tell me why you're holding my mother's money in your grubby hands?

JOHN: I can explain...

RUTH: I'm listening.

JOHN: We'll all be so much better off, Ruth.

RUTH: We?

JENNY: His friend is building a magnetic laundromat.

RUTH: A magnetic laundromat?

JOHN: No. It's much more complicated than that.

RUTH: No, no. It's quite simple, actually...You're falling for another one of those "get rich quick" schemes--

JOHN: No. It's diff--

RUTH: I know. It's different this time, right?

JOHN: Yes. Magnetism is going to be a major source of energy all over the world. It will power our cars, our heaters and air conditioners--

RUTH: Are you quoting from the brochure?

JOHN: Look, I know things are tight around here. Wouldn't life be much simpler if you had some extra cash...to help take care of Mom?

RUTH: What do you know about taking care of her...? How many times have you actually come to see your mother in the last two years? How many times did you visit her in the hospital when she was suffering with cancer?

JENNY: He can't help it if they won't let him off work.

RUTH: Oh, the imaginary job. I forgot about that.
JENNY: What are you talking about? Johnny, what is she talking about?
JOHN: Nothing, Momma.

> (Ruth walks over and yanks the roll of cash out of her brother's hand...)

RUTH: (STARING HIM DOWN) When Dad died, he left me his handgun...for protection. If I ever catch you in my house again, I'm going to treat you like an intruder.

> (John stares back at her, trying to call her bluff, but she does not back down...he walks over to Jenny, kisses her on the cheek and walks toward the front door...)

JENNY: Johnny?
> (He exits…)

JENNY: (TO RUTH) What the hell is wrong with you?

> (Ruth places the roll of cash back under the mattress and walks over to the console table...)

That's your brother...my son...Have you completely lost your mind?

(Ruth picks up the college application and stares down at it for a moment...she shakes her head, then drops it into the trash...)

Answer me.

(As Ruth exits through the hallway, she passes Stew, who enters, wearing his boxers...)

STEW: What's going on out here?
JENNY: Your mother has lost her mind.

(Stew plops down on the couch...)

STEW: You got the remote?

(Jenny feels down in her rocker and hands it to him.)

JENNY: Here.

(Yelling back toward the hallway...)

I wasn't finished talking to you yet!
STEW: It's not time for your show yet, is it?
JENNY: I don't care about my show. (TOWARD THE HALLWAY) Ruth, get back in here! I'm not through talking to you about this!

(Ruth returns, carrying a light jacket...)

RUTH: (HOLDING IT OUT TO JENNY) Put this on. There's a chilly breeze out today.

JENNY: I'm not going anywhere.

RUTH: You haven't had your exercise yet today, Mom. The nurse said--

JENNY: The nurse? I don't give a good god damn what that "nurse" said. He's the reason my daughter's running around, pretending like she's a school girl...the reason my son will probably never come see me again...

STEW: What's going on?

RUTH: (LIFTING JENNY'S ARM) Here. Let's get this jacket on you.

JENNY: (YANKING HER ARM BACK) That was my son you just threatened to shoot!

STEW: What? Uncle John was here?

RUTH: (LIFTING JENNY'S ARM MORE FORCEFULLY) I said, we need to get this jacket on you.

(Jenny resists... there is a determined scuffle...)

JENNY: I said I'm not going anywhere with you...you...you whore!

> (Ruth slaps her mother hard across the face...Ruth backs up, her eyes wide... Jenny holds her head down, her hand to her face.)

STEW: (TO RUTH) What the hell is wrong with you? This woman's almost 90 years-old!

RUTH: (DEFENSIVE) Don't you judge me, you ungrateful, lazy asshole!...I'm so sick of your lounging and your...your sponging...your sarcastic comments...oh, you're smart alright...smarter than I'll probably ever be. But, the way you're wasting your life makes you about the stupidest person I've ever known.

STEW: Coming from the mouth of the lunch lady.

RUTH: Yes. The "lunch lady" who made sure you had everything.

STEW: Everything? Do you realize that for the last thirty years you've lived your life on automatic-pilot? That's why he left, you know that, right...? I'm surprised that he stayed as long as he did.

RUTH: (WEEPING AND SHAKING HER HEAD) That's not true. He knew I loved him.

STEW: He didn't want to be your cell-mate anymore.

RUTH: No! He was mad at me because I kept taking you back in. He told me--

STEW: You made all of us feel like we had nothing, NOTHING to offer you!...and all because you lost the one person who meant the most...(BEAT)...you killed her...you killed her and you've spent the last thirty years making the rest of us pay for it.

RUTH: (GUARDED IMPLOSION) Get your fucking pants on and get out of my house.

(Ruth exits through the hallway and we hear a door slam... Stew leans over and tries to move Jenny's hand…)

STEW: You okay, Grams?

(She shoves his hand away and covers her face again...)

(The lights fade…)


## ACT II

### SCENE THREE

(Jenny is lying in her bed asleep. Ruth enters through the front door, wearing a pair of old sweats and carrying a couple of grocery bags…She sets them down on the dining table, then walks over to the laundry hamper and opens it…She reaches under the mattress and pulls out a number of blouses and panties, which no longer seems to faze her…There is a knock at the door...She tosses the clothes in the hamper and walks over to answer it. Wes stands on the other side...)

WES: Good Morning.

(He steps inside and kisses her...)

RUTH: (WAVING TOWARD THE COUCH) Hi.
Come on in.
WES: I see you've been to the store already this
morning.
RUTH: Yeah. I wanted to get back before she
woke up.
WES: You're a good daughter.

(Ruth lowers her head...)

You look tired.
RUTH: I think I'm just getting old.
WES: I can relate.
RUTH: Would you like some coffee or
something.
WES: No, thanks. I'm fine.
RUTH: So, do you have a lot of patients to visit
today?
WES: Four.
RUTH: That's not bad, I guess.
WES: No.

(There is a moment of silence. Then, they
both begin to speak at the same time...)

RUTH: Listen, I--
WES I wanted--
RUTH: You go first.

(Wes takes her hand.)

RUTH: This seems serious.
WES: I got the test results on your mother...

RUTH: And it's not good, is it?

WES: The cancer's back...I'm so sorry.

> (Ruth lowers her head and begins to sob. WES puts his arms around her and pulls her to him.)

RUTH: I'm a terrible person.

WES: No, you're not.

RUTH: Yes, I am.

> (Ruth sniffs and wipes her eyes with the back of her hand...Wes looks around and spots a kleenex box on the table next to Jenny's bed...)

WES: Let me get you some tissue.

> (He brings the box to her...)

RUTH: Thank you.

WES: Now, why are you so down on yourself? Do you realize how many people are dropped off at nursing homes and never hear from their children again? She's very lucky to—

RUTH: I hit her.

WES: What?

> (Moment of silence...)

RUTH: I did. I hit her.

WES: Do you want to talk about it?

RUTH: What's there to talk about? She called me a whore, and I slapped her...I slapped her really hard.

WES: And then what?

RUTH: She just sat there...for the longest time...holding her face. She wouldn't look at me.

WES: You're human. We've all lost our cool.

RUTH: Really? You?

WES: Of course.

RUTH: You just seem so damned perfect.

WES: That's the front I've been putting on to win you over. If you had to live with me, you'd see it differently.

(Moment of silence...)

RUTH: Listen, I haven't slept much the last couple of days, so I've had a lot of time to think.

WES: About?

RUTH: About us.

WES And?

RUTH: I can't see you anymore.

WES: (BEAT) Can you tell me why?

RUTH: My life wasn't so happy before I met you, but...it was comfortable. A sort of comfortable numbness...And then you came along and...well...

WES: And what?

RUTH: You made me feel things.

WES: And that's bad?

RUTH: If I had met you under different circumstances--

WES: Why does that matter?

RUTH: Because I have responsibilities....Look, I think you're a wonderful man with so much to give, but...you shouldn't waste your life with someone who's not able to give back.
WES: What about you? What about the application I brought you?
RUTH: I filled it out...

(Pointing toward the trash...)

then, I threw it in there.
WES: Why?
RUTH: It was a nice fantasy, but I have other things I need to focus on...and I can't do that if I'm...distracted.
WES: I don't understand. Don't you want some happiness for yourself?
RUTH: (TAKING HIS HAND) I had some...and I thank you for that.

(Wes motions toward the painting...)

WES: What about the Cherokee Princess? What about letting her breathe?
RUTH: She's called the "Wind Whisperer."...There were never any Cherokee Princesses. That's a myth.
WES: There are other options. You don't have to shut the world out. Let someone help you. Let me--
RUTH: Wes...

(She stares at him as if to make sure he's paying attention…)

She's my mother.

(He nods his head. After a moment he speaks...)

WES: I've made an appointment for her this afternoon with her oncologist...at 2 o'clock...I just thought she should get in as soon as possible.
RUTH: Thank you.
WES: Karen's coming back on Monday, and that's...probably for the best.
RUTH: I don't know...I bet her Benny impersonation isn't as good as yours.
WES: Your mom didn't seem to like it so much.
RUTH: Yes, she did. She just didn't like that she liked it.

(He hugs her, then pushes back and stares into her eyes, shakes his head, walks over to the trash can, pulls out the application, and holds it up to her as if to say, "I'm not giving up on you." He tucks it under his arm, and walks toward the door… When he gets there, he turns back...)

WES: By the way, I really think you should continue writing...you've got a gift for it.
RUTH: (AS WES EXITS) How did you--?

(She closes the door behind him, takes a deep breath, then walks over to the dining table... She begins to remove several non-perishable items from the bag, including toilet paper and two boxes of lotion kleenex. As She pulls out a bag of peanut M&Ms, She stops suddenly and stares down at it for a moment, then walks over and drops it into the trash can--a sign of "letting go." She grabs the grocery bags and carries them out to the kitchen...Jenny, still asleep, begins to thrash and scream...)

JENNY: (FLAILING HER ARMS AND LEGS) Get away from me! Stop it! Don't touch me! Get away!!

(Ruth reenters and rushes over to her mother...)

RUTH: Mother? What's wrong?
JENNY: Ruthie?!
RUTH: (GENTLE TONE) Yes, Mom. It's me. I'm here.
JENNY: (PUTTING HER ARMS AROUND HER) Get them away from me.

(Ruth pulls Jenny in close and begins rocking back and forth...)

RUTH: They're gone now. Everything's okay.

JENNY: They were trying to hurt me.
RUTH: No one's going to hurt you. I'm here
now...

> (Realizing, herself, that this is finally
> true...)

I'm here now...I'm here.

> (The lights fade...)

End.

# Salvage

A Play

By

Diane Glancy

CHARACTER LIST:

WOLF- 32, son of WOLFERT, husband of MEMELA

WOLFERT- 63, father of WOLF, father-in-law of MEMELA

MEMELA- (Me'-mah-lah or Me-me), 32, wife of WOLF, daughter-in-law of WOLFERT

WOLF and his father, WOLFERT, run the tow truck and salvage yard called, Blackfeet's. MEMELA is a grade-school teacher. WOLFERT is a medicine man. WOLF and MEMELA are general Indians who have lost some but not all of their traditions. They have two sons, ages 15 and 16, who do not appear in the play.

PHOEBE, WOLFERT'S dead wife, also does not appear in the play. She can be represented by lights when she appears as an apparition to WOLFERT. Maybe she's actually there. Maybe she's an animal. Wolfert may bring a sandwich to eat while he's in the cemetery. Maybe an elk or some animal comes for the crumbs.

*Salvage* was performed as a staged reading during the second annual Oklahoma City Theatre Company's Native American New Play Festival in 2011. It was selected as the featured production for the third annual festival and performed June 1-10, 2012. It was a regional premier directed by Sarah dAngelo with the following cast:

WOLFERT:    Michael Edmonds
WOLF:        Jeremy Tanequodle
MEMELA:    Tiffany Tuggle

Other parts played by the company

Lighting, Set Design by Jamie Wilson
Costume Design by Rachel Irick
Sound Design by Kory Kight Pagala
Projection Design by Sarah dAngelo
Stage Management by Kory Kight Pagala

*Salvage* was developed with support from a MAP (Multi-Arts Production) Grant, the Creative Capital Foundation and the Rockefeller Foundation by Native Voices at the Autry during their 2005-2007 annual playwrights retreats and Festival of New Plays. In 2008, Native Voices facilitated readings at the Public Theater's Native Theater Festival in New York and the Literary Managers and Directors National Conference at La Jolla Playhouse. *Salvage* had its world premiere at Native Voices at the Autry, Los Angeles in March 2009 and the full production was chosen for the Origins Festival at Border Crossings Theatre in London, England later that year.

### Diane Glancy (Playwright)

Glancy is a Cherokee novelist, playwright and filmmaker. Her film, *The Dome of Heaven* was featured during the Oklahoma City's deadCenter Film Festival in 2012. The Native Voices at the Autry has produced four of her plays, *The Bird House, Salvage, Stone Heart,* and *Jump Kiss.* She received a 2007 MAP (Multi-Arts Production) Grant with Native Voices at the Autry for the development of *Salvage.* The play went on to be the featured production during the Oklahoma City Theatre Company's Native American New Play Festival in 2012.

A short play, *The Mask Maker,* was part of the 2013 Two Worlds Theater Staged Reading Festival in Albuquerque. Glancy also is one of 25 commissioned playwrights to write a Civil War monologue for Our War: Final Project at Arena Stage, in Washington, D.C.

She has published two collections of plays, American Gypsy, University of Oklahoma Press, 2002, and War Cries, Holy Cow! Press, 1996. Her work appears in several anthologies including Telling Stories Our Way and Seventh Generation Anthology. She also has a chapter, "Native Dramatic Theory in a Bird House," in Twenty First Perspectives on Indigenous Studies: Native North America in (Transmotion), edited by Birgit Daewes, Karsten Fitz and Sabine Meyers, Routledge, New York, 2015.

She was included in the TCG Blog Salon, Artistic Leadership: How We Change the Game, June, 2015. http://www.tcgcircle.org/2015/06/direct-the-light-of-reason

Glancy is professor emerita at Macalester College in St. Paul, Minnesota.

In 2009, Glancy received an Expressive Arts Grant from the National Museum of the American Indian to research another project, the 1875-78 Fort Marion prisoners. She wrote a play, *The Catch*, which she turned into a new book of nonfiction, Fort Marion Prisoners and the Trauma of Native, published by the University of Nebraska Press in 2014. She has a new poetry collection, Report to the Department of the Interior, University of New Mexico Press, 2015.

In 2014, Glancy received the Wordcraft Circle of Native Writers' Lifetime Achievement Award. She also is the recipient of the 2016 Arrell Gibson Lifetime Achievement Award from the Oklahoma Center for The Book.

**NOTES ON THE PLAY:**
Of *Salvage*, Glancy says, "I was traveling on Highway 2 in Montana researching Stone Heart, a play about Sacajawea and the 1804-06 Lewis & Clark expedition, when I passed a salvage yard, and the characters of *Salvage* got in my car.

They were quiet as I worked on Sacajawea, and when I was finished, they began to speak.

*Salvage* is about the swift and irrevocable change in the way of life.

TIME:
Present

SETTING:
Cut Bank, a small town off the Blackfeet reservation near Browning in northwestern Montana, where Blackfeet Salvage Yard lines the north side of Highway 2. The back of the stage is a corrugated fence. There are shells of old cars and other accoutrements of a salvage yard. There are table and chairs for the kitchen.

## SCENE 1

### THE HOUSE

(Early evening…Wolf enters, visibly shaken…)

WOLF: I have to talk to you, Meme.
MEMELA: What's up?
WOLF: Trouble.  Where're the boys?

MEMELA: Pasted to the computer screen with their video games. What did you do? You're hurt—

WOLF: I can hardly talk about it yet. I want you to keep out of it. I want to say, it's my business. I want to hide it from you.

MEMELA: Hide what, Wolf? —Other than that bruise on your arm—that lump on your forehead.

WOLF: Wolfert and I were riding, talking about the old days. My brothers—killed. My sister— dead. My mother, Phoebe—there now with the rest of them. I was looking at Wolfert—telling him he can't camp out in the cemetery. I worry about him choking up—The road was straight open—

MEMELA: I haven't heard your dad choke up.

WOLF: I could see several miles. Who needs to watch every minute? —I hit a car coming from the other way.

MEMELA: Who was driving?

WOLF: Me, of course. Do you think I would ride with Wolfert?

MEMELA: Who was driving the other car?

WOLF: A family farther west on Highway 2— toward Browning.

MEMELA: Where's Wolfert?

WOLF: In the Indian clinic.

MEMELA: Where're the others?

WOLF: In the clinic with Wolfert.

MEMELA: All of them?

WOLF: I think the father was released.

MEMELA: Who's still in the clinic with Wolfert?
WOLF: The wife. Two children.
MEMELA: What condition are they in?
WOLF: Serious and critical.
MEMELA: Which one is Wolfert?
WOLF: Serious.
MEMELA: I can't believe you weren't hurt.
WOLF: I'm a little beat up—my shoulder
hurts—

(Her hand on his shoulder with
concern...)

MEMELA: Who are they?
WOLF: No one I knew.
MEMELA: Are they from the rez?
WOLF: Yes.
MEMELA: What're their names?
WOLF: Stover.

(Her shoulders drop...she's silent a
moment...)

MEMELA: Are they related to William Stover?
WOLF: I don't know. His name is Harry Stover.
MEMELA: What were you thinking?
WOLF: It was an accident, Meme. I didn't let it
happen. It happened by itself. That's what an
accident is—I didn't plan it. I can't always
control what happens. Things aren't always
clear. I was listening to Wolfert—a car suddenly
in front of me—clipped me—we spun. It
crossed the center line—It wasn't my fault.

MEMELA: (MEMELA TRIES TO QUIET HIM)
Sssshuu. Sssshuu.

(Black out...)


## SCENE 2

### THE CLINIC

(Later that night...Memela and Wolf
visit Wolfert who is in bed. Memela
holds a Bible. There is the steady hiss of
an oxygen tank and the green waves of a
heart monitor behind Wolfert. He is
stunned from both the accident and the
medication.)

WOLFERT: She comes to me wearing an elk-
skin robe—carrying an elk-tail bag—an antler on
her chest—
WOLF: Dad—
WOLFERT: Phoebe—my old wife—a young
woman again.
MEMELA: Wolfert—
WOLFERT: She comes to the place where she
rose into the sky—
WOLF: The boys are here to see you too.
WOLFERT: Wolf calls me away.
WOLF: You got to live in the present, Dad.
They're all dead.
WOLFERT: Look, son, look out!!—

MEMELA: You were in a car accident, Wolfert.
WOLFERT: It's all been an accident. Our story is one long accident.
WOLF: Not all of it, Wolfert.
WOLFERT: I was talking to Winston—
WOLF: Uncle Winston's been dead a long time—
WOLFERT: Maybe to you, son—but not me.
WOLF: I only believe what I can see—

(Memela is looking at the waves of the heart monitor that now resemble the waves on a shore...)

MEMELA: There's a story in the Bible, Wolfert—I know you don't want to hear, but it's helped me—The disciples were in a boat in a storm. They were afraid. Jesus came walking across the water. Maybe there were flashes of lightning. He was a holy man, after all. They let him on the boat and they immediately were on the other side. Or I think of that feeling when the car tosses in a storm, and I know someone is there with us though I can't see. I felt someone on the road in Hector's Plymouth when he used to drive like wildfire.
WOLF: I got you out of Hector's Plymouth, didn't I? You're riding in my Plymouth now.
MEMELA: Your heart monitor looks like waves coming to the shore, Wolfert.

(She hands the Bible to Wolfert...)

This is the bread that comes from heaven.  If any
man eats this bread, he will live forever.
WOLFERT: I hated this book—This Bible—This
loaf of bread.

(Wolfert takes the Bible from Memela.
He tears out a page...)

WOLFERT: This is what I think of it.

(Black out...)


## SCENE 3

## THE CAR

(Evening...Wolf and Memela are driving
back from the clinic...)

WOLF: The sheriff used our tow truck to pull
the two wrecked cars to our salvage yard.
I stood by the cars trying to think of how it
happened.
MEMELA: I saw them curled around each other
like an embrace.
WOLF: There'll be no embrace from Harry
Stover.
MEMELA: William Stover and my father got
into an argument when he sold Stover a car. My
father didn't have papers. I remember them
yelling in the yard. William stalked him.
WOLF: There won't be any stalking.

MEMELA: You can't know that.

WOLF: You stayed with me through our bad times, Meme.

MEMELA: (NOT ACCUSATORY, BUT WITH COMPASSION) Your bad times.

> (Wolf puts his arm across the seat and rests his hand on Memela's shoulder...)

As soon as Wolfert is out of the clinic, he'll be in the cemetery again.

WOLF: If you were gone, Meme, I would come after you.

MEMELA: If I was gone, I would take the first falling star back.

> (Black out...)


## SCENE 4


### WOLFERT'S HOSPITAL ROOM

> (The middle of the night...Hospital sounds...Hiss of oxygen...Phoebe visits Wolfert...)

WOLFERT: You've got them all with you, Phoebe. All but Wolf our youngest, born when the others were grown. He used to Pow Wow beside me. I can still see him circling. I can't tell you what happened—though I think you know. You were there with me—shielding us. I didn't

tell them — They had enough trouble
understanding. Winston was there too. I've
dreamed of you beside me. You should see
Wolf's boys — One of them looks more and more
like Frank — who was starting to look like
Winston. The clinic's got medicine now for
fever. I wish I could say the same about
alcohol — though it's the accidents still getting
us. Sometimes I look at the constellations and
see the shape of cars. Have Winston take you
back — I don't want you crossing the stars by
yourself.

(Black out...)

## SCENE 5

### THE HOUSE

(Morning...The moon still visible in the
dawn sky...A few days later...Memela
hangs up the phone as Wolf enters
through the back door...)

WOLF: (RILED) Stover rammed the gate of
Blackfeet Salvage Yard — He pulled his wrecked
car to his house — The sheriff said it's parked in
front for everyone to see.
MEMELA: Harry Stover's wife is still critical.
One child, the daughter, is worse.
WOLF: I told the sheriff it wasn't my fault. They
said Harry Stover told them it wasn't his fault

he said I was the one who crossed center line —
but maybe it wasn't me —
MEMELA: What're you saying, Wolf?
WOLF: What if both cars crossed the line? What
if Harry Stover was looking at his wife — They
were talking about stopping for some rocky
road ice cream. What if they were arguing about
their financial problems?

(Memela turns her back to him...)

What if their kids were fighting and Harry
turned to straighten them out?
MEMELA: (SHE TURNS TO HIM ANGRILY) I
worked all my life to get out of the mess my
family made — To not look back — or ever be in
trouble again.
WOLF: I fought for you, Meme. Don't you
remember Hector jumped me — drinking from
the hose after the dodge ball game? But I beat
his tail lights. It was you who did the dodging.

(Memela hears something, crosses to the
kitchen window...)

MEMELA: They're out there again, Wolf. I see a
car — it stops — then it drives off. Sometimes I
think someone is following me. The boys said
someone followed them.
WOLF: From now on, tell the boys to be in
before dark. Take the dogs with you.
MEMELA: Muffler and Tail Pipe? They're used
to the salvage yard. They'd tear up my car.

WOLF: I want them with you.

MEMELA: Will they sit at a school desk?

(Wolf goes out the back door. Memela
looks after him. She stands at the kitchen
window by herself...)

MEMELA: There's a moon in the sky, Wolf—
torn in half. The other half is discarded, torn
away. There's a little, ragged edge on the half
moon where the other half was torn.

(Black out...)

## SCENE 6

### THE HOUSE

(A few days later. Memela and Wolfert
sit at the table. Wolfert is still on oxygen;
the small tank hisses. Memela reads
through her lesson. Wolf enters with
bad news to deliver...but stops to listen
to Memela...)

MEMELA: DeSoto landed in Florida in 1539 and
traveled as far as the Mississippi River. He
thought the Pacific coast was just beyond the
river. DeSoto caught fever and died. Dona
Isabella, his wife, died from sorrow after his
death.

WOLF: Would you die from sorrow at my death?

MEMELA: You planning on dying this afternoon? DeSoto hoped for a trade route to China—imagine his disappointment.

WOLF: Why're we in grade school here?

MEMELA: The principal comes around this time of year and sits in back of the class. I'm just practicing.

WOLFERT: I feel like I'm looking for China—

MEMELA: You still got spirits coming out your ears?

WOLF: They call them hallucinations—You had a reaction to your medicine.

MEMELA: (PUZZLING OVER HER QUESTION) Should we go to the clinic and visit the Stover's?

WOLF: No.

WOLFERT: No.

WOLF: The sheriff won't make Stover remove the wrecked car from the front of his place.

MEMELA: Over the black waves—they let Jesus in the boat—immediately they were on the other side.

WOLF: It may take a while for us to get to the other side of this. Harry Stover's wife got worse. She died last night.

(Black out...)

## SCENE 7

## THE HOUSE

(Afternoon….the day of Stover's wife's funeral…)

MEMELA: (AT THE WINDOW INCREDULOUS) Mrs. Stover's funeral—today.
WOLFERT: (ASSURING HER) Relatives and friends are with us. Nothing'll happen.
WOLF: Fred. Butania. Uncle Winston's second wife—nephews, nieces—Where's Frances?
MEMELA: She's subbing for me at school.

(The phone rings…)

WOLF: Uncle Butte, his two girlfriends. Cousins Grover, Cleveland, Hoover.
MEMELA: Hello. Hello? They hung up.
WOLF!!! They're calling on the phone—They'll be coming into our house—
WOLF: How do you know it was them?
MEMELA: The phone rings. It stops. It rings again.
WOLF: Unplug the phone. Turn the cell phones on vibrate.
MEMELA: What have you opened, Wolf?—The unending revenge of the Stover family? What's this head-on wreck we've gotten into?—This side-swipe of vehicles that carries us where?—Where?

WOLF: Here, Meme—That's where. I could tear out of here— I could be out looking for auto parts—I could be scouting for the shells of old cars—but I'm here. It'll pass—For us it was an accident. For them, it was intentional.

MEMELA: Not us, Wolf, but YOU. YOU were driving when you hit the Stover's. YOU should have just driven into our house and torn it down on purpose. YOU ripped up our lives—that was never going to happen again—

WOLF: I didn't drive into their car by choice, Meme.

MEMELA: Someone held your hand on the wheel?—Some bad spirit took possession? I want to leave the house—but I'm afraid the Stover's will be there to follow me. I can't go outside.

WOLF: Be quiet—NOW!!

WOLFERT: In boarding school, we swallowed our bread like stones.

MEMELA: I worked forever to make this solid place—this Plymouth Rock—It's something you always had.

WOLFERT: Am I in a dream?

WOLF: No, Dad, you were in an accident—an accident caused by your son. Is that what you want to hear, Memela? Your husband made a terrible mistake. For one moment HE TOOK HIS EYES OFF THE ROAD. He caused an ACCIDENT and KILLED someone—

MEMELA: Not just someone—the Stover family.

WOLF: Who would you rather I hit?

MEMELA: Someone not as vindictive.

WOLF: What do you mean?
MEMELA: I had a dog.

(She shakes her head…doesn't answer
Wolf…)

We should keep Muffler and Tailpipe in the
garage at night.
WOLFERT: I hear thunder.
WOLF: My phone's buzzing on my leg. It's
technology Dad—not the ancestors. What do
they want?
MEMELA: Revenge—Wolf, his wife is dead—
You injured his children—Injured your father
and got yourself in trouble. You have a court
hearing. You'll have to pay for the Stover's
injuries as well as your father's.
WOLF: Stay out of this, Meme.
MEMELA: How can I? I'm your wife. They'll
come after us. They'll come after everything we
have. They'll take our wages. Yours and mine.
I'll have to get my clothes from the church barrel
again. We could lose Blackfeet Salvage Yard to
pay for their medical bills. Of course, they didn't
have insurance. Your accident affects my
teaching job—I'm the wife of someone in
trouble. The boys ask what's going to happen.
Wolf, you jump in your sleep. It startles me
awake—
WOLF: You got to back off.
MEMELA: I think you've got to go forward. Get
your foot off the brake. We have to deal with
this now. Call Stover. Meet with him—

WOLF: (INTERRUPTS) Where's your blessed
Savior?
MEMELA: (CONTINUES HER THOUGHT)
Wolfert could have a healing ceremony.
Otherwise, we'll come to nothing—
WOLFERT: Well—We could live in Winston's
old van—
MEMELA: It doesn't run.
WOLFERT: Our ancestors lived in tepees
covered with snow on open land.
WOLF: Would you live with me in a tepee?
MELEMA: That open land is sectioned off.
Owned by others.
WOLF: You didn't answer—
MEMELA: (HE KISSES HER SHOULDER)
We're two sides of the same moon, Wolf.

(Black out...)


## SCENE 8


## THE HOUSE

(Morning... A few days later. Wolfert is
at the window, steadier now. He holds a
rifle. Wolf sits at the kitchen table.
Memela enters, startled that Wolfert has
a rifle...)

WOLFERT: Someone let loose with a can of
spray-paint.

WOLF: They spray-painted KILLER on the corrugated fence at Blackfeet Salvage Yard while we were gone. They'll hunt us down. They'll wait for the sheriff to be asleep. They'll wait until we're off guard. These reservation wars— Us against us.

WOLFERT: We're on guard. We have to be. Harry Stover may be planning an attack. If we could see the danger, we would be terrified. First, the bow and arrow—then the rocket-propelled grenade—then the ballistic missile. You got in Stover's way, Wolf. You gave them a cause—Harry Stover and family—We have stepped into something not ours.

MEMELA: We stepped into a religion that settles our conflicts. We have to think about forgiveness. Wolfert's got his gun. I've got boys in the house.

WOLF: Memela's got her Savior. Her lightning in the storm. They killed in the name of their God—

MEMELA: —Who has become our God?

WOLF: Not all of us.

MEMELA: But mine. But mine.

WOLFERT: We are explorers—trying to find a way through this.

WOLF: Harry Stover taunts me.

MEMELA: The sheriff will stop you in a minute if you even look at him.

WOLF: He hasn't arrested me yet—

WOLFERT: Did Hernando DeSoto get arrested for what he did?—Did any of them?

    (Black out...)

## SCENE 9

## THE CEMETERY

(Night…Wolfert talks to his dead wife…)

WOLFERT: Phoebe my wife, Phoebe—Now the stars look like used auto parts. Are the heavens a salvage yard? Is that what we are? The boys computerized the inventory—the makes of cars—the parts available. I hear them at the keyboard. I peck also. It sounds like old motors trying to turn over. The sky is an internet—full of communication—Order after order for fender, door, grille, piston, tie rod, wheel bearing, tail light—parts for rebuilding—for restoration. Our salvage yard is a landing zone. I know you don't like me with a gun, but I carry one now. I don't want you to leave, but I know you have to go, Phoebe. No one wants to stay—once they've been in the heavens.

(Black out…)

## SCENE 10

## THE HOUSE

(Day…MEMELA has a bucket…)

WOLF: What are you doing, Meme?

MEMELA: The other teachers look at me in school. People look at me at the grocer's. They look at me in church. KILLER is STILL WRITTEN on the salvage yard fence!! Now I find someone wrote, WHO IS THE before KILLER and added a question mark. I'm sure it was the boys—I hope it wasn't you.
WOLF: Stay out of it, Meme. Keep them out of it too.
MEMELA: You're not doing anything.
WOLF: It's not going to wash off. Wolfert's going to paint over it.
MEMELA: I am tired of goodness. I got used to war as a child. I would get run-over if I didn't stand up for myself. I want to lift the fish-fins from that old Dodge in the salvage yard and slam them against the fence. (SHE SLAMS THE BUCKET ON THE FLOOR)

(Black out...)


## SCENE 11


## THE TOW TRUCK

(Day...Wolf and Wolfert are driving...)

WOLF: Another accident near Browning.
WOLFERT: You know what we're going to find—A tow-truck could have come from Browning.

WOLF: (IGNORING HIS FATHER) It's that jack-knife curve. Kids think they can make it without slowing.

WOLFERT: The jack-knife is only there if you're going fast enough—Another white cross by the road.

WOLF: Look at that new Hoop Bark fence.

WOLFERT: It's the Swafford's place.

WOLF: Look, Dad—(POINTING AHEAD) There it is—the Stover's house Look at his wrecked car in the yard!!—The one we hit—He parked it right against the highway—Just like we heard.

WOLFERT: Shit.

WOLF: They got OUR NAME painted on it, Dad.

WOLFERT: I told you to let Browning handle it.

(Wolf nearly swerves off the road...)

WOLFERT: STEADY, Wolf.

(Wolfert reaches over to keep the steering wheel straight...)

We got to pick up a wrecked car—not have another accident ourselves.

WOLF: Damn it! I'm going to turn around. Go back and get him.

(Wolf hits the steering wheel of the tow truck...)

Fuck—They can't leave our name on the road.

(Wolf pounds the steering wheel in
rage…)

What am I going to do, Dad?
WOLFERT: Pull over, son. You got a court date
coming up—Don't make it worse.
WOLF: The docket is full of rez wars.
I want to tear his head off.
WOLFERT: Get off the road. You got to cool
down. NOW!!
WOLF: Are you going to start talking to the
dead? Are you going off in space?
WOLFERT: I'm here, Wolf. I'm here.

(They stop by the road – Wolf rocks back
and forth, eating his anger…Wolfert
does not release his grip on his son…)

(Black out…)


## SCENE 12


## THE HOUSE

(Day. Wolf, Memela, and Wolfert…
Wolfert cleans his gun…)

WOLF: Sometimes when I was a boy, there was
no food—Wolfert would hunt. The venison

would be so stringy and tough, and the greens and bark my mother boiled so bitter and coarse, we could hardly eat. But then she would have somehow made custard—or a form of it—from some sort of commodity milk who knows how she did it.

WOLFERT: I didn't ask.

WOLF: Why were you a poor hunter?

WOLFERT: I just couldn't get a feel for it. I would aim at the deer, and the sapling next to it would fall over.

WOLF: You should have aimed at the sapling and maybe the deer would have fallen.

MEMELA: Maybe you should have aimed for Stover's car and then you would have dodged it.

WOLF: (TAKEN ABACK FOR A MOMENT) There's a difference of opinion that can't be reconciled. I'm riled. I feel like I got a furnace in me. There's no thermostat. I can't turn it down. What if Stover hurts you, Meme?

MEMELA: I think sometimes in the night, I hear someone in the yard.

WOLF: (ANGRY) Wake me, Meme.

MEMELA: I don't want you going out there.

WOLF: What I do is not your decision. I feel like I'm walking on fire. I feel like I'm touching flames.

WOLFERT: You got to get outside this world, Wolf. Let's go sit in the old Dodge—

WOLF: It's got 175,000 miles on it—

MEMELA: Nearly the distance to the moon.

WOLFERT: Look to the old ways, Wolf—

WOLF: (REFUTING HIS FATHER) Tradition is
a salvage yard.
WOLFERT: Let the spirit world bring you back
to yourself.

> (They speak a few syllables in the old
> language)

The brush beyond the boulder off Hibbard
Road—
WOLF: (NODS HIS HEAD) Where I killed my
first deer.
WOLFERT: Three miles off Highway 2 on the
old Browning Road.
WOLF: (NODS) Where you found the first car
you sold as salvage.
WOLFERT: It was the old ways—gave us the
idea for the salvage yard.
WOLF: (JERKING AWAY FROM WOLFERT)
I'm not floating into the past. My breath itches.
I got to beat the walls. I got to throw rocks
against the corrugated fence of the salvage yard.

> (Black out...)

## SCENE 13

### THE CAR

> (Night...Memela is alone on the road...)

MEMELA: Those headlights are blinding. Why
are they following so close? What are you

doing? Where are the dogs when I need them?
Where's the phone. Jesus. Wolf—you never
have your cell phone with you. You've
unplugged the phone at the house—the boys
might answer anyway.

(The car BUMPS hers...she cries
out...reaches for her cell phone, dials...)

911? (FRANTIC) A car is following me. It's
Memela—Wolf's wife—You know—Millie— it's
me!!!! Send the sheriff—Get Wolf for me. I don't
know where I am. Now the car is passing. I
don't know what mile marker. Highway 2.
They're ahead of me now—going slow— they're
almost stopped. I AM CALM. I am passing—
now they are BEHIND ME AGAIN!!

(BUMP...she cries out again when the
car hits hers...)

Get away from me. SEND SOMEONE!! Wait—
a mailbox is ahead—Jacobs—

(BUMP...she cries out again...)

Hello—Hello?—

(She tries to dial again...drops the
phone. She feels for it on the floorboard,
but can't find it. The car passes again...)

Where's a paper and pencil—

(She digs in her purse. The pencil pokes holes in the paper. The car nearly stops again. MEMELA passes...then it passes her...)

THE CAR'S BESIDE ME—GET OVER!! YOU'RE RUNNING ME OFF THE ROAD!!

(Memela is driving on the side of the road... the tire explodes...she wobbles to a halt, sobbing...soon she sees the red lights of the sheriff pull up behind her)

The sheriff!!—He's pulling up behind me?— how can he be so stupid? Get them—GET THEM—NOT ME!!

(Memela huddles in the car. Wolf and Wolfert drive up. Wolfert has a rifle. The sheriff drives off. Wolf pulls Memela out of the car. She's still frantic...)

I couldn't get the license number—
WOLFERT: (LOOKING UP, HE WHISPERS) Phoebe?—
MEMELA: (CRYING IN FRUSTRATION) 9-72— no—9-27—
WOLF: It's all right, Meme—Was it the same car you've seen?
MEMELA: (SOBBING AGAIN) I don't know— It's dark—It was a blur. The car was covered with dirt—

WOLF: (HE WORKS TO QUIET HER) Sssssssh.
Sssssh.

MEMELA: 7-29—

WOLF: (HE HOLDS HER) Let it go, Meme. I couldn't remember either. Come back to me—I counted the buttons on your cardigan once. 10. 9. 8. 7—I can't remember how many. I'm here with you now. No one else.

(Black out...)


## SCENE 14

## THE CEMETERY

(Night...Wolfert talks to his dead wife...)

WOLFERT: You were on the road with Meme. You left as we arrived. Why didn't you stay? Phoebe—What is happening? Did a space ship land? Did it suck us up and carry us away to a distant place? What world is this? Do we sit and receive it like bread?

(Black out...)


## SCENE 15

## THE HOUSE

(Day...Memela, Wolf, Wolfert...)

MEMELA: Wolfert found the boys posting messages on the web—

WOLF: I remember when I thought he heard messages from space on the aerials of the old cars in the salvage yard. Now he's an internet whiz. Maybe he can tell us the outcome of the court hearing tomorrow.

WOLFERT: The boys' messages were to the Stover's.

WOLF: (ALARMED) We can't let the boys get into this too—

MEMELA: They're already in it—The messages were threatening. The boys can only leave the house to go to school. The relatives will camp out at our house if we need them. Who knows if another Stover will take up the cause.

WOLF: Did you say the car that followed you was covered with dirt?—

(Memela turns to him, alarmed...)

I heard the boys talking about a car they called, the mud ball—

MEMELA: He's following them too—

WOLF: I'll take the boys to school. I'm going to follow you also.

WOLFERT: Our war has moved into cyberspace—It copies the way the spirits work. In the old days, we could send a thought to someone far away. We could read the stories in the wind. We could send a curse and someone would be sick.

MEMELA: When Hernando DeSoto died, his men bound him with stones, and buried him in the river. They feared the Indians would know their leader was dead—and attack.
WOLF: What're you talking about, Memela?
MEMELA: I'm reviewing my lesson plan.
I tied stones around the past. I was going to bury everything—but I feel it breaking loose.

(Black out...)


## SCENE 16

## THE CAR

(Day...Wolf, Memela and Wolfert on the way home from the courthouse...)

WOLF: It's going to be all right, Meme.
WOLFERT: (HAS HIS HAND ON WOLF'S SHOULDER) Charges against you were dismissed. The investigation was incomplete.
WOLF: Inconclusive—old man. My car crossed the center line more than his.
MEMELA: Harry Stover was furious. I saw his anguish.
WOLF: He saw mine when I talked about the night you were followed on Highway 2.
WOLFERT: (PATS MEMELA ON THE SHOULDER, KEEPS HIS HAND THERE) The judge told Stover to stay away from our place. He warned him against following us.

MEMELA: It's starting to snow. I hope the boys take care on their way home. The reservation is dressed in a white cardigan—with pearl buttons—

WOLF: (PULLS MEMELA TO HIM IN THE FRONT SEAT, BRUSHING WOLFERT'S HAND OFF MEMELA'S SHOULDER) You wore a sweater the first time I asked you out. "What's that called," —I asked—"a sweater that buttons up the front?"—

MEMELA: "A cardigan." Sometimes I actually found clothes I liked in the barrel at church.

WOLF: I knew you would keep it buttoned to the neck. "I like your brown cardigan," I said. "It's maroon," you answered. Thus, began my lesson in the slight variations of color.

> (Looks in the rear-view mirror…pushes Memela away…)

Put on your seat belt, Meme.

MEMELA: Why?

WOLF: Just do it.

WOLFERT: (TURNING AROUND) Oh, shit.

> (The sound of a car. Wolf looks in the rear-view mirror at the four-way stop in Cut Bank…)

It's Harry Stover—

(Wolf starts to get out of the car...
Memela and Wolfert put their hands on
him to stop him...)

MEMELA: Wolf—you'll start a fight.
WOLFERT: Hold on, Wolf. Keep your head—
Harry's trying to get you riled.
WOLF: (JUMPING OUT OF THE CAR,
YELLING) You follow my wife to the grade
school where she teaches. You follow my boys
to high school. You came up behind her on the
highway at night. GET AWAY FROM US!!!
Yeah—I crossed the center line. I ran into your
car. I injured your family. I crippled your
children and filled them with terror—but you
keep coming like the 7th cavalry.

(Black out...)


## SCENE 17

### THE HOUSE

(Night...Wolf, Wolfert,
Memela...Memela stands in the
moonlight at the kitchen window. Wolf
enters. He stands beside her. He moves
her hair and kisses the back of her
neck...)

MEMELA: I hear something, Wolf.
WOLF: The wind.

MEMELA: I thought I heard the dogs.
WOLF: They're barking at rabbits.

> (A dim light goes on in the hallway.
> Wolfert enters with his rifle and nearly
> trips over something...He groans...)

WOLFERT: Oh, for crying out loud!
WOLF: What are you doing, dad? You got the gun?
MEMELA: The boys all right?
WOLFERT: They're asleep.
MEMELA: Wolfert will kill us if he trips again—
WOLFERT: The dogs were barking. Then they were quiet.
WOLF: That's what they're supposed to do.
MEMELA: Go with him, Wolf. Get him out of the house.

> (The men leave. There are noises.
> Memela goes to the door in the dark.
> Wolfert is whimpering. Wolf comes in,
> nearly bumps into Memela. He covers
> her mouth with his hand...)

WOLF: Don't scream. The dogs are dead.
Someone left them at the back door. Wolfert
slipped in the blood. Help me get him in.

> (They pull Wolfert in the door...)

WOLF: Don't wake the boys. They'll see the
dogs. Get Wolfert's shoes off, Meme. He'll

track blood in the house. I'm going to bury the dogs. Keep Wolfert here.

MEMELA: Don't leave me, Wolf.

(Wolfert is sobbing. Memela holds him...)

WOLF: The boys can't see those dogs.

MEMELA: (STIFLING HER FURY) STOVER!!!

(Black out...)


## SCENE 18

### THE CEMETERY

(Dawn...Wolfert limps into the cemetery. He talks to Phoebe...)

WOLFERT: They're walking toward you now, Phoebe. If you look up, you should see them coming over the cloud bank. Muffler is the one that sounds like he's backfiring when he barks. Tail Pipe's always been thin as the center line on Highway 2. Wolf buried them with their noses to the east. I offered tobacco to the Maker for their journey. We've had them since Wolf found someone living in an old car in the back of the salvage yard. Take your elk-sinew, Phoebe. Sew up their throats that were slit.

(Black out...)

## SCENE 19

## THE HOUSE

(Morning…Several days later…Wolf
looks from the kitchen window.  Memela
stands beside him. Wolfert sits at the
table with a hand-full of order forms…)

WOLF: I called the sheriff about the dogs.
WOLFERT: He did nothing.
MEMELA: He was at the accident, Wolf. He saw
what you did to the Stover's.
WOLF: You've got it wrapped up, Meme—An
eye for an eye.
MEMELA: (SHE CALLS OUT) Boys!!  Let's go!!
Your father has to catch up on his orders.
WOLFERT: Losing the dogs makes me think of
the soldiers killing our buffalo.

(Black out…)

## SCENE 20

## THE SALVAGE YARD

(Night…A fire burns in a barrel. Wolf
and Wolfert…Wolfert is making a drum
from an air filter from the salvage yard.
His rifle is by his side…)

WOLF: What're you doing, Dad?

142

WOLFERT: Making a drum.

WOLF: (IMPATIENT) What will that do? You think it'll help?

WOLFERT: In boarding school, one of the teachers was mean. They were all mean—but this one was meaner. We didn't like any of the teachers, but we hated him. Then we knew he was sick. He walked bent over. He turned yellow around the mouth. We heard him vomit. At night he howled. When we first knew he was sick, we were glad. It kept him away from us. He deserved to suffer. It was what he had caused us. But in chapel, they had us pray for him and something broke in me. Somehow, I found compassion. Winston did too. We took a wooden bowl from the kitchen. We stretched a deer skin across the top of it and secured it with sinew. We sat in his room singing and drumming. Not loud. You hardly knew we were there. But it filled the room with a sense of presence. Anything was bearable because of the drum. Sometimes he opened a crusted eye to see who was there. Maybe he hoped we would shove a knife into him and relieve him of his suffering. But we sang. I think he rose to his heaven on the road of our song. Somebody that sick is going to die, Wolf. Someone that full of rage—the bile is going to get him.

WOLF: You helped him die.

(Wolfert lifts his rifle. Wolf pushes it down)

No pot shots. They'd scare Memela. The boys were shooting cars in the salvage yard—she broke down crying.

(Short pause...)

You think he wants to die?
WOLFERT: There wasn't any clinic. Nothing would save him—
WOLF: I mean Harry.
WOLFERT: It was what I had to do.
WOLF: I think Harry's asking for it—

(Black out...)

## SCENE 21

A FIELD BETWEEN THE HOUSE AND THE
SALVAGE YARD

(Night...Wolf hears a noise in the yard. He picks up the rifle and leaves...)

WOLF: He must watch our house from here.

(Wolf hunkers down...)

Harry—I hear you there in the grass. What are you doing? Scaring a woman and two boys? I could kill you. You got my name painted on your car for everyone to see. But I'm throwing down my rifle.

(Wolf places his rifle on the ground…)

Let's talk. Someone's going to get hurt. I smell the alcohol. My wife says I have to forgive—we have to forgive—Don't push me. Stop!! I couldn't help it, Harry. STOP!!! I can't hit you again.

(Black out…)


## SCENE 22


### THE HOUSE

(Night. Memela and Wolfert wait. Wolf enters…)

MEMELA: Thank God.
WOLF: Memela, I have to talk to you.
MEMELA: What now?
WOLF: I tried your way. I tried to forgive. I found Harry Stover between the salvage yard and the house. He wouldn't leave. I tried to talk. I tried to stop him—We wrestled. He held me down—I got the upper hand—Hit. Hit. I held him down— strangled—I stumbled away. He stayed on the ground—I didn't mean to. He came after me—

(Wolfert nods in agreement…)

I think another man rose to his heaven by my
hand—

> (Wolfert lays his hands on Wolf's
> shoulders. They stand together silently
> for a moment…)

MEMELA: The sheriff will have to come after
you now.  What will I do without you?  How
will I get into our bed by myself?
WOLF: I should turn myself in.  If I don't, it'll be
worse.

> (Wolfert nods…)

MEMELA: I can get up in the morning, go to
work, stay in the classroom all day with lesson
plans and construction paper.  I can fix supper
for Wolfert and the boys.  But it's still you, Wolf,
I want to be with.
WOLF: It's you Harry Stover came after on the
highway.  It was not all my fault—
WOLFERT: He won't come again.
WOLF: I'm going to call the sheriff to come and
get me.

> (Wolfert agrees…)

MEMELA: No, Wolf. NO!!!
WOLF: I have to, Meme. You know what I have
to do.

> (They embrace…)

WOLFERT: Everything turns on its side.

MEMELA: (ANGRILY TO WOLFERT) This is not the other side I wanted to be on.

WOLFERT: I see the accident in my sleep. I see Mrs. Stover step into the other world from a white field of snow.

MEMELA: We've torn ourselves in half.

WOLF: Ask Mrs. Stover for her version of the accident in one of your visions in the cemetery, Wolfert.

WOLFERT: She won't talk to me.

(Black out...)


## SCENE 23


### THE HOUSE

(Next day...Memela and Wolfert. Memela folds laundry. The boy's t-shirts have logos of basketball and the internet...)

MEMELA: I was going to get as far away from my family as possible. I was going to discover normal life. Do you know what it's like to be a child with nothing to hold onto riding in the backseat of a car driving wildly on a road? Do you know how many times I felt that way? They all went wild.

WOLFERT: Not Frances, your sister. Look at your boys—still interested in school.

MEMELA: Do you think the school will let Frances teach? Do you think they will let me? I had the Stover boy in my class two years ago. I recognized the name. I thought it was a different Stover. I looked on the chart. The girl will be in my class next year. Do you think the Stover family will let that happen?

WOLFERT: Their house in Cut Bank is empty. The boy is with relatives someplace else. The girl is still in the clinic. The sheriff pulled the Stover's wrecked car back to our salvage yard. The boys painted over our name.

MEMELA: The Stover's are not going to disappear. There is no more court hearing. Now we have a trial.

WOLFERT: I dreamed—

MEMELA: (PLEADING) Get over it, Wolfert.

WOLFERT: I saw a woman on the ground. I reached down, but my hand was a rag—the kind you see waving on a fence. The woman took my hand like a handle—She looked at me with horror—like I had the face of a bad spirit. What was she seeing? The land was all dream-like—its edge lit to pure white—then it grew dim.

(He chokes up...)

It wasn't the land that changed color, only the way it was perceived.

MEMELA: I've never heard you choke up.

WOLFERT: The woman on the ground was you, Memela. If Wolf could make some sort of restitution to the family —

MEMELA: NO! Not now — those Stover's — those trouble-causers, those DOG-KILLERS!!

WOLFERT: It's our tradition, Meme.

MEMELA: My tradition is supposed to be forgiveness — When I was a girl, a neighbor took me to church. I heard something there. In all the noise and upheaval at my house, something stuck. There was a small voice I've carried with me. That night on the road when Stover followed me — I saw someone — a Savior dressed in animal skin wearing string lights —

WOLFERT: I thought I saw Phoebe.

MEMELA: (IGNORING WOLFERT) I have shown my wounds to Christ — the wounds I hid from Wolf. How could he remove the life I made? How could he wreck everything?

WOLFERT: He didn't mean to —

MEMELA: (WITH A FLASH OF ANGER) Yes, protect him like you always have.

WOLFERT: He's the only one I have left.

MEMELA: I have to make supper. The boys'll be home soon. What's this on the table?

WOLFERT: Some car parts I was cleaning before I sent them out. I had orders for them today.

MEMELA: Clean them someplace else. Do it at your house in the salvage yard. You bring your junk in here — You and Wolf — you tear up my place. I can't see what I'm doing for these hubcaps and carburetors. These manifold blessings from God —

(Memela flings them across the room in a
fit of anger. Wolfert grabs her and tries to
hold her, but she beats her arms against
him... soon she grows calmer. Wolfert
holds Memela as she cries against him...)

MEMELA:  Dad.

(Black out...)

## SCENE 24

### THE CEMETERY

(Night...The moon is full. WOLFERT
talks to his dead wife...)

WOLFERT: I'm going to go back to our house in
the salvage yard, Phoebe—As soon as I can face
it without you. Wolf and Memela keep me in
their house because they think I spend too much
time in outer space. They think I need to be
watched. How can they know what it's like
when they haven't been? They don't know it's
the voice of the ancestors I hear. Don't tell them
what the earth is like now. They would be filled
with grief. They would melt with rage. I'm in
the way.  Even with Wolf in jail. He can't hear
the past I hear. Visit him in his dreams. Bring
Winston. Wolf's sentencing is ahead. Phoebe—
Sing us the old songs.

(Black out...)

## SCENE 25

### COUNTY JAIL

(Early morning...Memela and Wolfert
visit Wolf. The bars on the window of
the jail cast shadows similar to the grilles
on the old cars in the salvage yard...)

MEMELA: Wolfert and I placed a cross on the
road where the accident happened.
WOLFERT: You placed a white cross—
MEMELA: The scarred place was there—the
land remembers—it still carries the thump of the
impact—
WOLFERT: One of the Stover family called.
They took that cross down. It wasn't their way,
they said. It wasn't mine either, I said.
MEMELA: The spirits come around at night—
putting that cross back.
WOLFERT: Harry Stover's daughter left the
Indian clinic—she went to live with a relative—
her brother's there too—
WOLF: I killed their parents. I still hear Mrs.
Stover stuttering to her children. After the
accident I went to their car—
WOLFERT: The boys said we should go into the
scrap metal business. That's where the money
is—once we know what we have to pay to the
Stover children—
WOLF: No—I don't want to see those old cars
crushed—I used to sit in the cars in the salvage
yard and pretend I was driving. I used to

wonder who drove them—What kind of accident they had—who they hit—and why. Who died? Who lived? Insurance and culpability—accomplice to another's suffering never occurred to me. You know, Dad, sometimes I think about the salvage yard. I hear the voices of the cars behind the corrugated fence. An old car remembers where it's been. An old car remembers who drove it. An old car longs for the road again. I want to say, we run a prison at Blackfeet Salvage Yard. Open the gates. Let them all go free.

(Black out...)

## SCENE 26

### LOBBY OF THE COURTHOUSE

(Day...Wolfert finds Memela...)

WOLFERT: Wolf's sentencing was a banger, Meem.
MEMELA: I couldn't stay in there. Where are the relatives?—
WOLFERT: They're back home holding a ceremony for Wolf. It looked like the Stover family came from around the world—There were more relatives than it looked possible to have—all teary and crying and weeping and saying what a pity Harry and his wife were murdered—leaving two broken children—the

boy—and the girl who limped into the court room on crutches. Did Wolf have a chance? We will be responsible for their medical bills—and whatever rehabilitation it takes—(hesitates to tell her) Wolf got the full 12 years for involuntary manslaughter.

(Memela collapses…)

I give you the rag of my hand—just like my dream.

(Black out…)


## SCENE 27

### MONTANA STATE PRISON

(Day… Memela faces Wolf…)

MEMELA: Here I am on the other side—We crossed from the county jail to Montana State Prison. What did a man do in the old days when he killed another?
WOLF: If a man killed another man's wife, he gave him his own wife.
MEMELA: You killed the man too—as well as his wife. Don't you read the newspaper? It's supposed to be people different from one another who are fighting—Muslims, Christians, Jews. The terrorists from other places. We're fighting our own kind.

WOLF: Wolfert brought the boys. I didn't know what to say—I never meant—I'm sorry—I was—I was—

(Nearly stutters as he tries to apologize...)

MEMELA: (RISES FROM THE CHAIR AND BACKS AWAY FROM WOLF) I taped the page Wolfert ripped from my Bible—I did not come to bring peace, but a sword. Matthew 10:34. I am in the right religion. I choose to believe—though I don't understand—What kind of God is this? I can't stay with you, Wolf. I have to leave.

WOLF: You can't do that, Meme.

MEMELA: Love was a box I hadn't opened. I should have left it wrapped, but there was something about the ribbon that made me want to pull it. I opened the box—I folded up the paper, and rolled the ribbon in a coil, and put them in the box— but the box opened and the ribbon crawled out.

WOLF: I never know what you're talking about—

MEMELA: I will visit you—Wolf—I've got the boys to worry about. They'll be marked by what's happened. The school won't renew my teaching contract.

WOLF: You don't know that yet.

MEMELA: I can't live in a house where a man was murdered in the yard outside my kitchen-window.

WOLF: Where would you go?

MEMELA: —Frances.'

WOLF: Your sister doesn't have room for herself in that house. The boys are in school. They don't want to go someplace else—

MEMELA: I will tell them to get over it. I have to take care of them.

WOLF: You don't have any place to go, Meme. Stay in the house.

MEMELA: No.

WOLF: The Stover's will line up every time I'm up for parole—You think Butania has room? Do you think Cousin Hoover would take you?—

(Memela starts to leave...)

Where's your song about forgiveness? Can't you hear your own words? It's you who can't cross to the other side. (CALLS AFTER TO HER WHEN SHE'S GONE) Meme—(PAUSE) Memela—

(Black out...)


## SCENE 28


### THE HOUSE


(Night...Memela sits with her Bible...)

MEMELA: What is this religion I believe? What has it turned into? I open this Bible. The pages feel soft as a dog's ear between my fingers. What is it tonight? (WITH SARCASM) John 3:14— As Moses lifted up the serpent in the wilderness, even so must the Son of man be lifted up. What does that mean? What is it like to be lifted on a cross like a serpent? What little cramped heart can believe that? Look at you peering at us from your cross—Do you take only the hurt ones on your war path? Christ—I am bitten by your love.

(Black out...)

## SCENE 29

### THE HOUSE

(Day...Wolfert and Memela...Memela is packing some dishes to take with her...)

WOLFERT: You can't leave him, Memela. What if I went to the cemetery and Phoebe wasn't there?
MEMELA: Don't do this, Wolfert

(Memela turns from Wolfert...)

WOLFERT: He needs you now—
MEMELA: (IGNORING WOLFERT) I saw Wolf fight Hector. Someone wanted to be with me.

(She turns back to Wolfert...)

MEMELA: When I wanted Wolf's attention, I talked to Hector. I brought Wolf to my house—I showed him to my dad. I was not the unloved one who would never have a father's attention. I couldn't be in a family again, but I married Wolf—My jaw quivering as I said the vows. I saw you and Phoebe together. Wolf might not know what it was to hurt someone. But he did.

WOLFERT: Leaving Wolf is against everything you believe.

MEMELA: The boys came right away. Phoebe helped me with them. I was in school. I wanted to teach. There was a teacher who told me I could. We lived with you, Wolfert. Do you know how important that was to me? Phoebe taught me how to talk to the boys—to listen to their words before they could even talk. I could be a parent. I learned that from you and Phoebe.

WOLFERT: I'm moving back to our house in the salvage yard.

MEMELA: It's a shack. You can't stay there.

WOLFERT: It's where my life was. You stay here, Memela, in this house. You don't have any where else to go.

MEMELA: Yes, I do, Wolfert. I can apply for teaching jobs other places where they don't know what's happened.

WOLFERT: The boys belong here—on this land.

MEMELA: The boys live in cyber space. It goes where they go—just like the old ways.

(Black out...)

# SCENE 30

## MONTANA STATE PRISON

(Day...Wolfert visits Wolf...)

WOLF: Talk to her, Dad.

WOLFERT: I passed a family on the street in Browning with a lot of children. One little girl was walking behind the others. She was crying. No one wiped her tears. No one showed concern for her. I thought of one hurt piled on top of another. I looked down and saw Memela as a girl. I think Meme had wounds you never felt. Maybe you'll learn compassion.

WOLF: Maybe our wounds will embrace on the other side of this. Maybe I will know the boys again.

WOLFERT: Maybe you could listen to what Memela says—

WOLF: (INTERRUPTING) I can't tell what's real anymore. Lift me from here—I've seen it in a movie. A helicopter lands in a prison yard. The prisoner runs out, gets in, and rises into the air. I want a space ship to land. I want to take their stringy white hands. I want out, Dad. I can't stay in here all those years. There will be nothing left. Take me with you when you leave—

WOLFERT: I can't—

WOLF: I received Phoebe's and your love. It was all about me. Even Memela loved me. She came forward. She drew back. I liked her little dance. She didn't know it yet, but she was part of me. What can I do? —Feel compassion? —Is that what you want, Wolfert? Or is it sorrow I feel? Sorrow for myself. Is that the splendor on top of the world?

WOLFERT: I can't get you out, Wolf. There are laws bigger than us. You have to serve time.

WOLF: NO.

WOLFERT: It's killing me too. I have taken care of my family. I have provided—Yet it has come to nothing. What have I done wrong?

WOLF: Nothing.

WOLFERT: I will tell the boys what I didn't tell you.

WOLF: We've talked all our lives. What haven't you told me?

WOLFERT: Even when we're centered, sometimes we come away broken. We're up against a power greater than us. I think it's always moving too—

WOLF: They'll like that news. Let them live a little before you tell them.

WOLFERT: It's about alignment. It's a dance. Listen to your dreams, Wolf. Dreams and stories are medicine.

WOLF: (IMPATIENTLY) Yeah, yeah.

WOLFERT: Something will come to you. Maybe someone dressed in elk-skin.

(Black out...)

## SCENE 31

## MEMELA, WOLFERT and WOLF ARE IN SEPARATE PLACES

(Night...MEMELA is at the house.
Wolfert is in the cemetery. He puts on a
radiator for a breast plate and talks to his
dead wife. He holds his drum made
from an air-filter. Wolf is in Montana
State Prison. In the dark cell, the weight
of prison falls upon him. Wolf draws up
into a ball...)

WOLF: I can't sleep! Terror is here. Men cry out.
Dad—I hear angry shouts.
MEMELA: I dreamed of Mrs. Stover. I saw her
once at parents' day—Now I hear her from the
next world—
WOLF: This place is haunted. How can I stay
here?
MEMELA: Should I write down what she said?
Should I teach it in class? —Forgiveness comes
through understanding the ones who harmed
you.
WOLFERT: Send Muffler and Tail Pipe,
Phoebe—to chase away the dark spirits that
bother Wolf. Let him see them run. He hardly
mentions your name— but he knows you're
here.
MEMELA: Has Mrs. Stover been floating over
our house, watching us, studying our sorrows so

she could let go of her anger? Is that what she has to do to continue her journey?

WOLF: I'm held with four-point barbed wire. GET ME OUT OF HERE, DAD!! Sing me to the next world with your drum.

MEMELA: I hear Mrs. Stover choking on the stones of forgiveness. I am choking too.

WOLFERT: Phoebe—Is it you? —Is it something else?

MEMELA: Is that old car in the salvage yard in a different place each time I look? Is someone moving it? Or am I'm imagining it—

WOLFERT: Who knows the mystery of what we see?

(He beats a drum he made from an air-filter...)

(Black out...)

## SCENE 32

## MONTANA STATE PRISON

(Dawn. Wolf, alone in his cell...)

WOLF: It's a slide show in here—Splinters fly into me—I've got slivers in my skin—I remember when there were gradations. Shadings. Things seen from different ways. I remember when things weren't one way or

another—but could vary—They were looser—
not so tight against the wind pipe.

(Pause...)

I look from the prison window through snow
falling. There's a figure walking in the
distance—I press my face to the glass—She
continues walking toward the gate. Something's
happening—The snow falls in pieces of light—I
look at her again—She comes to me wearing a
white cardigan—a white cardigan covered with
pearl buttons.

(It starts to snow on Wolf in his cell. He
lifts his arms up to it...Black out)

End.

# Chalk in the Rain

A Play

By


Bret Jones

CHARACTER LIST:

MELEA TIGER - She is 22; however, the play is filled with flashbacks to earlier ages. She is a Muscogee (Creek) Indian who spends a few years in the Deep Water Foster Home.

ANGELINA BIBLE – She is 17 years old. A friend of Melea's in the home. She has been an orphan since she was 12. She is Muscogee (Creek).

COLIN FOWLER - We see him at different ages—mainly mid-20s. He is seven years older than Melea. He is charming, charismatic, and manipulative.

MS. SANDRA HAYES She is in her 40s and runs the Deep Water Foster Home. She is stern but fair to the children. She is universally loved and respected.

*Chalk in the Rain* was performed as a staged reading during the third annual Oklahoma City Theatre Company's Native American New Play Festival. It was selected as the featured production for the fourth annual festival and performed April 11-21, 2013. It was a world premier directed by Carly Conklin with the following cast:

MELEA TIGER:      Rachel Morgan
ANGELINA BIBLE:   Tiffane Shorter

COLIN FOWLER:     Jeremy Tanequodle
SANDRA HAYES:     Misty Red Elk

Other parts played by the company

Set Design: Doug Van Liew
Lighting Design: Paul Mitchell
Costume Design: Nicole Zausmer
Stage Manager: Paul Mitchell

### Bret Jones (Playwright)
Jones is Muscogee Creek and serves as the
Program Director of Theatre at Wichita State
University, Wichita, KS. He is a novelist and
playwright, as well as a film maker. His play,
*The Isolation House,* ran at The American Theatre
of Actors in New York City; *Thee and Thou*
premiered at The Jewel Box Theatre in
Oklahoma City. Two of Bret's Native American
plays—*Kindred* and *War Paint* have won the
Garrard Playwriting Award sponsored by The
Five Civilized Tribes Museum. Another of his
plays, *Native Skin* had a workshop staged
reading at the Native Voices Theatre in Los
Angeles. Bret lives in Goddard, KS with his
wife, Julie, and their three children: Lauren,
Austin, and Emma.


TIME:
The present and flashbacks to six and four years
before.

PLACE:
The Deep Water Foster Home and various
locations.

SETTING:
The play takes place in multiple locations. The
main area is the Deep Water Foster Home
outside of Muskogee, OK, which consists of
MELEA's bedroom that she shares with
ANGELA; an office area for MS. HAYES; an
area outside the foster home and other places.

## ACT I

(Melea Tiger enters and takes her place
at center stage…She is carrying a suitcase
and a bag over her shoulder…)

MELEA: I hadn't planned on coming back. Not
that it was necessarily a bad place to live. It
wasn't. There were other things…and those
other things are now associated with this place.
The birds' song in the trees outside the foster
home remind me…the cold wind in through the
willows near the pond. It's all a backdrop to the
moments that I've driven a stake through and
buried. But now…now, they are flooding back
into me. So many images all at once…and in the
back of it he is there. You are there.

(Ms. Hayes appears behind Melea…)

MS. HAYES: Melea! Melea!

MELEA: Ms. Hayes. Hello.

(They hug...Ms. Hayes holds Malea at
arm's length...)

MS. HAYES: You are so beautiful. So... (HUGS
HER AGAIN)
MELEA: You know, I haven't been gone that
long.
MS. HAYES: I know that, but— (LETS IT HANG
IN THE AIR BETWEEN THEM)
MELEA: I've got to tell you, I'm just a little –
MS. HAYES: – Yes. I understand. You didn't
have to be here.
MELEA: I did.
MS. HAYES: I want you to know how much it
means to me--to all of us.
MELEA: When I heard that they were thinking
about closing this place up.
MS. HAYES: Heartbreaking.
MELEA: That's why I'm here. I'm not sure what
all I can do.
MS. HAYES: But you're here.
MELEA: The radio station said that you could
have all the air time you wanted.
MS. HAYES: Bless them. Bless you.
MELEA: Is Mr. Dryden here?
MS. HAYES: Oh, no, hon, he's retired. I miss
him.
MELEA: Me, too. He'd kill me if he saw how
dirty I kept my place.

(They share a quick laugh...)

MS. HAYES: That man knew how to run a clean ship.

MELEA: He did.

MS. HAYES: I guess, really, Vicki and myself are the only ones left when you were here.

MELEA: But that's only been--

MS. HAYES: – A few years. Yes, yes, I know. Folks move on.

MELEA: Wow.

MS. HAYES: Come on in. Let me get your suitcase.

MELEA: (GETS IT BEFORE MS. HAYES CAN) I got it.

(They go into Ms. Hayes' office…)

MS. HAYES: You want a cup of coffee? Tea?

(They set the luggage down...)

MELEA: Tea would be great. Thanks.

(Ms. Hayes pours her a cup...)

MS. HAYES: Four years.

MELEA: What's that?

MS. HAYES: You've been gone four years.

MELEA: Yeah.

MS. HAYES: You graduated just last May.

MELEA: Yes, I did. Were you there?

MS. HAYES: I couldn't make it this year. I know the Creek radio station is glad to have you.

MELEA: I hope.

MS. HAYES: A real journalist is an asset to the tribe.

MELEA: I don't think I've been out long enough to be called a real journalist.

MS. HAYES: You have the degree and that's what counts.

MELEA: (SIPS TEA) Yes.

MS. HAYES: Sugar, honey? Any milk?

MELEA: Honey, please.

(Ms. Hayes gets it for her…)

MS. HAYES: There you go, hon.

(Melea works on her tea...)

MELEA: How many kids are here now?

MS. HAYES: Twenty-three.

MELEA: A handful.

MS. HAYES: At times.

(Quick pause…)

MELEA: As much as I was?

MS. HAYES: Oh, please, you were a joy to have here.

MELEA: Ms. Hayes--

MS. HAYES: – Let's not. All right? Now, "no one at the plow looking back is fit – "

MELEA: – (LAUGHS) "for the kingdom of God." I remember.

MS. HAYES: It's the Baptist in me. Sorry.

MELEA: Don't be.  I know more Bible than anyone else I know thanks to you.

MS. HAYES: I hope that's a good thing.

MELEA: It is. (LOOKS INTO HER TEACUP)

MS. HAYES: Sadness is catching, you know.

MELEA: Sorry.  Are the Baptists still interested in supporting the home?

MS. HAYES: Oh, yes, but they can't provide for all of it.  The tribe gives us about a tenth of our budget and we've had to hit up federal programs for a while now.

MELEA: What happened?

MS. HAYES: It's just a strain.  More kids than we really can handle, not enough money to give them everything they need, and so many other things.

MELEA: I promise you we'll keep it afloat.

MS. HAYES: Thank you, Melea.  I'm so thankful you're back.

MELEA: I'm not sure if I am or not.  It may take a while.

MS. HAYES: So, how do you like radio?

MELEA: Love it.  I really do.  I've found my niche.  I get weekend shifts on the air and I get to go around Indian country all over the place interviewing folks, going to bingo –

MS. HAYES: – of course! (LAUGHS)

MELEA: Yeah!  And I've met so many people.  So many good people.  So many that want to do well and be well.  That means a lot to me.

MS. HAYES: It should.  What about your grandpa?

MELEA: He passed away.

MS. HAYES: Oh, I'm so sorry to hear that. Bless your heart.

MELEA: It's okay. He didn't feel any pain in the end.

MS. HAYES: And for that you're blessed.

MELEA: Yes, ma'am. I just hated seeing him go like that...with my family situation and all.

MS. HAYES: What about your cousins up in Tulsa?

MELEA: Still there.

MS. HAYES: Your aunt, too?

MELEA: She moved down to Eufala. She got a trailer house near the lake down there. She loves it.

(A pause...)

MS. HAYES: I know we're dancing all around...things here, but I hope you'll make the best of it while you're here. You want to stay here in your old room?

MELEA: Really?

MS. HAYES: Sure. It's vacant. We had a girl in there recently that graduated high school and has moved on. An uncle came and got her and took her to New Mexico.

MELEA: Good for her.

MS. HAYES: So?

MELEA: Yes, I would love to.

(They gather her luggage... Melea puts her cup on the desk...They move to

another part of the stage that is her old
bedroom...)

MS. HAYES: I got a letter the other day--
MELEA: – A letter?
MS. HAYES: Surprised?
MELEA: I didn't think anyone actually wrote on
paper anymore.

(They laugh...)

MS. HAYES: I know.  I was surprised it wasn't a
bill, or something.  It was from Angelina.
MELEA: You're kidding me.  How is she?
MS. HAYES: Fine.  I thought you two kept in
touch.
MELEA: Not anymore.

(Quick pause...)

MS. HAYES: Oh.
MELEA: Too long of a story.
MS. HAYES: They usually are.

(They stop in the room...)

MELEA: Oh, wow.
MS. HAYES: Seem small?
MELEA: Tiny.
MS. HAYES: Yeah.  You have an apartment
now?
MELEA: I'm renting a two-bedroom house just
outside of Muskogee.

MS. HAYES: Good for you. I always wished we could give you girls more room in here, but we were packed back then.

MELEA: And now.

MS. HAYES: That's right. Still are. I've got a girl waiting to move in late next week. She'll get this room.

MELEA: She'll love it.

> (Melea puts her bag on one of the single beds... Ms. Hayes puts the suitcase by the bed...)

MS. HAYES: Will you want to talk to any of the children?

MELEA: I'd love to. But I think I'd feel a whole lot better if you were there with me when I did. I don't want to ask anything that's touchy.

MS. HAYES: I understand. The baggage the poor kids bring with them breaks my heart sometimes.

MELEA: All the time, probably.

MS. HAYES: All the time. Yes.

MELEA: For some, Ms. Hayes, this is the only home they ever had. Don't forget that.

MS. HAYES: I try not to. Listen, how about I treat you to dinner back in town tonight?

MELEA: You don't have to be here?

MS. HAYES: I can sneak out. I'm not really needed during meal times. I slip in and out a lot.

MELEA: I'd love to.

MS. HAYES: Anywhere you want. It's on me.

MELEA: Okay, great. I'll think about it.

(Ms. Hayes is about to leave...)

MS. HAYES: Thank you again, hon. I can't tell you what it means to me.
MELEA: Don't worry. We'll raise plenty of money.

> (Ms. Hayes exits... Melea walks around the room – puts the bag near the suitcase...)

> (A change of lights: flashback to Melea at 16... Angelina enters... She is 17 and fun-loving...)

ANGELINA: Hey, hey, hey!
MELEA: Hello.
ANGELINA: (STICKS OUT HER HAND) Angelina Bible.
MELEA: Melea Tiger.

> (They shake hands...)

ANGELINA: (LAUGHS) Nice Creek name.
MELEA: You, too.
ANGELINA: No folks?
MELEA: No.
ANGELINA: No grandparents?
MELEA: One.
ANGELINA: Oh.
MELEA: He can't--

ANGELINA: Gotcha, gotcha. I hear ya.

MELEA: Diabetes.

ANGELINA: Ouch! Sorry to hear that. How old are you?

MELEA: Sixteen. You?

ANGELINA: Seventeen. I guess that's why Ms. Hayes stuck us together. They're a few other girls here, too, but they're younger. Twelve, I think, and a few under ten years old.

MELEA: I'm glad there's someone else here my age.

ANGELINA: Yeah. It's been pretty dull around here with all the youngsters. My folks are dead.

MELEA: I'm sorry.

ANGELINA: Car accident on I-44 just outside of Tulsa.

MELEA: I'm sorry.

ANGELINA: They were on their way back from seeing my brother.

MELEA: Oh.

ANGELINA: He's in college up there. Tulsa Community. He can't really take care of me, so I ended up here.

MELEA: No other family?

ANGELINA: Not really. I got an uncle somewhere. Don't know where.

MELEA: My grandpa is all I have.

ANGELINA: (FLOPS BACKWARD ON THE BED) And that's why you're here!

MELEA: (SITS ON THE OTHER BED) When do we eat?

ANGELINA: Dinner time! Hey! You don't smoke, do you?

MELEA: No.

ANGELINA Ever tried it?

MELEA: No.

ANGELINA Good!  I've got plenty for both of us

> (Angelina lifts a pillow and reveals a
> couple packs of cigarettes...)

MELEA: Where did you get those?

ANGELINA The smoke shop, hello.  Where else?

MELEA: You aren't of age.

ANGELINA I'm seventeen, but I look a good eighteen.  Nineteen, really.

MELEA: That's okay.

ANGELINA: What's that?

MELEA: I don't want to smoke anything.

ANGELINA: Neither do I, that's why I do it!

> (She curls up on the bed...)

MELEA: Okay.  Whatever.

> (A quick pause...)

ANGELINA: Melea.

MELEA: Yeah?

ANGELINA: Uh...it's like this...well, look, if I yell out in the night, don't worry about it too much, okay?

MELEA: Okay.

ANGELINA:  Sometimes I have night terrors. Ever have those?

MELEA: No.

ANGELINA: You don't want them. Believe me. If I wake you, just ignore me, or make sure I don't fall off the bed and whack my head on the floor or anything.

MELEA: Gotcha.

ANGELINA: A night terror is the worst kinda terror you can have...

(Angelina disappears...the lights shift back to the present...)

MELEA: Night terrors are the worst kind of terror you can have. (WALKS TO CENTER STAGE) I feel like praying all the time, but I don't know what to pray for. I wrote a list and keep it in my purse as a reminder. Every one of them has something to do with me. I need this, give me that, I have to have more...whatever. At sixteen, with no parents, my grandpa not able to raise me, and in a new place with new people I prayed for something to take me away. It sounds trite now, but a man on horseback with hair waving in the wind...paint on his face...arrows strapped to his back...named Tecumseh. I had this all planned out. So did Angelina. And those plans intersected. So much the worse for the both of us. He didn't have paint on his face and he wasn't named Tecumseh. But he did have--well, I'm looking behind me, aren't I?

(The lights shift: Melea walks into Ms.
Hayes' office – picks up a microphone
that is hooked up to a recorder. Ms.
Hayes is sitting answering a question
that Melea has put to her…. She is
speaking nervously into the
microphone...)

MS. HAYES: (NERVOUS) And the foster home
was built right after that.
MELEA: After the flood of '56?
MS. HAYES: Yes. So many youngsters lost their
parents and had nowhere to go. A coalition of
Creek Baptist churches rallied together and built
the original home, which we now use as storage
for the children and for some lawn equipment
and other odds and ends.
MELEA: When was the current structure built?
MS. HAYES: In 1974. The tribe came through
with some funds and so did the coalition. We
also got some grant money from the federal
government.
MELEA: How many children have come
through these doors, Ms. Hayes?
MS. HAYES: I can look in the files if you want
me to.
MELEA: No, that's all right. I just –
MS. HAYES – So many, Melea. Clean faces,
dirty faces, scared, horrified...I've seen them all
walk through our doors. But we give them a
roof over their head. Food to eat. And
hopefully love. "Love covers a multitude of
sins." Oh, I'm sorry. I –

(Ms. Hayes breaks out of the interview
and waves for Melea to cut the recorder
off. Melea stops it...)

MELEA: What?
MS. HAYES: I shouldn't have said that. Can you
erase that, or edit it out. Whatever you do...
MELEA: Sure. Why didn't you mean to say –
MS. HAYES: It implies that sin was behind them
being here in the first place. And I don't mean
that at all. That's the last thing I meant.
MELEA: Folks will know what you meant.
MS. HAYES: I'd rather take it back, if that's all
right. I don't even want to imply –
MELEA: – Sure. Don't worry about it.
MS. HAYES: Thank you.
MELEA: It's okay. We weren't live. You're
jittery.
MS. HAYES: Just the thought of my voice
broadcasting all over the place out there sets me
on edge. Do you want some tea?

(Ms. Hayes gets up to get tea...she's
getting edgy...)

MELEA: No, I'm fine. I can fix you some if you
want.
MS. HAYES: No, that's okay.
MELEA: What is it?
MS. HAYES: Oh, Melea.

(Ms. Hayes slumps into her chair...)

MELEA: It's okay. I promise this fund-raising drive will give you what you need to keep the doors open.

MS. HAYES: It's not that. I got an e-mail this morning.

MELEA: From who? Angelina?

MS. HAYES: No. She only sends letters. I don't even know if she owns a computer.

(A quick pause...)

MELEA: Oh.

MS. HAYES: I can call him, but he's going to be hard to persuade not to come. He counts this place as his only home.

MELEA: No, it's fine.

MS. HAYES: I know I said all that about looking back yesterday, but I didn't know –

MELEA – No. I'll be busy interviewing some of the staff today.

MS. HAYES: He wants to come and give me a check. I asked him to mail it, but he wants to put it into my hands. That's what he said, anyway. I didn't know how to tell you.

(A pause…)

Melea?

MELEA: Did you know that every March I go into a...I don't know what to call it: a funk, I guess. I walk for hours with nowhere in mind to go. I skipped classes a lot. I changed my hair style. Once I changed my hair color. I eat a lot of junk that's bad for you. It's this overwhelming feeling of sadness. It's oppressive.

MS. HAYES: I didn't know that. Have you talked to anyone about it?

MELEA: You. Just then.

MS. HAYES: I mean really talked.

MELEA: I'm not going to.

MS. HAYES: You seem so sad now. I didn't want to say anything –

MELEA: – I've been sad a long time. Really, before all of...it...I did have a flash of it. Of happiness. You and Angelina gave that to me.

MS. HAYES: Look, go on back to the radio station for the day. I'll take care of business with him and I'll call you when he's gone.

MELEA: No.

MS. HAYES: Melea.

MELEA: (GETS UP TO LEAVE) And if he so much as lays a hand on me, Ms. Hayes, I'll kill him!

(Lights shift: flashback to Angelina and Melea in their room... Angelina is looking out the window into the dark holding a flashlight... Melea enters with a cup of ice cream. She has one for Angelina...)

ANGELINA: (JERKS AROUND QUICKLY) Whoa, you scared me!

MELEA: Sorry. (HANDING TO ANGELINA) I got you some ice cream.

ANGELINA: Thanks. Do you have homework?

MELEA: I finished it downstairs. What's the flashlight for?
ANGELINA: To see where it dark! (CLICKS IT ON AND SHINES IT IN MELEA'S FACE)
MELEA: Hey! Thanks a lot!
ANGELINA: It's bright, huh?
MELEA: Yes, it's bright. Who's out there?
ANGELINA: Who said there's anybody out there?

(Angelina opens her ice cream and starts eating it...Melea is finishing hers...)

MELEA: I didn't. I just asked.
ANGELINA: Nobody.
MELEA: Is that his name?

(A quick pause...)

ANGELINA: (LAUGHS) No. It's just a friend.
MELEA: A guy friend.
ANGELINA: Yes. A guy friend.
MELEA: That guy that was here earlier today?
ANGELINA: You saw him?
MELEA: Only from the other room. He was talking to Ms. Hayes.
ANGELINA: He used to be an orphan here. A few years back.
MELEA: He looked older to me...from a distance.
ANGELINA: Depends on what you think is older.
MELEA: Yeah. Right.

ANGELINA: What?

MELEA: Nothing.

ANGELINA: What?

MELEA: Have you...?

ANGELINA: Have I what?

MELEA: You know what.

ANGELINA: No. Why don't you say it?

MELEA: This is ridiculous. I'm going to bed. Hop off and let me go to sleep.

ANGELINA: Wait! Wait, come on. He wants me to sneak out later tonight.

MELEA: And do what?

ANGELINA: Melea.

MELEA: How much older is he?

ANGELINA: Does that matter?

MELEA: Does it to you?

ANGELINA: Why are you asking so many questions?

MELEA: Am I?

ANGELINA: Stop it. Come on! He likes me.

MELEA: What's that mean?

ANGELINA: (FLICKS MELEA WITH THER SPOON) Another question!

MELEA: I've never had a boyfriend.

ANGELINA: Really?

MELEA: Not one that counted, anyway. There was Sam Harjo back in fourth grade.

ANGELINA: (LAUGHS) Well, this guy is no fourth grader.

MELEA: What's that mean?

ANGELINA: He's no fourth grader.

MELEA: Oh. Does Ms. Hayes know?

ANGELINA: Are you out of your mind? Of course not! She'd kill me, then him! That's why we have to sneak –

(Melea looks out the window...sees a light flashing...)

MELEA: There's your signal.

(Angelina crawls over Melea to look out the window...)

ANGELINA: Two o'clock.
MELEA: Is it Morse code or something?
ANGELINA: No, two flashes means two o'clock.
MELEA: Where can you go at two o'clock?
ANGELINA: I don't know. Maybe we'll just talk.

(Melea smiles...)

What? Stop it!

(Melea flicks Angelina with her spoon...)

MELEA: We're supposed to be asleep at two o'clock in the morning.
ANGELINA: You did see him from a distance, didn't you? There's no other guys around, Melea.
MELEA: Thomas.
ANGELINA: He's fourteen! Sick!
MELEA: How old is this guy?

ANGELINA: I told you: older.

MELEA: What's his name?

ANGELINA: Who says he has one?

MELEA: Is it Tecumseh?

ANGELINA: Nooo. Tecumseh? We study that at school and you've got it on the brain.

MELEA: He was majestic.

ANGELINA: Sure. Okay. But he's also dead.

MELEA: So let me guess: he's a Harjo.

ANGELINA: No.

MELEA: Just guessing. It seems like every Creek around here is a Harjo or Bible or –

ANGELINA: – Tiger.

MELEA: Right!

ANGELINA: He kissed me.

MELEA: Where?

ANGELINA: On my mouth! Where else?

MELEA: There are a lot of places to be kissed.

ANGELINA: How would you know?

MELEA: I don't, but I can imagine it, can't I?

ANGELINA: He kissed me on my mouth. He just put his lips over mine and just held his face there. No open mouth. No tongue. Just soft. Sweet.

MELEA: How did he taste?

ANGELINA: Girl, you ask the craziest questions! How did he taste? I don't know!

MELEA: How?

ANGELINA: I have no idea: salty! How should I know?

MELEA: You were kissing him.

ANGELINA: He was kissing me. I held my breath. My head started pounding. My fingers tingled.

MELEA: What did he say?

ANGELINA: I'm not telling you. Go to bed.

MELEA: You're sneaking out?

ANGELINA: Yes.

MELEA: Let me come with you.

ANGELINA: Uh, no.

MELEA: Tell me about it tomorrow.

ANGELINA: Maybe. We'll see.

MELEA: When he kisses you this time, kiss him back.

ANGELINA: Don't worry. I will.

(Light shift: Angelina disappears. Melea walks back to center stage...)

MELEA: I wish I had some great story or anecdote from when I was a child and my mother told me about boys to share that would help illustrate the mind set of those days. I don't have any. Mom was dead. Dad, too. And I wasn't about to ask Ms. Hayes. Not that she wouldn't have had an answer. I'm sure she would have. I tried to stay awake that night when she left. I couldn't. But I dreamed about it. And it wasn't a night terror, either. It had texture and substance and things in it I hadn't dreamed about before. And I wasn't an orphan anymore. And then the rain came down.

(Light shift: Melea walks into Ms. Hayes' office. It is present again. It is the moment before the flashback. Ms. Hayes and Melea are in their original spots...)

MS. HAYES: I hope you don't mean that.
MELEA: What? Oh, the –
MS. HAYES: – Yes. The threatening to cut off his –

(She can't finish. Melea finds this funny...)

MELEA: I should've done it. Or Angelina. Someone should have.

(Ms. Hayes is about to open her mouth...)

Don't. No verses.
MS. HAYES: I wasn't.
MELEA: You were.
MS. HAYES: Well, I had one ready.

(They smile. Ms. Hayes touches Melea's hand...)

MELEA: I need to run back into town.
MS. HAYES: I thought you were staying?
MELEA: I've thought better of it. I need to go back and load what we've recorded into the computer and start editing.
MS. HAYES: I hope you have what you need.

MELEA: I have enough to get started. Don't worry. I'm coming back.

MS. HAYES: I know you are. I just feel like I should tell you –

MELEA: (PICKS UP HER BAG AND EQUIPMENT) I'll be back.

MS. HAYES: The other day – the other day, the day before yesterday, I saw something. I've never been one for omens, or anything, but this was something you don't see every day. I got up early, earlier than I usually do. I guess it must've been about six o'clock. I made coffee and had it sitting on the back porch facing east. The sun was just beginning to come up. And I know it sounds funny, but as I sat there watching the sun come up I saw a cluster of clouds, dark ones, float across the horizon next to the sun. I mean, not next to the sun, they couldn't right? You know what I mean. And it's the strangest thing: one seemed to break off from the rest. And you know how clouds look like things...images? This looked like a horse riding right at the sun. I couldn't take my eyes off of it. And then the cloud changed. I guess the wind blew into it. It then looked like a hand. And just for a moment, a brief second, it looked like it was choking the sun. Just choking the life right out of it.

(A quick pause...)

I'm not one for omens, but I know you are. I
know you see those kind of things all the time.
Or, you used to.
MELEA: That wasn't until after.
MS. HAYES: Oh.
MELEA: I wouldn't worry about it if I were you.
MS. HAYES: You're not, though, are you?

> (Ms. Hayes touches Melea on the
> shoulder, then exits. Melea stands there
> holding the bag on her shoulder. Looks
> out the window of the office...looks back
> across the stage at her old room...)

> (Light shift: flashback. Angelina is on a
> cordless phone...)

ANGELINA: (ON THE PHONE) You are not!

(Pause...)

Uh-uh. No way. I don't believe you. I don't.

(Pause...)

Yeeess. Okay.

> (Melea walks into the room. Angelina
> waves at her...)

I don't know, sure. Let me ask.
She puts a hand over the receiver.

Ms. Hayes said I could go have pizza. Wanna come?

MELEA: I have some homework to do. Is that him?

ANGELINA: Yes. Come on. I want you to meet him.

MELEA: And Ms. Hayes--

ANGELINA: She said it was all right. Come on. Free pizza.

MELEA: All right.

ANGELINA: Really? Good. (BACK ON THE PHONE) We'll be there in a half hour.

(Pause…)

Ms. Hayes will drop us off.

(Pause...)

No. I don't know. I'll ask her.

MELEA: Ask what?

(Angelina puts a hand on the receiver...)

ANGELINA: He wants to know if he can drive us back after we eat.

MELEA: I don't know if Ms. –

ANGELINA: – I'll ask her. Okay. Okay. 'Bye.

(Angelina hangs up the phone…)

MELEA: Since when do you get to take the phone into our room?
ANGELINA: Since I asked.
MELEA: You asked Ms. Hayes?
ANGELINA: Not exactly.
MELEA: Who then? Mr. Dryden, wasn't it?
ANGELINA: So. What if it was?
MELEA: You better go put that right back where you found it or you won't be having any pizza and I'll have to go in your place.
ANGELINA: Uh, no you won't. Come on.

(She gathers up her purse and the phone...)

MELEA: You know what?
ANGELINA: What now?
MELEA: You've never even told me his name.
ANGELINA: It's Colin Fowler.

(The lights shift: Melea appears at center stage...)

MELEA: Art therapy is what I heard it called the first time I went there...this was after...I'd been gone from the orphanage for a couple of years. I kept seeing the same image in my dreams, in my day dreams, and in my own night terrors. I'd like to blame Angelina for that, but it was my own doing. So, anyway, I started painting the images in my mind. The guy running the sessions encouraged me to do it. I took him the finished product. He asked if he could have it.

He actually paid me for it. It wasn't to be the last one. I've painted the same picture four hundred and sixteen times since then. During the month of March a couple of years back I was averaging three canvases a day. I read somewhere that Picasso did that: averaged three a day. The painting is a rider on a horse. He's heading straight for the sun. His hands aren't on the horse. They're reaching out toward the light. The fingers aren't outstretched. They're curled. It's as if he wants to grab the sun and put it out forever. I start number four hundred and seventeen tonight.

      (The lights shift: A flashback to the pizza place. Angelina is sitting at a table...Melea walks over and sits down...)

ANGELINA: I thought you fell in.
MELEA: I was just fixing up.
ANGELINA: I can tell.

      (Colin Fowler walks over with a pitcher of soda pop. He sits down in between the girls. He is a very handsome Creek Indian. He is 23 years old in this scene. He is in control of himself and knows how to be in control of others...)

COLIN: I got the pizza ordered. What did you say you liked...uh –
MELEA: Melea.

COLIN: Right, Melea. What kind?

MELEA: Whatever. Pepperoni.

COLIN: You're in luck. They had it. (HE LAUGHS)

ANGELINA: Did you order a sausage?

COLIN: I did. Of course. (HOLDS ANGELINA'S HAND)

MELEA: It's noisy. They're a lot of folks out tonight.

COLIN: Dirt track races outside of town. My buddy has a car that he races. Me, too, sometimes.

ANGELINA: I didn't know that.

COLIN: I hadn't mentioned it?

ANGELINA: No.

COLIN: You should come out and watch me race. I won second last time. Woulda won first, but the jerk cut me off.

ANGELINA: I'd love it.

COLIN: Melea?

MELEA: Yeah, sure. Sounds fun.

COLIN: It is. Maybe I can talk him into letting you girls ride a round in the warm-up laps.

ANGELINA: Really? That'd be great.

(She leans into him for a kiss...)

COLIN: What?

ANGELINA: Give me kiss!

(He leans away from her...)

COLIN: How bad you want one?

(She leans in closer. He pulls back
further. Melea is watching intently...)

ANGELINA: Colin!
COLIN: What do you think, Melea? Does she
get one?
MELEA: Sure. Why not?

(He kisses Angelina hard on the mouth.
Melea is mesmerized by it...)

COLIN: (TO MELEA) And what about you?
MELEA: What about me?
ANGELINA: Yeah. What about her?
COLIN: Nothing. Not a thing.

(He kisses Melea's hand. Angelina
playfully slaps Colin's shoulder…)

ANGELINA: Not funny, you know.
COLIN: It wasn't meant to be. So, Melea, how
do you like the home?
MELEA: It's fine.
COLIN: My only home all my teenage years. I
love that place. And Ms. Hayes is the mom I
never had 'cos mine was hooked on crack.

(A quick pause…)

ANGELINA: You didn't tell me that.
COLIN: There's a lot you don't know about me,
sweetheart. There's time. I promise.

(He kisses her again...)

MELEA: Is she still alive?
COLIN: Who? Oh, my mom? If you call being cranked out of her mind all the time alive, then yeah, she is. But don't ask me where. I don't know. And my dad.
ANGELINA: What about him?
COLIN: Don't ask.
MELEA: Dead?
COLIN: Nope. But he oughta be.

(Their number is called out...)

That's ours. I'll be right back.

(Colin leaves...)

ANGELINA: So?
MELEA: I'm not sure.
ANGELINA: What's that supposed to mean? You're not sure. He's hot, right?
MELEA: Yes.
ANGELINA: And his eyes. His hair. And his sense of humor.
MELEA: All right.
ANGELINA: Sometimes I wonder if you're not half dead. I can barely get a rise out of you about anything.
MELEA: I'm just watching. That's all.
ANGELINA: What's there to watch? I think I'm falling for him.
MELEA: Already?

ANGELINA: Yes!  I want him to –

(Colin comes back with the pizzas
cutting her off…)

COLIN: And here we are.  A pepperoni for the
lovely lady.

(He gives one to Melea…)

MELEA: Thank you.
COLIN: And one for this lovely lady.

(He puts the pizza down and steals a kiss
from Angelina. They begin eating…)

MELEA: I hear they have good pizza.
COLIN: The best.  I know the manager.  We got
'em for half price.
ANGELINA: Awesome.
COLIN: I thought so.  If he doesn't stay too
busy, I want you girls to meet him.  He's a good
friend of mine.  I met him after I got out of the
home.  He first got me into sales.  Got me a job
selling cars at the Ford place.  And then he
introduced me to the guy I'm working for now.
MELEA: Doing what?
COLIN: I sell auto parts for him.  I've got a trip
coming up to Dallas in a couple of months to
our annual sales conference.  You girls oughta
come.  It'd be fun.
MELEA: Uh...?
ANGELINA: Colin, there's no way.  Hello.

COLIN: Sorry. Just thinking out loud. It'd be great if you could come down there with me. The hotel's got a pool, sauna, and a hot tub. All the amenities, as they say.
ANGELINA: How do you know?
COLIN: I made sure it did before I agreed to go.
ANGELINA: Could you pass me the cheese? There isn't any.
COLIN: No can do, lady, we don't have any. I'll go get you some.

(He begins to get up. Angelina stops him…)

ANGELINA: I got it. I bet they have some up at the front. Anybody need anything?
COLIN: I'm fine.
MELEA: Me, too.

(Angelina leaves...)

COLIN: Man, she's great, isn't she?
MELEA: She is.
COLIN: You're awfully quiet.
MELEA: Well. Uh. Things are new these days.
COLIN: With the home?
MELEA: Yes. And my grandpa...
COLIN: What? Is he sick?
MELEA: Very sick.
COLIN: I'm sorry to hear that. At least you got him. Listen, Melea, I don't know you from anybody, but I can tell a thinker when I see one. And my advice is: don't. I did that for years out

there with Ms. Hayes and it didn't help. You're
alone, but you're not alone. Okay? You've got
Angelina and Ms. Hayes and everyone else out
there at Deep Water. You'll get used to it.

(Melea cracks a little...)

MELEA: I'm so tired of being alone.
COLIN: I know, I know. Come on now.

(He hands her a napkin and holds her
hand...)

MELEA: I see the world moving around me and
I can't seem to go along with it.
COLIN: You will. Trust me. You will. You're
tough. And you're smart, I can tell. And on top
of that, you're beautiful. You're gorgeous.

(A quick pause...)

MELEA: I'm what?
COLIN: You heard me. You're beautiful.
MELEA: I've never heard –

(Angelina comes back with the grated
cheese...)

ANGELINA: Hey, am I interrupting a moment
here, or what? It better be or what.

(She taps Colin on the shoulder and he
lets go of Melea's hand...)

COLIN: Melea needed a pick-me-up. And that's what I do best.
ANGELINA: What's wrong?
MELEA: Nothing.

(Melea looks at Colin. He smiles at her...)

COLIN: She's fine. She's just a little down, that's all.
ANGELINA: Well, not tonight, she's not. We're out of the zoo for a night and I want to enjoy it.

(Angelina sprinkles cheese on her food and begins eating. All action freezes except for Melea who turns out to the audience...)

MELEA: It didn't take an expert to see where this was going. That night Angelina slept with him for the first time. He wasn't her first, but he might as well have been. She talked about it – in great detail – for days. But then I got into the equation somehow and so did Ms. Hayes. She didn't know about them sleeping together – if she did, she would have put an end to it right there. But Colin lived there under her roof and he knew just what to say – every single time.

(The lights shift: Ms. Hayes office. Colin is there waiting for Ms. Hayes to finish reading a card.  He is holding a vase of roses...)

COLIN: So you see –

(Ms. Hayes holds up a hand as she is still reading...)

Sandi – Ms. Hayes?

(She finishes reading the card...)

MS. HAYES: This is very sweet, Colin.  Put the flowers on the desk. (HE DOES)
COLIN: I didn't know what to say, Ms. Hayes, but I thought I could at least try with that card.
MS. HAYES: And these flowers.  You're buttering me up.  I thought you just wanted to take Angelina out to get her exposed to other people.
COLIN: That's true.  And you have to believe me that was my only intention.  But –
MS. HAYES: Yes, but.  It seems to suggest quite a bit, doesn't it?
COLIN: I didn't plan it.  She didn't either.  You can ask her.
MS. HAYES: I will.  Colin, you're so much older than her.
COLIN: Please don't use that on me, Ms. Hayes.  You've known me practically all my life.  You saw me grow up around here.  You raised me.  You know what's in my heart.

(He pauses waiting for a response. Ms. Hayes doesn't say anything...)

It's this place that made me what I am. Can you imagine if I had been raised away from here by some distant relative. Can you?

MS. HAYES: No. You were here so long, I just count you as a permanent resident even though you've gotten older and moved on with your life.

COLIN: And I wouldn't have had that if I hadn't been here. With you, Mr. Dryden, and everybody else. When I came back for a visit and met Angelina for the first time, I just saw her as another me. You know? Not knowing where to go. Not knowing what my future might be outside of this place. And I didn't have anyone to mentor me out of that. I had to do it on my own...and with your help, too.

MS. HAYES: She's only seventeen.

COLIN: Yes. She is. And I am very respectful of that every time we go somewhere. Public places only. Crowds of people. Why would I want to betray your trust? Why would I want to do that?

MS. HAYES: She's very pretty, Colin. You're older and you're in a position to take advantage of her.

(He stares at her...)

COLIN: Ms. Hayes. Isn't what I wrote in that card – isn't it...?

MS. HAYES: Isn't it what, Colin? It's just a card with words. Your actions speak a lot louder than flowery words in a card.

COLIN: I realize that. You drummed that into me a thousand times. I understand that. I live it out every day.

MS. HAYES: And on top of everything else, she's vulnerable right now. She's got some issues to deal with.

COLIN: I know that. She's told me everything. I know about the night terrors and all the rest. I'm trying to help her through it. Didn't you always say that the heart speaks the loudest? That we should never be deaf to it, but listen?

MS. HAYES: Yes, but that's just something nice and inspirational to say, Colin. When it becomes a practical matter, it's something else in entirely.

COLIN: I'll only see her here then. How about that?

MS. HAYES: That's a good place to start.

COLIN: And maybe every once in a while we can go into town for a burger or something?

MS. HAYES: We'll see.

COLIN: And how about Melea?

MS. HAYES: Wouldn't she be a third wheel?

COLIN: Not at all. She's great. And we like having her around.

MS. HAYES: All right, Colin, all right – (TOUCHES HIS HAND) You didn't have to get the flowers, you know.

(The lights shift: the girls' bedroom. It is present day. Melea is sitting on the bed – looking through a scrapbook...stops at a page and is reading. Ms. Hayes enters and is holding a letter...)

MS. HAYES: Where did you find that old thing?
MELEA: In the library. I had no idea you kept every scrap we ever wrote on.
MS. HAYES: Almost.
MELEA: We're ready to broadcast from here all day tomorrow. I hear that the chief is coming as well as some of the tribal town mekkos.
MS. HAYES: That's wonderful. What are you reading?
MELEA: A letter I wrote to you on the day I left.
MS. HAYES: Speaking of letters, I got this just now in the mail. (HANDS IT TO MELEA)
MELEA: Who's is from?
MS. HAYES: Guess.
MELEA: (LOOKING AT THE LETTER)
Angelina. What's it say?
MS. HAYES: Go ahead. It's not strictly for me. Read it.

(Melea opens it and reads quickly...)

MELEA: She's doing great. I wish I heard from her more often.
MS. HAYES: You should go see her.
MELEA: I wish I could.

MS. HAYES: I wish we both could. You think we could plan a trip after the fund-raiser is over?

MELEA: Can you leave?

MS. HAYES: Sure. I get vacation time now and again. What do you say?

(Melea puts the letter back in the envelope...)

MELEA: I say let's do it. I can take a couple of days off and we can drive up there and maybe stay for a while. She'd love to see us.

(Ms. Hayes sits beside Melea on the bed...)

MS. HAYES: You can go with it a long ways, can't you?

MELEA: Go with what?

MS. HAYES: (POINTING AT THE LETTER) This.

MELEA: I don't follow.

MS. HAYES: I know, Melea. I've known from the first letter I got from her. You should've worked harder on copying her handwriting.

(Melea jerks up from the bed...)

MELEA: Copying her –? What are you talking about?

MS. HAYES: You can drop it, hon. I don't know where she is any more than you do, but I will say this: even though you've lied to me with these letters from her, I do appreciate what you were trying to do. And how you worked out getting them sent from Flagstaff I'll never know.

MELEA: What are you –?

MS. HAYES: The mailing stamp the post office puts on the letters to tell you where they were posted out of.

MELEA: I have a college buddy who's been doing it for me.

MS. HAYES: And all to keep up the ruse that Angelina is still –

MELEA: – Ms. Hayes--she's gone!

MS. HAYES: I know she is.

MELEA: She's gone! I don't know where to find her.

MS. HAYES: I know.

MELEA: When she – I – I tried tracking her down.

MS. HAYES: She can't be found. I know. I've looked, too.

MELEA: Why didn't you say something?

MS. HAYES: I just did. You had your reasons. I waited until now because I thought that enough was finally enough.

MELEA: You know as well as I do that I'm the one responsible for her disappearing.

MS. HAYES: We all make our own decisions. You didn't make that one for her.

MELEA: Yes, I did. When Colin and I –

MS. HAYES: – you're only going to get yourself worked up over it, Melea. Let's just say I appreciate your thoughtfulness, but not your lying.

MELEA: Lying was never my intention.

MS. HAYES: But that's what you did.

MELEA: So, now you're going to preach to me about needing to face reality.

MS. HAYES: Do I need to, hon? Is that a lesson I really have to give?

MELEA: Ms. Hayes –!

(She runs out of the room...the lights shift and follow her as she walks across the stage to Ms. Hayes' office. The lights come up on the office. Colin is standing there holding a vase of roses. Melea bursts into the office. Colin turns to face her. A pause...)

COLIN: Melea! I didn't expect to see you here. Hello.

(Blackout...)


## ACT II

(Melea is standing at center stage. She has her microphone and recording equipment. She is recording a segment for the radio station.)

MELEA: The grounds haven't changed that much in the past few years. Storage facilities, a few cottages, and the main building which houses most of the children here. Deep Water has been in existence since 1956 and has housed Native children who didn't have anywhere else to go. Although a private agency, it depends greatly on donations and outside funds to keep its doors opened. The home started as an outreach of the Baptists by taking in homeless Native Americans in the area. Land was eventually donated by the tribe and countless children have graced the doors of this beautiful place. With staff educated in Native culture, children learn about their language, arts, and history – (SHUTS OFF THE RECORDER) And some of us learned other things.

> (The lights shift: the girls' room. Angelina is in bed. She jerks up suddenly, yells out, and falls out of bed onto the floor. She is crying and moaning. Melea enters...)

MELEA: Angelina! I heard you all the way in the library!
ANGELINA: Melea! Melea!

> (Melea holds her...)

MELEA: Okay. Okay. Come on now. It's okay.
ANGELINA: I don't wanna go back to sleep, I don't wanna go back to sleep, don't make me go back to sleep.

MELEA: Shhhh.  Shhh.

(She rocks Angelina back and forth…)

ANGELINA: Why does this have to happen?
MELEA: Don't.
ANGELINA: Why?
MELEA: Shhh.
ANGELINA: Melea.  There has to be a reason.
Ms. Hayes says there's a reason for everything.
I'm being punished.
MELEA: You are not.
ANGELINA: I'm a sinner.
MELEA: You are not.  Shhhh.  Stop that.
ANGELINA: I am.  And sinners get punished.
MELEA: Angelina, you're only getting yourself
worked up.
ANGELINA: You don't know.
MELEA: I can guess.
ANGELINA: You can't.
MELEA: How long?

(Angelina suddenly jerks up…)

ANGELINA: How long what?
MELEA: How long have you been sleeping with
Colin?

(A quick pause…)

ANGELINA: A month or so.
MELEA: Your first?
ANGELINA: No.  I had a third cousin who –

MELEA: Angelina!

ANGELINA: Yeah. But we were only thirteen, so that doesn't count.

MELEA: Are you scared?

ANGELINA: I was at first, but he is so – I don't know.

MELEA: Where?

ANGELINA: Melea, that's personal.

MELEA: Where?

ANGELINA: His truck – in the back. I saw stars. And the moon – (HOLDS HER HEAD DOWN AGAIN)

MELEA: Shhh. Don't think about your dream. Think about something else. Think about him.

ANGELINA: I don't want to. Not right now. I –

MELEA: What was it? Can you tell me?

ANGELINA: It's mainly pain. Mainly someone chasing me. Searching for me. I'm running. Constantly running. It's crazy.

MELEA: Who was chasing you this time?

ANGELINA: I don't know. Somebody. I couldn't tell. It was raining the whole time.

MELEA: Raining.

ANGELINA: Yeah. When I first came here, one of my first jobs was to clean the erasers from the chalkboards. Right before you came a lot of those were replaced by smartboards and other stuff. We still have a couple chalkboards left. Anyway, we got to write in all different colors on the board. White, yellow, red, orange, you name it. So I'd slam those erasers on the concrete in the parking lot. I liked it. I liked watching all those different colors float up into the air. And one day after I'd finished, it rained. I watched as all the colors of the chalk blended together and disappeared as the rain hit it. That's how my dream started.

MELEA: And that scared you?

ANGELINA: I can't explain it. I thought it was me.

MELEA: What? The chalk?

ANGELINA: I guess so. I don't know. I really don't.

> (She puts her head on Melea's shoulder...)

MELEA: Shhhh.

ANGELINA: Don't make me go back to sleep.

MELEA: I won't.

ANGELINA: Don't tell Ms. Hayes.

MELEA: I won't do that, either.

ANGELINA: Or Colin.

MELEA: Okay.

ANGELINA: I think I love him.

MELEA: Shhhh.

ANGELINA: Don't. Okay?

> (The lights shift: Melea stays there holding Angelina...)

MELEA: There were quite a few nights like that one. She couldn't seem to let go of whatever had ahold of her. Something. Somebody. And then it was Colin. Months passed like that.

She'd named their first two kids together. She'd drawn up a basic plan for their house. She had a dress picked out of a magazine and hid it under her bed. She did a thousand things she shouldn't have done. She puts Angelina back into bed and tucks her in. But then other things happened, too. More things that shouldn't have happened.

(Melea walks to center stage...)

Invincibility is something that plagues the young and haunts the old. And for a fleeting moment I felt myself to be impervious to anything. I was so wrong.

(She walks into office...Colin is standing there as he was at the end of Act One. The lights shift back to the present...)

COLIN: Hey, you.
MELEA: Colin.
COLIN: Wow, you look great. (NO RESPONSE) Ms. Hayes around?
MELEA: She is.
COLIN: I brought her flowers.
MELEA: I see that. And a card?

(A pause...)

COLIN: No.
MELEA: Not this time. I'm sure she's kept the others you've sent her.

COLIN: Maybe.

MELEA: She'll be here in a minute.

COLIN: It's great to see you. You really look good.

(No response...)

I wish I did. Too much frybread at the softball tournaments.

(He laughs-she doesn't...)

MELEA: I see that.

(He laughs again...)

COLIN: Same ole Melea.

MELEA: Not really, no.

(He takes a rose out of the vase...)

COLIN: Here.

(She doesn't move...)

It doesn't bite.

MELEA: But you do.

COLIN: Melea. Come on. Water under the bridge. We all make mistakes.

MELEA: Some more than others.

COLIN: Here, come on. I've done nothing but be nice.

(She takes the flower...)


MELEA: I hear you brought a check.
COLIN: I did. I called some of the old gang and told them what was going on out here. I gathered up as much as I could. It's not enough, but it's something. And I heard on the radio today that you guys are going to have a radio-thon, or something?
MELEA: Yes.
COLIN: That's great. This place is special.
MELEA: It is.
COLIN: A lot of memories here.
MELEA: A lot.
COLIN: I would love to have lunch and catch up.
MELEA: I have to do some recording. Some ad spots for the radio-thon.
COLIN: Oh, okay. A raincheck.


(No response...)


You know, this is the first time I've seen you since you lived here. Man, has that been a long time, or what?
MELEA: You saw me after.
COLIN: What? I did.
MELEA: You did.
COLIN: Where? In town? I don't remember.
MELEA: I do.
COLIN: Where was it?
MELEA: At the college.
COLIN: At Bacone? In town?

MELEA: Yes.

COLIN: I don't remember.

MELEA: I was eating at the cafeteria. You brought pizza. You made sure everyone that knew you had some. Saw you. You made sure you sat down next to me. That was the last time you saw me.

COLIN: Oh. Yeah, right. I remember. I thought I'd bring you something good to eat instead of that cafeteria food.

MELEA: There were other things you wanted to make sure of.

COLIN: Melea, come on. I'm trying to be nice.

MELEA: You always were, weren't you? I'm a grudge-holder. She moves to leave.

COLIN: What about Angelina? Is she coming down?

MELEA: Haven't you heard from her?

COLIN: No. Not since...man, it's been a few years –

MELEA: Yeah, I thought so.

COLIN: Not since she moved out. She moved up to Tulsa, right?

MELEA: No one knows where she is, Colin.

COLIN: Oh.

MELEA: She just fell off the face of the earth.

COLIN: I thought she might at least call.

MELEA: No. Not once.

COLIN: I'm sorry to hear that.

MELEA: A lot of us are.

(Ms. Hayes enters...)

MS. HAYES: Colin!
COLIN: Ms. Hayes, how are you? You look as pretty as you ever did.
MS. HAYES: Quit it.

> (Melea gives Ms. Hayes the flower...)

MELEA: This is for you.

> (Ms. Hayes takes it. Melea leaves.
> Colin's and Ms. Hayes' voices fade out.
> The lights shift: Melea is standing center
> stage. She is miming painting a picture
> on a large canvas...)

MELEA: He wasn't what I expected. If I had any expectations, I've forgotten them now. Blotted them out. This canvas is bigger than all the rest. And it's actually different. Somewhat, anyway. Down in the corner are colors running along the ground. They're blending together and disappearing in the rain that is now falling. The rest is the same: the Indian man on horseback racing at the sun. His arms outstretched. His hands ready.

> (She steps back from the canvas and
> looks at it...)

Now I know what Angelina felt. All of her – all of me – washed away in the torrent of the rain

> (She dabs a bit on the canvas...)

Some images refuse to die. We may try to get rid of them, but they just stay. They remain. They become a part of what you thought you'd be. (SHE GOES BACK TO PAINTING THE CANVAS)

>(The lights shift: Colin and Ms. Hayes are downstage center....they are outside the home. Melea enters with her recording equipment.)

COLIN: There she is.

MS. HAYES: I was beginning to wonder where you'd gone.

MELEA: I walked over to the storage building.

MS. HAYES: Why there?

MELEA: You don't want to know.

COLIN: Do tell.

MELEA: Angelina and I smoked a cigarette there once...maybe twice.

MS. HAYES: Oh, don't tell me. I don't want to know.

MELEA: (SETS UP HER RECORDER) I told you.

COLIN: After this, do you ladies want to go have lunch somewhere?

MS. HAYES: That would be nice.

MELEA: I've got to take what I've recorded and edit it at the station. I've still got a lot to do before we start this thing tomorrow.

COLIN: I think she's trying to avoid me, Ms. Hayes.

MS. HAYES: It would seem so, but if she's got work.

COLIN: Next time.

(Melea presses the record button and will follow the conversation with her microphone...)

MELEA: And we're recording. I'll just ask questions –
COLIN: – and we'll answer away.
MELEA: Fine.
MS. HAYES: I'm ready.
MELEA: This is Melea Tiger at the Deep Water Foster Home just outside the Muskogee city limits. I have with me the home's director Ms. Sandi Hayes –
MS. HAYES: – Hello.
MELEA: And Colin Fowler, a one-time resident of the home. Welcome.
COLIN: Thanks.
MS. HAYES: Thank you.
MELEA: Mr. Fowler, this is your first time back at the home since –?
COLIN: --oh, I don't know, I guess it's been about a year or so. Isn't that right, Ms. Hayes.
MS. HAYES: I think so, Colin.
COLIN: I like to come back and visit. You have to understand, this was really the only home I ever knew. This is where I learned about my culture –
MELEA: – and that would be?
COLIN: You know.
MELEA: Yes, but the listeners –

COLIN: – Oh, yeah, sorry. I forgot. I'm Muscogee-Creek.

MELEA: What did you learn here about your culture.

COLIN: Yours, too, Melea.

MELEA: Yes. What did you learn?

COLIN: Oh, you name it. Stickball. We actually had a team. You remember that, Ms. Hayes.

MS. HAYES: Yes. How could I forget?

COLIN: I remember getting banged up pretty good one time.

MS. HAYES: We had to take you to the emergency room. A broken nose, as I recall.

COLIN: And a rib or two out of place.

MS. HAYES: Scared me half to death.

COLIN: I loved playing stickball out here. Loved it. And we learned about her language and Creek history. The mounds back east and the tribal towns here in Oklahoma. We made a few visits as field trips.

MS. HAYES: We went all over.

COLIN: We sure did.

MS. HAYES: It was wonderful.

COLIN: It was. And we learned about the food. We made a lot of frybread. Ate a lot of frybread. Way too much.

(He and Ms. Hayes laugh...)

MS. HAYES: Here at Deep Water, Melea, we believe very strongly in teaching the children about where they came from. That's one of our main goals.

COLIN: And I wouldn't have learned any of that if I wasn't here.

MELEA: Any special memories about this place?

(A quick pause...)

COLIN: Too many. Way too many.

MELEA: Anything specific come to mind?

COLIN: Yes. When I came back when you and Angelina Bible were here.

MS. HAYES: Well, that was a long time ago.

COLIN: Not that long ago. Those were great times for me. A lot of fun.

MS. HAYES: It seems like a long time ago. Doesn't it, Melea?

COLIN: The radio listeners out there do know you lived here, too, for a while, don't they?

MS. HAYES: I'm sure they do.

(Melea can't find any words to speak...)

COLIN: I hope so. That's why you're here, right? Why the station is here? I think it's great what you're doing and what they're doing. This place has to keep its door open.

MS. HAYES: We'd like that very much. We've been here for over a fifty years and would like to keep doing the work we've committed to.

COLIN: It's very special, Melea. You know that. They fed us, taught us, and I didn't even mention about my spirituality. If it weren't for Deep Water, there's no telling what kind of person I'd be. I learned about God here.

219

MS. HAYES: Thank you, Colin.
COLIN: No, thank you, Ms. Hayes.

(Melea turns the recorder off...)

MELEA: That's good. I've got plenty to work with here.
COLIN: If you need any more, just let me know. Ms. Hayes, you ready for some lunch?
MS. HAYES: All right, Colin.

(Melea stares at her...)

COLIN: You sure you're not coming? It's on me.
MELEA: No. I've got work to do.
COLIN: Okay. Another raincheck then.

(Ms. Hayes touches Melea on the shoulder as she and Colin exit...)

MELEA: When it happened, it happened very quickly.

(The lights shift: Colin is sitting in his truck. He is looking forward. He is at a drive-in movie. Melea enters the vehicle and sits by the passenger door...)

COLIN: There you are. I thought you fell in.
MELEA: Nope. I saw a cousin of mine.
COLIN: Really? Who?
MELEA: Mike Atkins.
COLIN: Don't know him.

MELEA: I barely do. He's on my grandpa's side of the family.

COLIN: Have you seen this before? (POINTS TO THE MOVIE SCREEN)

MELEA: No. We don't watch a lot of movies.

COLIN: I remember. I love this place. You get to sit in your own truck while you watch a movie. It's great.

MELEA: There's a lot of folks out here tonight.

COLIN: Always is. There's a lot more to do than just watch the movie.

MELEA: Oh.

COLIN: I'm sorry Angelina couldn't come. Is she really feeling that bad?

MELEA: Pretty bad. She hasn't slept very well in a while and now she's got the flu.

COLIN: Bummer. I'm glad you got to come.

MELEA: Thanks for taking me.

COLIN: You seem better.

MELEA: What do you mean?

COLIN: Well, at the pizza place a few weeks back you seemed pretty out of it.

MELEA: I stay that way.

COLIN: It's confusing, I know.

MELEA: It's so hard. I never thought I'd end up where I am. I thought my grandpa would take care of me forever. But Ms. Hayes is all right. She seems to really care about me.

COLIN: She does.

MELEA: And Angelina is great.

COLIN: Yeah.

MELEA: I just feel so out of place no matter where I go.

COLIN: You don't have to feel that way. You don't.

MELEA: I daydream a lot. Imagine myself somewhere else.

COLIN: Where?

MELEA: You'll laugh.

COLIN: No, I won't. Promise.

MELEA: We studied about Tecumseh the other day.

COLIN: Oh, yeah. He's great.

MELEA: We talked about how he followed the words of the prophet and worked so hard to get the people together. He was charismatic and so many believed in him. I see him riding off with the sun shining behind him...I told you it sounded pretty funny.

COLIN: Not at all. Are you there?

MELEA: Yeah.

COLIN: Where?

MELEA: I see myself riding behind him, holding him close to me. And I keep telling myself: he's not even from my tribe. But then I think how he tried to bring all of the people together. How he tried to get everyone to think alike and stay focused on good living and unity.

COLIN: It's an awesome story. I can see why you daydream about it. We all have to have heroes. Some more than others. (TOUCHES HER HAIR)

MELEA: I don't want to be confused anymore.

COLIN: No one does.

(She notices him touching her hair...)

MELEA: What are you doing?

COLIN: I'm sorry. I couldn't help it. It's just that –

MELEA: – What?

COLIN: I have feelings for you. I don't know –

MELEA: – What about Angelina?

COLIN: I don't know about her. I don't. I'm with her, but want to be with you.

MELEA: I don't think that this is –

COLIN: – You're right. You're right. (PULLS HIS HAND AWAY)

MELEA: That's part of my confusion.

COLIN: I know it is. I see it in your eyes when I look at you.

MELEA: I don't want to hurt anyone.

COLIN: I don't, either. I can't help what I feel.

MELEA: Me, either.

(He reaches over and kisses her. She responds. The lights shift: Colin freezes with his face buried in Melea's neck...)

MELEA: And that's how it begins. From no family to loneliness to a new home to a new way of life to a new friend to...this. Of course I kept it from Angelina. Yes, I didn't breathe a word to Ms. Hayes. But now someone wanted me. I hadn't made my way in school. I hadn't had the chance yet. No one wanted me for my singing voice. I didn't play in the band. I wasn't on a team. My personality was a blank slate. But now someone wanted me. Forget that he was seven years older than me. I was wanted. I had something to offer. I could give something now. And I did. Two weeks later in the back of his truck, him laying down a towel, I saw stars for the first time. All I remember now is the hurt of it. Afterwards, he threw the towel into the trees and took me back home (GENTLY TOUCHES HIS FACE AND KISSES HIM LIGHTLY)

(The lights shift: Angelina and Ms. Hayes are in the girls' bedroom...)

ANGELINA: When's she coming back?

MS. HAYES: They were going to the concert and then to get some ice cream. They were going to bring you back some.

ANGELINA: I'm not hungry.

MS. HAYES: It's ice cream.

ANGELINA: Do I still have a fever?

MS. HAYES: No, you don't (SITS ON THE BED BESIDE ANGELINA)

ANGELINA: Why am I still sick? I've had this for going on two weeks now.

MS. HAYES: Have you thrown up?

ANGELINA: No.

MS. HAYES: That's good. You've just got the bug that's going around.

ANGELINA: I hurt all over.

MS. HAYES: Are you still not sleeping?

ANGELINA: I'm trying my best, Ms. Hayes. I just can't.

MS. HAYES: It's all right. Goodness! Try and relax

(She begins rubbing Angelina's neck…)

ANGELINA: That feels good.

MS. HAYES: Good. Do your legs still hurt?

ANGELINA: I ache all over. When are they getting back?

MS. HAYES: Before ten. Colin promised me.

ANGELINA: What do you think of him?

MS. HAYES: Of Colin? He was one of ours. I love him very much.

ANGELINA: Yeah, but you're supposed to.

MS. HAYES: Very funny.

ANGELINA: Well, you are.

MS. HAYES: I think he's got a lot going for him. He pulled himself out of a very difficult situation and made the best of it. He's always done that.

ANGELINA: I have to tell you something.

(A quick pause…)

MS. HAYES: All right, go ahead and tell me.

ANGELINA: I love him.

(A pause…)

MS. HAYES: You're infatuated with him. There's a difference.

(Angelina jerks away from her...)

ANGELINA: There isn't!

MS. HAYES: Angelina –

ANGELINA: – there isn't!

MS. HAYES: I was afraid this might happen. I knew this would be too great a temptation for everyone involved.

ANGELINA: I want to be with him.

MS. HAYES: You're only seventeen. You don't know what you want.

ANGELINA: I'm nearly eighteen! And I do, too!

MS. HAYES: Calm down. You're only going to get yourself worked up again and you won't be able to sleep.

ANGELINA: I need him!

MS. HAYES: Angelina –

ANGELINA: – I want him!

MS. HAYES: That is enough! I don't want to have to discipline you when you're not feeling well and not yourself.

ANGELINA: I am myself. Where is he?

MS. HAYES: They'll be back soon enough. I told you.

ANGELINA: He's with Melea?

MS. HAYES: Yes. I told you that, too.

ANGELINA: That's not good –

(She squirms on the bed, wrapping the pillow in her arms...)

MS. HAYES: All right, now. Just catch your breath. You're just making your flu bug even worse.

ANGELINA: We're going to be married.

MS. HAYES: Angelina! No more talk like that. You need to focus on something else. You're getting yourself all bent out of shape. Now, just breathe. We don't want any terrors tonight, now, do we? Do we?

ANGELINA: No, ma'am.

MS. HAYES: All right. Just breathe

(She begins lightly scratching Angelina's leg...)

ANGELINA: I'm sorry.

MS. HAYES: Don't be.

ANGELINA: But everything I said was true.

MS. HAYES: I know that. We'll have to talk about it later. And I'll have to talk to Colin.

ANGELINA: No!

MS. HAYES: Angelina.

ANGELINA: Yes, ma'am.

MS. HAYES: Go to sleep.

ANGELINA: I can't. I don't want to.

MS. HAYES: You know, you came here a little too late for me to tell you stories at bedtime. I do for all the littler ones here.

ANGELINA: Come on, Ms. Hayes, I don't wanna hear a story.

MS. HAYES: Okay. I'll tell you one, anyway. One that you'll like. Just breathe. I heard this from a Creek man who lived in Okmulgee. He could do a little medicine, too. He called this one: "The Orphan."

ANGELINA: Oh, great.

MS. HAYES: Just listen.

ANGELINA: It won't change anything.

MS. HAYES: All I'm interested in is getting you to sleep. All right, now – "The Orphan." There was an orphan going about one day shooting arrows. He came across a creek with the sound of thunder coming from it. He was curious and went to see. He saw a snake a being of Thunder fighting in the water. The snake tried to get the orphan to kill the Thunder, but the being of Thunder yelled for him not to. He told the orphan where to kill the snake with his arrow. And so the orphan did. And by doing this the orphan got the Thunder's power, but he was told not to reveal its source to anyone. This power gave him great wisdom and authority. He predicted what animals the hunters would kill. And he was right every single time. And then war came. A conflict between two tribes. He brought lightning and thunder on their enemies and scattered them. The orphan was renowned all over for his power and wisdom. And then one final war came. The orphan went out by himself and circled a tree. When he did, the lightning and the thunder came down and killed all their enemies. He spent his last bit of power and wisdom to save his people. But the orphan was never seen again after that. Some said he disappeared into the sky with the thunder. And that's why Thunder is proclaimed to be an orphan child.

(Angelina is asleep...)

Works every time.

> (Ms. Hayes lays her down and tucks her
> into bed. The lights shift: It is present-
> day with Melea outside on the grounds
> of the home. Colin walks up behind
> her...)

COLIN: It's quiet out here.

> (She turns to look at him...)

MELEA: It was.
COLIN: My only question is why?
MELEA: A very big question when you think
about it.
COLIN: You've been cold to me ever since I
came back.
MELEA: Well, don't ask why. That'd be stupid.
COLIN: Why?

> (He tries to laugh-she doesn't...)

MELEA: Some waters run very deep.
COLIN: That's funny. Deep Water Foster
Home--
MELEA: – I got it.
COLIN: Ironic.
MELEA: Whatever.
COLIN: I'm married now.

> (A pause...)

I've got a kid.

(She doesn't move...)

He's three. Name's Gabriel. After the archangel.
MELEA: Ms. Hayes would be proud.
COLIN: She is. We call him Gabe.
MELEA: Who'd you marry?
COLIN: You don't know her.
MELEA: From around here?
COLIN: Okmulgee.
MELEA: Oh.
COLIN: Whatever happened, it was –

(He lets it hang in the air...)

MELEA: The truth of the matter is I was young
and vulnerable and you took advantage of that.
COLIN: Melea –
MELEA: – You were allowed to be near me
when you shouldn't have been anywhere within
a hundred miles of the place.
COLIN: Don't blame Ms. Hayes –
MELEA: – I'm not. She got suckered in like
everybody else. You're a salesman, right?
COLIN: Yeah, still at it. I guess.
MELEA: You always were. Fox. Snake. You fit
in well with all our stories.
COLIN: You were beautiful. Still are. I couldn't
resist that.
MELEA: And Angelina?
COLIN: I don't know, Melea. It was so long ago.

MELEA: Four years is long ago?  Really?  When did you meet the woman you're married to?
COLIN: Right after I left here that last time.  I left town and started working at a car dealership in Okmulgee.  She was the secretary.
MELEA: I haven't seen or heard from Angelina since you left.
COLIN: You're kidding?
MELEA: I only wish I was.  We don't even know if she's dead or alive.
COLIN: But Ms. Hayes says she gets letters from her.
MELEA: She knows better now.
COLIN: Who are they from?  Oh.
MELEA: We saw you as something you weren't.  A wolf in sheep's clothing.
COLIN: Aw, come on.  You're getting a little melodramatic here, aren't you?
MELEA: You don't have any idea, do you?  Not one clue.  I was confused.
COLIN: But you weren't for long.  You knew what you wanted.
MELEA: You put that thought in my mind.  I destroyed two lives out of that ordeal.
COLIN: Two?
MELEA: Never mind.
COLIN: What –?
MELEA: Never mind.  Look, I've got to go –
COLIN: – Let me guess:  record something for the radio-thon.
MELEA: I do.

(She begins to leave...)

COLIN: I still believe you're doing a great thing here.

(She is gone…)

I do (LOOKS AROUND THE GROUNDS)
What'd you –? Aw, forget it. (LEAVES)

(The lights shift: Melea is at center stage…)

MELEA: In the end my heart was swallowed up whole. Completely devoured. I now had a life. I had something to give someone else. But then it went wrong. It usually does in situations like this. Ms. Hayes knew before I did. I didn't know. And what was decided is the reason why March is so bleak. It's why Angelina is gone never to return. I want something to put my finger on and claim as my own. I want to hold something down and say that's mine. Hands off. The sun always rises. It always sets. In my darkest hours I want that man on the horse to kill the light. Just kill it and get it over with. I had just turned seventeen. Angelina was about to graduate from school and move out of the home.

(The lights shift: flashback. Melea walks into Ms. Hayes' office.)

MS. HAYES: You sick again?
MELEA: I threw up.

MS. HAYES: Here, sit down.  You want something to drink?

(Melea sits down...)

MELEA: I don't think I could keep it down.

(Ms. Hayes touches Melea's forehead...)

MS. HAYES: No fever.  It's not like the flu bug that Angelina and some of the other kids had a couple of months back.
MELEA: At least she sleeps now.
MS. HAYES: What about you?
MELEA: Not so much.  I'll be all right.
MS. HAYES: You've been doing this – what?  Two days?
MELEA: Three.  Yeah.  I think that's right.  Three.

(Ms. Hayes sits down...)

MS. HAYES: Melea.
MELEA: Yes, ma'am?
MS. HAYES: Look at me.

(Melea won't...)

Melea.
MELEA: I can't.
MS. HAYES: You better.  Right now.

(Melea does...)

MELEA: I don't feel good.
MS. HAYES: And you're going on not feeling
good.

(Melea cracks a bit...)

MELEA: Ms. Hayes –
MS. HAYES: Colin?
MELEA: Yes, ma'am.
MS. HAYES: Melea.
MELEA: I know.  I know it.  You don't have to
say a word.
MS. HAYES: I put my trust in you.  And him!
MELEA: I know.  Please don't!
MS. HAYES: Why would you do something like
that?  Why?

(Melea turns away...)

Look at me.
MELEA: I don't want to.
MS. HAYES: You will!

(Ms. Hayes stands up...)

MELEA: What am I supposed to say?
MS. HAYES: Nothing.  Not a thing.

(Ms. Hayes moves to the front of the
desk and stares down at Melea...)

MELEA: I'm so sorry.

MS. HAYES: In the years I've been here this has never happened. Did you know that? I'm sure you had no idea. And Colin! What was he thinking?

MELEA: I'm sorry.

MS. HAYES: Stop saying that! It isn't doing either of us any good. I can't call your grandfather.

MELEA: No, don't!

MS. HAYES: I won't. Hush. Oh, Melea. Melea, Melea. Why didn't you use some kind of protection –

MELEA: – I don't know! He didn't want to! He said that it felt –

MS. HAYES: – Never mind what he said. Just never mind. Melea, this has never happened here at Deep Water. Never. How am I going to report this to the board? What are they...?

MELEA: I'm just another statistic, aren't I?

MS. HAYES: Melea. Please, hon, don't talk like that.

MELEA: We just studied it in class the other day.

MS. HAYES: All right, all right now. Goodness. Calm down. Just breathe

(She touches Melea on the shoulder...)

MELEA: I am so sorry.

MS. HAYES: Have you told Colin?

MELEA: No. I'm not going to.

MS. HAYES: You'll have to.

MELEA: We're finished. I don't want this.

MS. HAYES: I know you don't.

MELEA: I don't!

MS. HAYES: Are you sure?

MELEA: Yes, I'm sure.

MS. HAYES: I don't know if this is something--
do you trust me?

MELEA: Yes, ma'am.

MS. HAYES: Okay, then. We'll get through this.
We will.

(The lights shift: back to Melea and
Colin standing on the grounds...)

COLIN: Aw, never mind.

(Melea walks back to him...)

Did you forget something?

MELEA: I think you ought to know that I've
carried a burden for a very long time. Ms.
Hayes and I have. And now I want to give it to
you.

COLIN: What are you talking about?

MELEA: The past.

COLIN: It's long gone.

MELEA: For you maybe. Not for me. Not for
Ms. Hayes, Angelina. There are some things
that young girls can't take no matter what the
research says.

COLIN: Where is this going?

MELEA: To the last night we were together.

COLIN: I loved you so much.

MELEA: Forget that. My question is why?
COLIN: A very big question. Your words.
MELEA: Did you want me to get pregnant?

(A pause...)

COLIN: Melea, that was so long ago.
MELEA: Did you want me to?
COLIN: I don't know.
MELEA: It's a yes or no question. Did you?
COLIN: Yes.
MELEA: You did?
COLIN: Yes.
MELEA: You wanted me pregnant?
COLIN: I said so, didn't I?
MELEA: Why?
COLIN: Why, why, why! Stop asking!
MELEA: Why!
COLIN: I thought it was the only way I could keep you. I didn't want Angelina anymore. She knew that. But I knew that the only way I could have you was to –
MELEA: – I see.
COLIN: And when you miscarried, it devastated me. We should've been together. You shouldn't have pushed me away.
MELEA: I have to tell you...something now.
COLIN: What?
MELEA: I didn't miscarry.

(A long pause...)

237

COLIN: Ms. Hayes would never have let you get an abortion –
MELEA: – she did.
COLIN: No way!
MELEA: She did. She took me.

(Another pause...)

COLIN: No.
MELEA: I thought you ought to know.

(She leaves. Colin stares out at the sky. Melea enters Ms. Hayes' office. It's the day of the radio-thon. Melea picks up her equipment from the desk.)

MELEA: Are you ready to do this?
MS. HAYES: I'm ready. Are you?
MELEA: Yes, ma'am. We are gonna raise that money.
MS. HAYES: I hope so. I really do. I love this place.
MELEA: Me, too.
MS. HAYES: Even after – I mean, I know it's been so hard coming back and seeing me...and Colin. And not knowing about Angelina.
MELEA: We were so young. We didn't know any better.
MS. HAYES: Wounds turn into scars, but the scars still remain, I've heard it said.
MELEA: They do. (WALKS TO THE DOOR)
MS. HAYES: Melea –
MELEA: Yes?

MS. HAYES: (NOT ABLE TO SAY
ANYTHING) The words...they just won't come,
hon. I wish I could...

MELEA: There's no need. We'll just leave it that
way.

> (Melea leaves and walks to center stage.
> A special comes up on her. Angelina
> walks into the light.)

ANGELINA: I would say I hate you, but I don't
think I have to!

MELEA: She said to me the last time we saw
each other. I never said a word.

ANGELINA: I've been thinking all night and all
day what I would say to you. What I'd try to do
to you!

MELEA: She didn't know that I'd had already
been done. Well, she did. She knew. She found
out. She listened outside the door that night
when Ms. Hayes found out.

> (Melea enters their room for the final
> confrontation from years before...)

MELEA: There are only so many ways I can say
I'm sorry, Angelina.

ANGELINA: We were going to be married!

MELEA: He doesn't want that. You know he
doesn't.

ANGELINA: He does so!

MELEA: Colin doesn't know what he wants.
But he's hurting a lot of people while he tries to
find out.

ANGELINA: Do you know how many
nightmares I've had because of this?
MELEA: Do you want to know how many I've
had?
ANGELINA: Saying I hate you isn't enough!
MELEA: But I'd understand. I would.
ANGELINA: Stop being so understanding,
Melea! It makes me sick!
MELEA: What can I say that would make this all
better? I mean it. What do you want me to do?
I'll do it.
ANGELINA: I don't want you to do a thing.
Not one single thing. I want to something –
MELEA: – Angelina, please, come on--
ANGELINA: – I want to do something cruel!
You know? I want to hurt you. I want to crush
you. To do to you what you've done to me.
(PAUSES TO THINK ABOUT) The worst thing I
can do to you is just leave. Just like Thunder.
MELEA: I wanted to ask her what she meant,
but my tongue stuck to the roof of my mouth.
ANGELINA: I want to bring down thunder and
lightning to kill all my enemies! But I'll just
disappear above the trees with the thunder –
leaves.

(Melea turns with microphone in hand...)

MELEA: This is Melea Tiger on the air for
KCRK, Creek radio. We're here at the Deep
Water Foster Home just outside of Muskogee
and we're going to be here all day for this radio-
thon to save this wonderful place. So dig deep

in those pockets and be charitable to young people that are displaced. They need a home and Deep Water has been that home for more than a hundred years...

(Thunder echoes all around. Melea freezes. Ms. Hayes appears in a special in her office. Colin appears in a special at the pizza place. A spotlight comes up on the girls' bedroom, but Angelina isn't there...)

MELEA: I would love to be able to paint the thunder in my pictures, but I can't. I still have my warrior chasing after the sun ready to smother the light. And all I can think is that the feelings will fade with time, that the detachment will lessen, that all of this – Ms. Hayes, Colin, and Angelina--will all become memory, and then that will fade. And finally the last remnants will turn to dust. And then, and only then, the sun will be choked of its light. But the orphaned thunder – it remains.

(The lights fade...)

End.

# Jacobson and the Kiowa Five

A Play

By

Russ Tall Chief

CHARACTER LIST:

SPENCER ASAH - Kiowa artist/college student in his 20s; His Kiowa name is Lallo meaning "little boy."

JAMES AUCHIAH - Kiowa artist/college student in his 20's

SOPHIE BROUSSE - French writer/scholar, Oscar Jacobson's wife; she sometimes calls him her "dad"; her pen name is Jeanne D'Ucel; she is in her 40s

YOLANDE - Jacobson's toddler daughter

JACK HOKEAH - Kiowa artist/college student in his 20s

OSCAR JACOBSON - Swedish artist and professor in his 40s

SAVOIE LOTTINVILLE - Student editor of University of Oklahoma daily newspaper in his 20s

STEPHEN MOPOPE - Kiowa artist/college student in his 30s

SUSIE PETERS - American field matron for Kiowa Tribe in her 40s

LOIS SMOKEY - Kiowa artist/college student in her late teens

MARTHA TSATOKE - Monroe Tsatoke's wife in her 20s

PEGGY - Tsatoke's toddler daughter

MONROE TSATOKE - Kiowa artist/college student in his 20s

*Jacobson and the Kiowa Five* was performed as a staged reading during the fourth annual Oklahoma City Theatre Company's Native American New Play Festival on April 21, 2013. It was directed by Chad Anderson with the following cast:

| | |
|---|---|
| SPENCER ASAH: | Matt Cross |
| JAMES AUCHIAH: | Matt Cross |
| SOPHIE BROUSSE: | Emanuelle Chiocca |
| JACK HOKEAH: | Aubrey Murphy |
| OSCAR JACOBSON: | Rob May |
| SAVOIE LOTTINVILLE: | Tia Lasiter |
| STEPHEN MOPOPE: | Bobby Barron |
| MONROE TSATOKE: | John Greer |
| PEGGY/YOLANDE: | Tia Lasiter |
| SUZIE PETERS: | Tia Lasiter |
| LOIS SMOKEY: | Katie O'Dell |
| MARTHA TSATOKE: | Maya Torralba |

**Russ Tall Chief,** (Playwright) is an Osage, and currently serves as the Director of Student Engagement, Inclusion, and Multicultural Programs at Oklahoma City University. Tall Chief has served as the Art Galleries Editor for Native People's Magazine. As an educator, he has taught at several institutions throughout Oklahoma. Tall Chief is a Taildancer and former Drumkeeper for the Greyhorse District of the In'lonshka Osage ceremonial dances. He served as the Head Man Dancer for the Smithsonian National Museum of the American Indian in New York City. Tall Chief went on to serve as Executive Director of visual art and cultural performance events for the Jacobson House Native Art Center in Norman, OK. Additionally, Tall Chief curated Native art exhibits and was the featured dancer at the Grand Palais in Paris as part of the annual Art en Capital exhibitions. Tall Chief is the great nephew of the renowned Osage ballerinas Maria and Marjorie Tall Chief.

## NOTES ON THE PLAY:

Although this story is dramatized, much of the dialogue is conveyed in the artists' actual words as recorded between 1927 and 1937. Tall Chief assembled their quotes and stories from memoirs, newspaper articles, interviews and books, and tried to present their words verbatim as often as possible throughout the script. Some passages of the dialogue maybe spoken in Kiowa although the current dialogue is written in English with a bit of French and Spanish. Translations may be projected as supertitles throughout the play, if needed. Images of the artists' paintings will be projected onto a screen along with historical photos of the artists, their families and important people in the story as the images relate to the character and narrative of a particular moment. While the artists are painting in the scenes, the screen will appear as if it were their canvas magnified with the images of the paintings emerging in real time using graphic design software that simulates painting. The effect is to bring the painting into full view of the audience as if it is taking place on stage at that precise moment.

The Kiowa Five's work marks the genesis of contemporary Native art in Oklahoma as well as Native arts as its own American art form. The art which emerged from this group of determined and passionate Kiowa's was a visual memoir of their own religio-cultural experiences as well as the preservation of the cultural memories of their Kiowa elders, of life before the reservation, government schools and assimilation. While the art of the Kiowa Five is important in its artistic merit, the Kiowa aesthetic preserved in their paintings is also a vitally important archive of Kiowa culture. Kiowa and other American Indian artists that have followed the Kiowa Five to the University Of Oklahoma School Of Art continue to preserve the history of contemporary Native art while also evolving Native art in their own artistic voices.

TIME:
1927

SETTING:
Various locations in Kiowa country, the University of Oklahoma in Norman, Oklahoma, and Prague, Czechoslovakia.

## ACT I

### SCENE ONE

### KIOWA DANCE GROUNDS

(Monroe Tsatoke sings as Spencer Asah, Jack Hokea, Stephen Mopope, Martha Tsatoke and Lois Smokey dance. Susie Peters watches as they dance. At the conclusion of the song/dance, Martha Tsatoke and Lois Smokey present Susie Peters with a beaded bag. She carries this bag with her at all times.)

## ACT I

### SCENE TWO

### OSCAR JACOBSON'S OFFICE

(Oscar Jacobson's office is adjacent to the art studio at the University of Oklahoma in Norman, Oklahoma. He grades papers at his desk. There is a knock at the door...)

OSCAR JACOBSON: Come in, please.

(Susie Peters enters...)

SUSIE PETERS: I hope I am not disturbing you, Professor Jacobson.
OSCAR JACOBSON: Not at all. Some of my students' art submissions, on the other hand, are quite disturbing. If only I could teach fearlessness then art could evolve.
SUSIE PETERS: I am happy to hear that, professor. I may be of some help in that effort.
OSCAR JACOBSON: If you have some idea of how to get art students to paint from their hearts and not their heads then I am all ears, Ms....
SUSIE PETERS: Ms. Peters, professor. My name is Susie Peters.
OSCAR JACOBSON: Welcome, Ms. Peters. Please, have a seat. How can I help you?

(They sit...)

SUSIE PETERS: I am the field matron for the Kiowa Indian community in Anadarko.

OSCAR JACOBSON: Oh yes....fascinating landscape. I have travelled the area a bit myself since I have been here in Oklahoma.

SUSIE PETERS: Oh? Have you been here long?

OSCAR JACOBSON: I began the art program here at the university about ten years ago in 1915. My wife and I built a house just a couple of blocks away from here. You may have walked by it on the way over.

SUSIE PETERS: The quaint stucco house with the flat roof?

OSCAR JACOBSON: That's the one. I designed it myself. The architecture is quintessentially Swedish in honor of my heritage. I challenge you to find one hallway!

SUSIE PETERS: It is very unique for this part of the country.

OSCAR JACOBSON: Thank you, Ms. Peters.

SUSIE PETERS: As a scholar of aesthetics I believe that you should appreciate the work I bring you today. It is very unique as well.

(Susie Peters presents artwork to Oscar Jacobson...)

SUSIE PETERS: These drawings and paintings are the works of Kiowa students that I have been mentoring. A few years ago, I was impressed by their drawings in my home economics class. So, I formed an art club and encouraged the young artists, providing them with art supplies. The students attended St. Patrick's Mission School in Anadarko during the week and met on Saturday mornings at my house in Red Stone to practice their artwork. Some of the students showed tremendous artistic promise, so I took them to study with Willie Baze Lane, an art instructor in Chickasha. Willie gave them lessons in color theory, perspective, and the use of line and form. They are about to graduate from St. Patrick's, so I am here at the encouragement of not only Willie Baze Lane, but also Father Al and Sister Olivia at St. Pat's, who also see great potential in these young Kiowa artists.

OSCAR JACOBSON: Well, this is certainly the first portfolio of art I have reviewed on paper bags and shoe box tops.

SUSIE PETERS: I am afraid we are short on art supplies on the reservation, professor. The students have been known to even draw in the sand when supplies were scarce.

OSCAR JACOBSON: That is most certainly a good sign of natural artistic inclination.

SUSIE PETERS: I agree, professor. These young Kiowas are artists in every sense; art is truly inherent in their culture. Besides expressing themselves through visual art, many of them dance, sing, and also tell dramatic stories at community gatherings.

OSCAR JACOBSON: The work appears almost petroglyphic. The images are fresh and the artistic voices appear to be nearly completely intact of Western influence. It is a bit parochial by university standards, however, Ms. Peters. Do you think that the students would be able to manage the academic courses as well as the art classes?

SUSIE PETERS: I would like to say yes, professor, but I believe we would be setting them up to fail. If there were a way for them to be enrolled as special students of some form or another I believe they could benefit greatly as artists.

OSCAR JACOBSON: I have to admit that I am intrigued by this work, Ms. Peters. I am also curious how you came to become so invested in these Kiowa students that you would make such a forthright effort on their behalf?

SUSIE PETERS: Oh, I have taken an arduous road to get where I am today, professor.

OSCAR JACOBSON: I don't doubt your integrity, Ms. Peters. I am always interested to know how my fellow Euro- Americans come to be transplanted out here to the great frontier.

SUSIE PETERS: I was born in Huntsville, TN, and came to Oklahoma by way of Texas. My parents settled near Alex, OK.

OSCAR JACOBSON: Having worked in law enforcement in the past I can tell you from experience that is dangerous country.

SUSIE PETERS: Yes, but had it not been for the criminal element around Alex I might not have met my first husband.

OSCAR JACOBSON: Your husband was a criminal?

SUSIE PETERS: I beg your pardon, professor. Like you, my husband was in law-enforcement. Unfortunately, he didn't live to see retirement.

He was killed after having the misfortune of meeting Carl Vincent and his son Charles. Between them and the Hudgins gang, my husband didn't stand a chance of seeing old age.

OSCAR JACOBSON: I heard plenty about those characters. They ran with a ruthless bunch.

SUSIE PETERS: I had my own run in with them riding home from school one day. They were very successful at cattle and horse stealing, as well as armed robbery. They got away with my beautiful gold watch, but I felt lucky to get away with my life.

OSCAR JACOBSON: Indeed, you were lucky, Ms. Peters. Those men aren't known for leaving anyone alive.

SUSIE PETERS: Their killing spree ended when they met a man named John Swain, a widower, who was leading a posse chasing the gang. He cornered the gang at their hideout in the Arbuckle Mountains. John said that the gang was so impudent that they played their fiddle during the shootout.

OSCAR JACOBSON: Perhaps they were playing the Funeral March.

SUSIE PETERS: That would have been apropos for their farewell performance. After two hours, 14 outlaws were either killed or wounded. John found my gold pendant watch on one of the gang members. He read my name inscribed on the back of the watch, at that time "Susie Ryan." He was curious as to what kind of girl would own such as beautiful little watch and decided to deliver it to me in person. He said to his law partner, Matt Cook, "if she is pretty, I'll buy her a new chain for the watch". He did in fact buy a chain for the watch on a cold, snowy winter night in 1891 and personally delivered it to me. We were married a year later.

OSCAR JACOBSON: He sounds like a romantic after my own heart.

SUSIE PETERS: John was like a perfectly ripened melon—underneath that firm exterior, he was sweet and tender. We settled on a ranch around Purcell. John desperately wanted to resign his commission in law- enforcement. One winter morning, John and my father went out early to brand some cattle. The day was bitterly cold, so John had bundled up in his heavy coat and thick gloves. His gun belt was tucked underneath his coat. Close to the pasture gate he was approached by three men, Carl Vincent, his son Charles, and Jim Colbert. My father was some distance behind him in a wagon. Dad couldn't hear the conversation, but he said the three men were obviously angry. Dad heard John say, "I'll see you men later," and he turned his horse to go. Then Carl Vincent pulled his rifle and shot John through the body. John fell to the road but managed to pull his glove off with his teeth and unbutton his coat to reach his gun. As Vincent ran toward him, John shot him through the heart and killed him. I heard the shooting and ran out onto the porch to find my father carrying my dead husband. I continued to live on the ranch—heartbroken.

OSCAR JACOBSON: I'm very sorry, Ms. Peters. Did you remarry?

SUSIE PETERS: Yes, I remarried a while later— James Peters, a railroad dispatcher. He was very handsome, but very jealous. He was a hard drinker—nothing like John. James was shot and killed in the red light district of El Reno.

OSCAR JACOBSON: My dear, you certainly have taken an arduous journey.

SUSIE PETERS: Oh, yes, professor. I am afraid I gave up long ago any notion of having a family of my own out here in the "great frontier," as you call it.

OSCAR JACOBSON: It is a difficult life, but I appreciate the simplicity here.

SUSIE PETERS: I suppose I had to leave Oklahoma in order to come to appreciate it.

OSCAR JACOBSON: I couldn't agree more, Miss Peters. I ran as far away as possible from these Great Plains only to find myself nearly right back where I started. I managed to find the love of my life on my journeys, however. So the effort was not entirely unsuccessful.

SUSIE PETERS: You are fortunate, professor. I don't know that my third marriage ever stood any more a chance of success that the previous two. Poor Shaffer—it must have been difficult for him to live with the ghosts of two dead husbands and a widow that wouldn't let them go. When I was offered a government job in Arizona at the East Farm Sanatorium, I felt like it was a much-needed change. But I only stayed seven months. I was offered a job back home in

Oklahoma by the Choctaws that was much more to my liking. When I was offered the job as the Kiowa field matron, the qualifications read: "The woman accepting this position must be robust, fearless, and able to hitch and care for her own team, and live alone in one of the thickest Indian settlements." Well, I was far from robust, but I was a fine horsewoman, riding side-saddle. I knew and loved Indian country and Indian people. So I accepted the position. I have lived among the Kiowa now for 10 years. They accept me as one of their own now, and I have come to think of them as my family. These young students are like my children, professor. Rest assured that my commitment to them is genuine.

OSCAR JACOBSON: I appreciate your honesty, Ms. Peters, and I don't doubt your generosity in the slightest. Unfortunately, we don't have funding at the moment for special students.

SUSIE PETERS: I recently met a member of the Oklahoma Legislature, Mr. Lewis Ware, who is himself a Kiowa. Mr. Ware is well-connected among the Oklahoma elite, professor. He might be able to help find a sponsor for the students.

OSCAR JACOBSON: I will contact Mr. Ware as well as a colleague of mine named Lou Wentz in Ponca City. Perhaps we can find a way to supply the boys with a modest stipend for the year. What an enchanting exercise to have American Indians as artists-in-residence, Ms. Peters. It's unprecedented!

SUSIE PETERS: They are the first artists of their kind around here, professor. I cannot thank you enough.

OSCAR JACOBSON: No, it is I who should be thanking you, Ms. Peters. Judging from this small sampling of Kiowa art it looks as if it will be I who will be the student.


# ACT I

## SCENE THREE

## THE UNIVERSITY OF OKLAHOMA ART STUDIO

(Stephen Mopope, Spencer Asah, Jack Hokeah paint, while Monroe Tsatoke watches and waits for his paints. Some of the dialogue may be spoken in the Kiowa language with supertitles translated into English on the screen. They speak English very well, although their first language is Kiowa...)

STEPHEN MOPOPE: Why aren't you working, Monroe?

MONROE TSATOKE: I ran out of paints. Professor Jacobson is bringing me some more. What are you working on, brother?

STEPHEN MOPOPE: A buffalo hunt—in honor of my clan.

SPENCER ASAH: Our clan, brother.

STEPHEN MOPOPE: Ha, Lallo. OUR clan.

MONROE TSATOKE: How about you, Lallo? What magic are you making?

SPENCER ASAH: A powerful piece, brother—a self-portrait.

STEPHEN MOPOPE: How are your hands?

SPENCER ASAH: Crooked...from baseball.

STEPHEN MOPOPE: I mean the hands in your painting, brother. Be careful not to give yourself paws again.

> (Monroe Tsatoke observes Spencer Asah's painting...)

MONROE TSATOKE: I believe it is too late, Stephen.

SPENCER ASAH: Paws? I don't have paws.

MONROE TSATOKE: No, Lallo. I believe you are correct. They look more like hooves.

SPENCER ASAH: My hands don't look like hooves. Jack, tell them I am not a horse.

JACK HOKEAH: Hunting Horse?

SPENCER ASAH: No, brother. Tell them I am not a horse.

JACK HOKEAH: Yeah, stealing horses.

MONROE TSATOKE: He can't hear you, Lallo.

STEPHEN MOPOPE: I don't know how he ever made it through St. Patrick's.

SPENCER ASAH: Jack was student of the year in 1919. Have you ever seen his handwriting? His penmanship is perfect. He writes like the President of the United States.

MONROE TSATOKE: Coolidge?
SPENCER ASAH: Like Abraham
Lincoln...or...Andrew Jackson.

(They all scoff...)

MONROE TSATOKE: You dare utter the name
of the devil himself?
STEPHEN MOPOPE: What did Grover
Cleveland do to have his picture replaced by
Andrew Jackson's on the $20 dollar bill?
SPENCER ASAH: I don't know, but it must
have been REALLY bad.
STEPHEN MOPOPE: Actually, Grover
Cleveland was the only president to serve two
non-consecutive terms.
MONROE TSATOKE: Someone paid attention
at St. Patrick's.
STEPHEN MOPOPE: Who picked Andrew
Jackson to replace him? Who decides that?
Shouldn't there be a vote?
MONROE TSATOKE: A vote? When did you
get so political?
STEPHEN MOPOPE: Now that I have the right
to vote I plan to exercise it.
SPENCER ASAH: From now on I'm going to
refuse to pay for anything with a $20 dollar bill.
MONROE TSATOKE: You've never had a $20
dollar bill.
SPENCER ASAH: Yeah, well, if I ever get one I
will trade it in for two sawbucks.
STEPHEN MOPOPE: Why don't you just paint
over Jackson's face on your twenties?

SPENCER ASAH: Let's paint Jacobson's face over Jackson's.

MONROE TSATOKE: How about painting pictures of chiefs over all the presidents' faces on ALL the money we earn from art.

ALL: Ha!

STEPHEN MOPOPE: I heard there is a Kaw brother running for Vice-President—Charles Curtis.

MONROE TSATOKE: Imagine that? An Indian Vice-President. Too bad he's not Kiowa.

ALL: Ha!

STEPHEN MOPOPE: At least we have Louis Ware in office. Every vote counts. Boy, Andrew Jackson is lucky Kiowa's couldn't vote back then.

SPENCER ASAH: I wonder where we would be today if not for Andrew Jackson.

STEPHEN MOPOPE: The White House.

SPENCER ASAH: I say we paint it red and call it the Red House.

MONROE TSATOKE: I think we would probably still be in the Black Hills.

SPENCER ASAH: I bet we would still be talking to the animals, flying with the birds, and dancing in the stars.

STEPHEN MOPOPE: We sure have come a long way from doing laundry at St. Patrick's, that's for sure.

JACK HOKEAH: St. Pat's? I don't miss it a bit—especially Sister Olivia's leather strap.

STEPHEN MOPOPE: That strap was so long she could hit three kids at once.

SPENCER ASAH: If I got one more whipping from Sister Olivia I wouldn't have any shape to my backside.

STEPHEN MOPOPE: There IS no shape to your backside, Lallo.

SPENCER ASAH: Yes, there is.

(Flexes his buttocks...)

Can't you see? These are dancing muscles.

STEPHEN MOPOPE: Your backside is as flat as a board, Lallo.

MONROE TSATOKE: You're all-back, Lallo—from head to toe.

JACK HOKEAH: That's right. I always start my paintings with the left toe. That's how I start to dance—left foot first.

MONROE TSATOKE: We're talking about Lallo in the cradleboard, Jack. Spencer!

JACK HOKEAH: Oh, right. His grandmother kept him in the cradleboard too long. When she let him out he was almost as tall as she was.

MONROE TSATOKE: Maybe that's why he is so clumsy.

SPENCER ASAH: I'm not clumsy. It's these white man shoes. They're slippery.

JACK HOKEAH: Was it the white man's shoes that made you dance in backwards at Medicine Park, Lallo?

SPENCER ASAH: I woke up late and forgot my bustle.

MONROE TSATOKE: He'd been up all night singing.

STEPHEN MOPOPE: What was the point of dancing grand entry backwards, Lallo?

SPENCER ASAH: I thought if I danced in backwards that no one would notice that I wasn't wearing a bustle.

STEPHEN MOPOPE: You didn't think that would make you stand out more?

SPENCER ASAH: I still looked good—even without my bustle. What was that crazy dance move you were doing this past weekend, Jack?

JACK HOKEAH: You mean the one I pulled out to beat you and Stephen in the contest?

STEPHEN MOPOPE: Ha, Jack. I let you win because I felt sorry for you always taking second place.

SPENCER ASAH: What do you call that move, Jack? The one where you look like a windshield wiper?

JACK HOKEAH: I don't know. Why don't you show me, Lallo.

(Spencer Asah mimics Jack Hokeah dancing the "windshield wiper." Monroe Tsatoke sings for him. Stephen Mopope keeps painting. Jack Hokeah stops them…)

JACK HOKEAH: Whoa, whoa, whoa…it doesn't look anything like that, Lallo.

SPENCER ASAH: Yes, it does. You look just like a windshield wiper on a Model-T.

STEPHEN MOPOPE: Pretty close, Jack. Only Lallo has more swing.

(Stephen Mopope begins to mimic Spencer Asah mimicking Jack Hokeah. Monroe Tsatoke sings for them. They stop...)

SPENCER ASAH: So what do you call that windshield wiper move, Jack?
JACK HOKEAH: I call it the windshield wiper...but it doesn't look like that. It looks like this...

(Monroe Tsatoke sings as Jack Hokeah dances. Spencer Asah mimics Jack Hokeah. Stephen Mopope mimics Spencer Asah mimicking Jack Hokeah. The door opens to the studio. Enter Oscar Jacobson, Sophie Brousse, Savoie Lottinville and Lois Smokey. Monroe Tsatoke stops singing. Jack Hokeah and Stephen Mopope stop dancing...startled, Spencer Asah slips on the rug and crashes to the floor, taking a table down with him...)

MONROE TSATOKE: Hello, Mr. Jacobson. We hope you enjoyed our "welcome dance."
STEPHEN MOPOPE: It's called the "windshield wiper."
OSCAR JACOBSON: That was quite a finish, Spencer.
JACK HOKEAH: Must be those white man shoes, aye, Lallo?

SOPHIE BROUSSE: Are you okay, Spencer?

(Spencer Asah has knocked the wind out of himself...)

SPENCER ASAH: Unkha.

OSCAR JACOBSON: While you summon some air, Spencer, I would like to introduce you gentlemen to some folks. I am sure you all know Lois Smokey. She is the newest member of our studio taking the count to five Kiowa artists in residence here at the University of Oklahoma.

SOPHIE BROUSSE: Extraordinary!

(Greetings all around...)

OSCAR JACOBSON: I know you will all make Lois feel welcome here at the university.

LOIS SMOKEY: I brought my mother with me. She will be living with me while I am taking classes.

ALL: Ha.

OSCAR JACOBSON: I would also like for all of you to meet Savoie Lottinville. He is the editor of the university newspaper.

SAVOIE LOTTINVILLE: I look forward to interviewing you all and writing about your art. By the way, is your art for sale? I would like to purchase one of your pieces for my father.

JACK HOKEAH: Mine's not for sale.

SOPHIE BROUSSE: Jack has a hard time parting with his work.

JACK HOKEAH: Why would I want to sell them?

MONROE TSATOKE: Someday when you have a family to support you will understand why you need to sell your art, brother.

SPENCER ASAH: Someday when you don't have Lou Wentz and his oil money to support you then you will need to sell your art.

MONROE TSATOKE: Someday I am sure one of your girlfriends will want a pretty ring, Jack.

JACK HOKEAH: All of them want a ring.

MONROE TSATOKE: Well, don't wait too long, Jack. The joys of fatherhood give my life meaning. My daughter, Peggy, gives my painting purpose.

OSCAR JACOBSON: I wholeheartedly concur, Monroe. My daughter, Yolande, represents the best of both Sophie and I. As God has seen fit to bless me with two muses I find myself painting twice as much.

SOPHIE BROUSSE: Thus I find myself cleaning twice as much. Our walls and floors have become canvases for our daughter's painting.

OSCAR JACOBSON: Yes, our toddler has turned our home into an art project. Even our dog, Napoleon, emerges from Yolande's room nearly every day a different color.

SOPHIE BROUSSE: Thank goodness dogs are color-blind. The poor thing has no idea as he growls at the postman that he looks like a circus clown.

OSCAR JACOBSON: What's worse, the dog has taken to following me all over campus like that.

SAVOIE LOTTINVILLE: I recall a dog that appeared onstage last week while William Howard Taft was speaking in the university theatre.

OSCAR JACOBSON: Oh, yes….I'm afraid that was our Napoleon. When Taft mentioned the name of the formidable French Emperor, Napoleon, in his speech, the dog thought Taft was calling him.

SOPHIE BROUSSE: He knows his name well, but I am afraid he doesn't know much more.

OSCAR JACOBSON: He behaved himself well on stage. I will give him credit for that.

SOPHIE BROUSSE: Yes, throughout the ENTIRE speech.

OSCAR JACOBSON: Fortunately Taft is a dog lover. We had a good laugh at our Yale alumni breakfast the next morning.

SOPHIE BROUSSE: Between Yolande and Napoleon we can't seem to keep up with Oscar's paint supplies.

OSCAR JACOBSON: I am convinced the dog eats my brushes.

MONROE TSATOKE: I sympathize with you more than you know. My paints and brushes tend to disappear daily now that my Peggy is walking. Then they reappear in the most unlikely locations. In fact, my toes at this very moment are painted cherry red after the insides of my shoes became my daughter's most recent paint palette.

SPENCER ASAH: We'll have to change your Indian name from Hunting Horse to Red Toe.

MONROE TSATOKE: My honorable grandfather, Red Tepee, would have been very proud.

OSCAR JACOBSON: Well, Red Toe, I have brought more paint supplies for you and your toddler apprentice.

MONROE TSATOKE: Thank you, professor. I shall give them a good time.

> (Monroe Tsatoke and Lois Smokey take their places in the studio and begin to work...)

OSCAR JACOBSON: Monroe and Stephen are such prolific painters, Savoie, we can hardly keep them supplied with paint. Spencer and Jack are much more contemplative about their work.

SOPHIE BROUSSE: You'll find that Lois is very careful about her work, too.

OSCAR JACOBSON: You must know, Savoie, that it is unprecedented to have American Indian students studying art here at the university.

SOPHIE BROUSSE: What's more, to have a Kiowa woman studying painting is highly unorthodox, especially to paint figuratively.

SAVOIE LOTTINVILLE: And what do you mean by painting "figuratively?"

OSCAR JACOBSON: Lois is the only Kiowa woman to paint "people" in addition to designs.

SOPHIE BROUSSE: Lois is also an accomplished seamstress and textile artist. Kiowa women traditionally make beautiful clothes adorned with beadwork and porcupine quillwork. Lois makes her own buckskin dresses as well as the men's dance outfits.

LOIS SMOKEY: I learned to make clothes at St. Patrick's Mission School in Anadarko. I went to class half of the day and then worked in the sewing room in the afternoon. For some reason sleeves and the French seam came very naturally to me.

SOPHIE BROUSSE: That must be why we get along so well.

STEPHEN MOPOPE: Lois also made our school uniforms at St. Pat's.

LOIS SMOKEY: My mother taught me beadwork, and I also learned embroidery and crochet from Father Hitto. Oh, I miss him. Father Hitto was such a jolly man—always smiling and laughing. All the students liked him. One time he brought me back some beads from Europe and I made a beaded bag with some of my friends. We all made different pieces and then sewed them together and put fringes on it. It was nice. We gave the bag to Susie Peters for all that she did for us.

OSCAR JACOBSON: I believe she was carrying the bag when she brought your art to me.

LOIS SMOKEY: Since we gave her the bag I have never seen her without it. It makes me feel good to see someone appreciate things I make.

SOPHIE BROUSSE: Lois, you may very well be the next Olinka Hrdy.

LOIS SMOKEY: Who is Olinka Hrdy?

OSCAR JACOBSON: Olinka Hrdy was one of our prize student artists here at OU. She painted numerous murals throughout the university campus.

SOPHIE BROUSSE: She left just before Lois came, unfortunately, otherwise she could have been a wonderful mentor to her.

SAVOIE LOTTINVILLE: What is your favorite subject to paint, Lois?

LOIS SMOKEY: I paint what is most important to me—family and children.

SOPHIE BROUSSE: I find it fascinating why most of your paintings are blue and yellow, Lois.

LOIS SMOKEY: The blue represents the sky and the yellow represents the yellow grass of the Plains.

OSCAR JACOBSON: One isn't often privileged to see women in Native art, which also makes Lois's depictions all the more endearing.

LOIS SMOKEY: I paint women to honor them. My mother especially inspires me. She is the last living survivor of the battle of Palo Duro Canyon.

SAVOIE LOTTINVILLE: What happened at Palo Duro Canyon?

MONROE TSATOKE: Palo Duro was the scene of a horrific attack on the Kiowa people.

(Historical photos and art are projected on the screen…)

LOIS SMOKEY: It was September 28, 1874. My mother Maggie was asleep when the attack began. Col. Mackenzie had been chasing Quanah Parker for three years before he and a band of Kiowas with the Quesadas were trapped in Palo Duro Canyon. They thought they would be safe in the canyon. In order to keep the light from the fires from being noticed from above, they killed horses and covered the coals with the carcasses. When the cavalrymen attacked, people ran in all directions. My great-aunt jumped on her horse, which was known to be very fast. She turned and saw my mother sitting alone—mom was still just an infant. My aunt gave a war whoop and ran to my mom. She circled her on the horse, stooped down and swept her up into her arms. The horse stumbled first and nearly fell, but they held on until the horse regained its footing. The horse was so fast that it outran the cavalry and the two were able to escape the battle. The cavalrymen shot all of our men before they could get to their weapons. After they shot the women and children they trampled them with their horses. Anyone left behind was butchered with sabers.
SOPHIE BROUSSE: How barbaric.
LOIS SMOKEY: If I have a son, I will name him Ksai (Keah-soy), "Fast Horse."
SAVOIE LOTTINVILLE: Would you ever attempt to depict the battle in your painting?
LOIS SMOKEY: No, but one of my brothers here might.

OSCAR JACOBSON: Another extraordinary aspect of these artists' work, Savoie, is that they never use models. They have never studied anatomy; out of the magic of their memories spring all their creations. They see instead of thinking about what they see. Their memory seems to retain all that their eyes have absorbed and they can manifest their memories visually whenever they wish. All that is irrelevant is omitted, only the essential quality remains. They do instinctively what the modern western painter is trained to do.

SOPHIE BROUSSE: I am particularly struck by the action and the rhythm with which their paintings vibrate— the dancer's dance, the deer leap; looking at them one seems to hear the drum and the flute; all the figures are remarkably, radiantly alive. Lines, mass, and color, all combine to make a whole that simply sings.

OSCAR JACOBSON: Speaking of singing, when we first met Monroe he was singing at a dance.

MONROE TSATOKE: Craterville Park.

SOPHIE BROUSSE: That's right. A musical quality permeates all of Monroe's work. His soul is music.

OSCAR JACOBSON: He paints not only his own people but also neighboring tribes, the Pawnees, Osage, Comanches, and others.

SOPHIE BROUSSE: We own one of his paintings where three women, a Comanche, a Kiowa, and an Apache, stand together seen from the back. Another of his works shows a warrior in a feathered bonnet, one knee lifted in the motion of the war dance. His flute player and the woman he has wooed is nothing short of a masterpiece.

OSCAR JACOBSON: Historically, Savoie, Kiowa art has a clear cultural tradition in painting on buffalo and deer hides. Thirty years or so ago there were two Kiowas, Hawgone and Silver Horn, who painted mostly on hides, and whose work shows some of the characteristics noticeable in that of these artists.

STEPHEN MOPOPE: My greatest honor was renewing the Battle Tepee with my uncle Silver Horn and Oheltoint.

OSCAR JACOBSON: For the benefit of our guest, would you indulge us with an explanation of what it means to renew a tepee, Stephen?

STEPHEN MOPOPE: When a tepee is given to a new owner it is repainted. After we got the tepee from the Cheyennes in 1840, we painted hatchets and yellow and black stripes on it. Then a little more than ten years ago in 1916, I renewed it, or repainted it, with my uncles.

OSCAR JACOBSON: Thank you, Stephen. Well, Savoie, we should let them get on with their work.

SAVOIE LOTTINVILLE: Certainly, professor. Perhaps I can interview each of the artists for an article in the newspaper— when it's convenient for them.

271

OSCAR JACOBSON: I will have my assistant, Edith, arrange some time for you to spend with each of the artists.

(All bid farewell to Savoie Lottinville as he exits...)

OSCAR JACOBSON: And what are you working on, Jack?

JACK HOKEAH: A war dancer.

SOPHIE BROUSSE: What else would Jack be painting?

OSCAR JACOBSON: You have a tremendous sense of movement in your dancers, Jack.

JACK HOKEAH: I danced this past weekend, so I am trying to show what I was feeling when I danced.

SOPHIE BROUSSE: I believe you illustrate your dancing with tremendous emotion, Jack.

JACK HOKEAH: Thank you, Mrs. Jacobson.

OSCAR JACOBSON: Monroe, my boy, what does your heart have to say today?

MONROE TSATOKE: I am painting the church service I attended last weekend.

OSCAR JACOBSON: Very powerful imagery.

MONROE TSATOKE: It was a very powerful service. When the Water Song was sung in the morning, I noticed a man's face gradually disappear and then in its place I saw a design where the Water Bird was singing, perched up on a staff with a peyote gourd or "rattle." The bird was brilliantly designed in the wing and tail. The fan was made of Water Bird. The Water

Bird's shrill cries are very musical to us. We regard him as predominate among birds who live on the water. In worship, when the time for the water comes, which is in the morning at dawn, the Water Bird fan is used. That is what this painting says today.

SOPHIE BROUSSE: Oscar, I would say there is as much difference between a Tsatoke and a Hokeah as between a Valasquez and a Rubens.

OSCAR JACOBSON: I am afraid I must disagree with you, my dear. Monroe possesses the religiosity of Valasquez, but certainly not the technique—nor should he. He should paint in his own style and in his own technique. I will, however, agree that Monroe is without a doubt a "painter's painter," as was Valasquez.

SOPHIE BROUSSE: I think the resemblance between these paintings is more superficial than fundamental. It comes mostly from the fact that much of their subject matter is dance and ritual, and from the fact that they seem to see the world, or at least prefer to paint it, in two dimensions only, thus securing not mere realism, but the decorative, synthesized quality which is their aim and for which I believe they unconsciously strive.

OSCAR JACOBSON: I would hardly consider Jack's work Rubenesque.

SOPHIE BROUSSE: I am not suggesting that Jack's work is Rubenesque in the Baroque sense. But look at how he handles the paint; it is thick in spots. Against the velvety texture from

273

washing it, the paintings show a jewel-like brilliancy that is arguably Rubenesque.

OSCAR JACOBSON: Arguably Rubenesque, but you would hardly see one of these Kiowa painters depicting a voluptuous nude woman, as Ruben did.

SOPHIE BROUSSE: If you married a 16-year-old girl at your ripe old age, as Ruben did, I bet you would turn from painting landscapes to nudes overnight. That would be like you marrying Lois, although I couldn't see Lois posing nude even for a Kiowa artist.

(Lois Smokey exits. Spencer Asah goes after her...)

OSCAR JACOBSON: I will not argue that point with you, my dear, but if I painted figuratively or nudes at all, you would be the subject of all of my works. Alas, I am a landscape artist.

(Stephen Mopope exits...)

SOPHIE BROUSSE: Perhaps one day I will appear in one of your works as a coyote.

OSCAR JACOBSON: Absolutely not, ma cheri. You would be incarnated in the form of an orchid, at the least.

MONROE TSATOKE: I beg your pardon, Mr. and Mrs. Jacobson. We consider nudity a private matter.

SOPHIE BROUSSE: Perhaps the female form in its most natural state is better appreciated by the French.

OSCAR JACOBSON: I have to disagree with you once again, ma cheri. We Scandinavians enjoy a robust appreciation of the female form—of any race or nationality—we do not discriminate!

MONROE TSATOKE: That being said, perhaps your appreciation of the female form is better left private.

OSCAR JACOBSON: Oh my, Sophie. It appears we have crossed a cultural barrier-

SOPHIE BROUSSE: ...a cultural barricade, in my opinion; one that needs crossing.

OSCAR JACOBSON: Spoken like a proud French woman.

SOPHIE BROUSSE: Merci.

OSCAR JACOBSON: However, we should probably be more careful about what we say in front of the Kiowas.

SOPHIE BROUSSE: Suit yourself. Perhaps they need some desensitizing.

OSCAR JACOBSON: In due time, Sophie. Let's unveil the nuances of nudity with a bit more discretion.

SOPHIE BROUSSE: Très Bien.

OSCAR JACOBSON: Let's go fetch the students, Monroe. How do you say "art for art's sake" in Kiowa?

MONROE TSATOKE: We don't have a word for art, professor.

OSCAR JACOBSON: We will have to do something about that, my boy.

> (Oscar Jacobson and Monroe Tsatoke exit. Jack Hokeah still paints…)

SOPHIE BROUSSE: Well, Jack, you don't seem to be as sensitive to salaciousness as your fellow Kiowas. Or is it because you cannot hear well enough to be offended?

> (Jack Hokeah ignores her and continues to paint...)

Well, my dear Jack, since you do not seem to hear a word I am saying, I would like to share with you that I greatly appreciate the grotesque in your work. I notice that your paintings are both more decorative and also more barbaric than those of the others. You speak very little, but I see that your eyes observe everything. Indeed, your piercing eyes, your hawk nose, and your slender face somehow brings to my mind images of Aztec warriors. Your quiet and shy smile is very winning, in my opinion. I can see why you have so many girlfriends, although I am quite content with my Swedish Viking warrior, Oscar.

> (Jack Hokeah turns to Sophie Brousse...)

JACK HOKEAH: Did you say something, Mrs. Jacobson?

SOPHIE BROUSSE: That is a lovely dancer, Jack. Is it a self-portrait?

(Jack Hokeah nods in the affirmative and continues to paint...)

Well, if you will excuse me, Jack, I will go tend to the other students.

(Sophie Brousse exits...)

JACK HOKEAH: Aztec warrior?

## ACT I

### SCENE FOUR

### JACOBSON HOUSE

(Monroe Tsakoke paints while holding Peggy. Oscar Jacobson attentively observes. Martha Tsakoke sits with Sophie Brousse. Yolande is working on an art project...)

MONROE TSATOKE: Thank you, once again, for allowing me to paint here in your home, Mr. and Mrs. Jacobson. There are very few distractions here save for my beloved daughter, Peggy, whose torment I could not work without.

OSCAR JACOBSON: You are always welcome here, Monroe.

SOPHIE BROUSSE: As are you, Martha. Our home is always open to you and your darling daughter.

MARTHA TSATOKE: Thank you...I mean, "merci," Mrs. Jacobson.

SOPHIE BROUSSE: Très bon, Martha. Did you hear that, dad? Martha is speaking French.

MONROE TSATOKE: Très bon!

SOPHIE BROUSSE: A-HO.

MARTHA TSATOKE: Actually, Mrs. Jacobson, when you say A-ho like that it means you want to kill me.

SOPHIE BROUSSE: Oh my...I assure you, Martha, that I would only count coup on you.

OSCAR JACOBSON: Learning French is fine, but I am determined not to let you or the other artists be "contaminated" by white studies, Monroe. I want you to always select your own subjects and use your own techniques. If you are looking for a career in art, don't attempt to work in the white manner—50,000 of them will always have some advantage over you. Instead, do what the white artists cannot do—paint in the Indian way; follow the traditions of your ancestors; draw inspiration from the culture and legends of your people. In doing that you will succeed and you will also make a real contribution to American art.

MARTHA TSATOKE: Are you sure you don't want me to hold Peggy, Monroe?

MONROE TSATOKE: I am absolutely certain, Martha. Peggy is my best critic. When I paint something she likes, her eyes light up like the morning sun. When I paint something she doesn't like, she grimaces as if she has just eaten a lemon. She has even destroyed some of my work she didn't like.

SOPHIE BROUSSE: Delightful!

MARTHA TSATOKE: Delightful for you, maybe, but cleaning up after her hardly leaves time for cooking for Monroe. He is too thin, as it is.

MONROE TSATOKE: We couldn't ask for a better mother and cook, Martha. I wouldn't trade you for a hundred horses.

SOPHIE BROUSSE: Awe, isn't that charming, Dad?

OSCAR JACOBSON: Très bon, my love. You are also a talented culinary artist—when you are not writing, that is.

SOPHIE BROUSSE: Yes, the more I write the less I cook.

OSCAR JACOBSON: I am perfectly content in maintaining a healthy hunger for knowledge and art, my dear. I proved in my travels as a youth that when food and money are scarce that man can in fact live on bread alone. There were also times when I couldn't even give away a painting that I actually lived on art. Once in Arizona I got so hungry that I painted a steak dinner and imagined that I was eating it. I tell you if canvas and paint were edible I would've eaten it before the paint was dry. I left the painting by the side of the road somewhere in the middle of Arizona in case some other hungry soul might find it that it would feed his imagine if not his stomach.

MONROE TSATOKE: That would be art for art's sake. Right, Mr. Jacobson?

OSCAR JACOBSON: Dear boy, your ears miss nothing uttered, do they?

MONROE TSATOKE: There is much to know in the world and I intend to learn as much as I can.

SOPHIE BROUSSE: You have quite an appetite for knowledge, too, Monroe.

MARTHA TSATOKE: I have known Monroe all of our lives and he has always been that way. When he was young and the other boys were playing games, Monroe was sitting with the elders, listening to stories and learning songs. He seems already like an old man to me sometimes, even though he is so young.

SOPHIE BROUSSE: I believe he has the soul of a poet, Martha, as does Oscar. Men like ours are not easy company, however, especially in times when practicality is considered burdensome and sensibility is boring. I often have to remind Oscar that art is often an ideal reality and not always the way of the real world.

MARTHA TSATOKE: I have always felt that Monroe lives in a different world than the rest of us. It is as if he has one foot in our world and one foot in the spirit world. He sees what others do not see or maybe what they cannot see. I think that is why art is so important to him. Art is the only way he can show the rest of us what he sees.

SOPHIE BROUSSE: I believe artists have a way of seeing not simply the world around us and all its beauty, but also its warts. They also seem to see the essence of the world — the spirit of the world, I suppose.

MARTHA TSATOKE: When Monroe looks at me, I believe that he sees the "me" that is on the inside, not just what is on the outside. He knows my spirit — the part of me that is real — the part of me that is silent.

SOPHIE BROUSSE: When I met Oscar it was love at first sight. Isn't that right, dad?

OSCAR JACOBSON: What are you two talking about, my dear?

SOPHIE BROUSSE: Le coup de foudre, mon chéri?

OSCAR JACOBSON: Oui, ma chérie. Like a bolt of lightning.

SOPHIE BROUSSE: When I came to America from France, I met the quaintest old gentlemen on board the ship. As he had a daughter my own age he appointed himself my guardian. He was most kind. During the two stormy days when I felt squeamish, he sent me oranges, which were rare on board. During dinner one evening, he asked me who was the young man I was going to marry. I told him I was not going to marry anybody; I was going to teach. At which he exclaimed "Oh! Now! Don't be so secretive." He and the other passengers kept asking me at every meal, to my intense embarrassment and annoyance, until I hit upon the idea of taking up the challenge. So I invented a suitor living in Boston whom I had to describe in detail. The next day, I sprang another beau, completely different, hidden away in New Orleans. I couldn't make up my mind, I explained. It became the standing joke at the table. As we were landing in New York, I said goodbye to the doctor, thanking him for his kindness. Then he asked, "Well! Out with it. Who is he?" "Honest" I replied, "I told you the truth in the first place, that I plan to stay in this country two years, and then return home." He wagged his finger at me saying "Ah! Ah! Ah! When you go back you'll already be married." And wouldn't you know it, his prophecy came true. When I met a young artist-teacher named Oscar Jacobson, it was love at first sight—"le coup de foudre," to give it its French name: a bolt of lightning. It was as his bride that I crossed the Atlantic again.

MARTHA TSATOKE: I would be afraid to take a boat that far away. I would never want to be that far away from my family.

SOPHIE BROUSSE: Oh, it's quite an adventure, Martha. Just think—had I not come all this way from France I never would have had the pleasure of meeting you.

MARTHA TSATOKE: We are very different, you know.

SOPHIE BROUSSE: Yes, and also not so different. Love is no different in any part of the world, in my observations; only the expression of love.

MARTHA TSATOKE: I love when Monroe brushes my hair.

SOPHIE BROUSSE: He brushes your hair? How alluring.

MARTHA TSATOKE: I get goose bumps every time.

SOPHIE BROUSSE: The beauty in that simple gesture, Martha, could rival the most passionate expressions of love in the world.

MARTHA TSATOKE: I don't know about that, Mrs. Jacobson, but I do know that it's not just how it feels on the outside, but also how it makes me feel on the inside. It's as if he is caressing my soul.

SOPHIE BROUSSE: You are very expressive, Martha. Have you ever considered taking up some form of art, such as painting, like Lois?

MARTHA TSATOKE: No, Mrs. Jacobson. What Lois is doing is considered man's work. A lot of people don't think she should be here painting with the men. It's not ladylike, especially being so young.

SOPHIE BROUSSE: But her mother is with her. Doesn't that make it more acceptable?

MARTHA TSATOKE: Not to me. My interest is only in my family. That is what is important to me; taking care of Monroe and Peggy. That is how I was taught. Doing anything else in my opinion would be disrespecting my elders.

SOPHIE BROUSSE: So then do you believe that Lois is disrespecting her elders by painting?

MARTHA TSATOKE: It's 1927; we are living in a modern age now. Time has changed us a lot. Even Kiowa women cut their hair, wear high heels, and also paint. That doesn't mean we all have to be that way. I want to be a good wife and a good mother. That is how I was taught and that is what I think is right.

SOPHIE BROUSSE: If being a wonderful wife and mother is your job, Martha, then you are outstanding in your field.

MARTHA TSATOKE: Yes, I am quite a scarecrow, Mrs. Jacobson. You are a great writer, too.

SOPHIE BROUSSE: How do you know? Have you ever read anything I have written?

MARTHA TSATOKE: No, but I can tell by the way you talk that you must be a good writer.

SOPHIE BROUSSE: You are a doll, Martha.

> (Monroe Tsatoke gives Peggy a paint brush...)

OSCAR JACOBSON: Are you sure you want to give little Peggy a paint brush, Monroe? She is awfully close to your painting.

MONROE TSATOKE: She likes to count coup on my paintings with the brushes. Besides, how else will she learn to paint?

OSCAR JACOBSON: Well, be careful she doesn't count coup on your Medicine Man.

MONROE TSATOKE: Too late. She just gave him a tail...and now he has wings.

MARTHA TSATOKE: PEGGY! You've ruined another one of daddy's paintings!

MONROE TSATOKE: It's okay, Martha. I think the Medicine Man looks better with a tail and wings. He looks more mystical.

OSCAR JACOBSON: It appears you have a painting partner, Monroe. Perhaps you are onto a new collaborative phase in your work.

(There is a knock at the door. Martha Tsatoke takes Peggy from Monroe Tsatoke. Sophie Brousse answers the door. Jack Hokeah, Spencer Asah and Lois Smokey enter carrying Stephen Mopope. He is barely conscious. They make their way to the couch…)

SOPHIE BROUSSE: Oh my goodness! What's happened to Stephen?

SPENCER ASAH: He entered the university boxing tournament.

LOIS SMOKEY: I told him not to, Mrs. Jacobson.

OSCAR JACOBSON: Boxing? Does he have any boxing experience?

SPENCER ASAH: No, but there was prize money so he couldn't resist.

(Jack Hokeah holds up two finger to Stephen Mopope's face...)

JACK HOKEAH: How many fingers am I holding up, brother? How many fingers do you see?

STEPHEN MOPOPE: Eight.

SPENCER ASAH: Oh no! He's gone cross-eyed!

SOPHIE BROUSSE: Lay him down on the couch.

JACK HOKEAH: Jeanette is going to kill us.

STEPHEN MOPOPE: (DELIRIOUS) Jeanette!

SPENCER ASAH: Someone get him some castor oil.

MONROE TSATOKE: What are we going to do with castor oil, Lallo?

SPENCER ASAH: Castor oil cures everything, they say.

MONROE TSTAOKE: Who are "they?"

SPENCER ASAH: White people.

OSCAR JACOBSON: Maybe we should get him some ice.

JACK HOKEAH: Jeanette is going to kill us.

STEPHEN MOPOPE: Jeanette!

(The phone rings. Sophie Brousse answers it....)

SOPHIE BROUSSE: Allo. Lynn! Hello, dear boy. How is the novel coming? Oh? Green Grow the Lilacs? I think it's a lovely title. I adore lilacs. We have some growing in our garden—well I should say they grow as long as Napoleon, our spirited canine, doesn't frolic in them. I think he loves lilacs more than I do. Yes, he's here. Just a moment. Oscar, it's Lynn Riggs, darling. He sounds upset.

OSCAR JACOBSON: Upset? He is so sensitive. I wonder what narrative is tormenting him now.

SOPHIE BROUSSE: All he needs is a poetic muse to inspire him. He needs love.
STEPHEN MOPOPE: I love you, Jeanette!
OSCAR JACOBSON: Please get Stephen some ice.

(He takes phone…)

Lynn Riggs! Hello, my boy. How is our aspiring poet—or should I say our "perspiring" poet? You sound distraught, my boy. Unbearable? How can you detest your life so much at such a young age? Trust me, Lynn, it could be much worse. Just ask this young Kiowa on my couch. He's been knocked cross-eyed. And don't even get me started on my sabbatical year in Algiers. Talk about unbearable. I contracted an illness of epic proportions.
SOPHIE BROUSSE: Oscar…please…
OSCAR JACOBSON: Now that was unbearable. I was so feverish and delusional in Algiers that I began speaking Arabic—which I had never learned, by the way.
SOPHIE BROUSSE: Oscar!
OSCAR JACOBSON: The doctors were astounded—even terrified at times—so I'm told. Today, I haven't the slightest recollection of the illness or the Arabic language.
SOPHIE BROUSSE: Oscar! We don't need to relive that fever.
OSCAR JACOBSON: New York can be very cruel, Lynn. Sometimes deadly. I think you should wait a while before going east. You would encounter there much the same

conditions that you find unbearable here. You are a Westerner, Lynn; derive your inspiration from the West. You need to find yourself just now; then you can safely face the east. My advice to you is to go to Santa Fe. There are enough artists and writers there to give you stimulation; yet there is a chance for you to go your own way. Contact my friend Witter Bynner. He is a poet whose friendship and criticisms would be very beneficial to an hysterical young writer, such as you. Alright then, Lynn. Good luck and God speed, my boy.

(He hangs up the phone...)

Lynn Riggs may turn out to be a great writer if he doesn't torment himself into insanity. How is Stephen?
LOIS SMOKEY: Stephen seems to be doing better.

(Jack Hokeah holds up two fingers again...)

JACK HOKEAH: How many fingers am I holding up, brother?
STEPHEN MOPOPE: Two.
ALL: A-ho!
SPENCER ASAH: His eyes uncrossed!
LOIS SMOKEY: Thank goodness.
JACK HOKEAH: If we would have brought him home like that...
SPENCER ASAH: Jeanette would have killed us.

OSCAR JACOBSON: Excellent! Keep that ice on your head, Stephen. Please make yourselves at home. Sophie and I will prepare dinner.

(Oscar Jacobson and Sophie Brousse exit...)

MONROE TSATOKE: How about a song while we wait.

MARTHA TSATOKE: That sounds fun. Let's dance, Spencer.

SPENCER ASAH: If you think you can keep up.

LOIS SMOKEY: Would you like to dance, Jack, or do I need to ask your girlfriend first?

JACK HOKEAH: Depends on which girlfriend.

MONROE TSATOKE: Stephen, why don't you stay on the couch, brother? Rest up for dinner.

(Monroe Tsatoke sings while the others dance. Stephen Mopope stays on the couch. Oscar Jacobson and Sophie Brousse return and join the dance. Song ends...)

MONROE TSATOKE: That was a couple's dance, Mr. and Mrs. Jacobson.

OSCAR JACOBSON: Now that we have learned the Indian couple's dance, I will have to teach you all a cowboy couple's dance called a Two-Step.

MONROE TSATOKE: What is the cowboy Two-Step, professor?

OSCAR JACOBSON: It's also a social dance and a lot of fun. I learned it when I was a kid and worked as a ranch hand. Did you know that I used be a cowboy? They called me Mustang Jake.

SPENCER ASAH: Mustang Jake? That sounds like a horse's name.

OSCAR JACOBSON: Well, I was given the name precisely because I worked with horses, Spencer. I rode the buck out of dozens of horses in my day. And I assure that I was also thrown higher than a barn roof many times, too. I cowboyed in New Mexico, Colorado, Arizona—all over the Southwest.

MONROE TSATOKE: Well, Mustang Jake, I for one will take you up on your offer to learn the cowboy dance.

OSCAR JACOBSON: Very well then, Monroe. I will teach you the cowboy dance after our cowboy dinner.

LOIS SMOKEY: Smells good. What's a cowboy dinner?

SPENCER ASAH: Hope it's not anything gassy.

JACK HOKEAH: Grassy?

SPENCER ASAH: Not grassy. GASSY, Jack.

LOIS SMOKEY: White man food makes Lallo gassy.

JACK HOKEAH: Oh, gassy. Not again. You can have the studio to yourself tomorrow, Lallo.

SPENCER ASAH: Fine with me. You guys need to work on your singing anyway.

JACK HOKEAH: And you need to work on your hands, Lallo.

MONROE TSATOKE: You mean hooves, right?

LOIS SMOKEY: You all stop teasing my cousin. Just because his name means "little boy" doesn't mean he is one.

SPENCER ASAH: Ha, cousin. You'll come paint with me tomorrow, won't you?

LOIS SMOKEY: Think I'll be getting ready for our church meeting tomorrow night.

JACK HOKEAH: Remember those Catholic Church services? I barely started praying before they were over.

LOIS SMOKEY: Except when Father Al was leading the service. Boy was he long-winded.

SPENCER ASAH: I liked Father Isadore's services—short and sweet. Remember how he used to make everyone take quinine and calomel when they were sick?

LOIS SMOKEY: Oh, that stuff tasted disgusting. One sip of it used to turn people's faces into prunes. Everyone made the same face after they took it.

(She makes a face)

SPENCER ASAH: We used to tell the younger kids that their faces would stay like that. That kept them from getting sick more than anything.

JACK HOKEAH: Even when I was sick I wouldn't tell anyone. That medicine tasted so bad that I would rather stay sick.

LOIS SMOKEY: Father Isadore used to have to take the medicine himself in front of the sick people so they would know he wasn't trying to poison them. I watched him take it one time and he never even blinked. I think he liked it.

SPENCER ASAH: When I was 14, I painted a picture of him called "Father Isadore Ministers to the Sick." He hung it on his wall until he left and Father Al took over.

LOIS SMOKEY: Remember when they gave all of you boys bowl cuts? They used the same bowl on all of you. You all looked so funny. The girls couldn't breathe from laughing!

(Silence...)

SPENCER ASAH: No, I don't remember that.

JACK HOKEAH: Nope, don't remember.

SPENCER ASAH: Remember when we snuck into the wine cellar and got the father's cat drunk on communion wine?

LOIS SMOKEY: You got the father's cat drunk?

SPENCER ASAH: More than once.

JACK HOKEAH: You ever seen a cat swagger?

SPENCER ASAH: Swagger? You mean stagger! We got the cat drunk so many times it became a lush.

STEPHEN MOPOPE: I heard it became a priest.

ALL: HA!

MONROE TSATOKE: Stephen's back among the conscious.

SPENCER ASAH: Welcome back, brother.

LOIS SMOKEY: Are you okay, Stephen?

STEPHEN MOPOPE: I'm okay as long as Jeanette doesn't find out.

JACK HOKEAH: What do you remember about the boxing match, Stephen?

STEPHEN MOPOPE: I remember the bell ringing to start the fight.

MONROE TSATOKE: That's it?

STEPHEN MOPOPE: Then everything went black.

LOIS SMOKEY: Kiowas weren't meant to box.

SPENCER ASAH: We weren't meant to be farmers either.

STEPHEN MOPOPE: Don't tell Jeanette I got knocked out. She'll kill me!

JACK HOKEAH: What did I tell you?

(The phone rings. Sophie Brousse enters to answer it…)

SOPHIE BROUSSE: Allo, Jacobson residence. The old man? You mean Oscar? No. Oh, really? Certainly. Stephen, your wife is on the phone for you.

STEPHEN MOPOPE: Nobody say a word…

SPENCER ASAH: You mean about you getting knocked out?

STEPHEN MOPOPE: Lallo! Shh. If Jeanette doesn't kill me her mother will.

SPENCER ASAH: So was boxing like a suicide mission?

STEPHEN MOPOPE: Quiet!

(He puts phone to his ear…)

Jeanette? Yes, I'm fine. Painting up a whirlwind. What? Boxing? Me?

SPENCER ASAH: Uh oh.

STEPHEN MOPOPE: Your mother? Where did she hear it? Who? And she heard it from…and she heard it from…boy, the moccasin telegraph is faster than the telephone. There was prize money, Jeanette. I was trying to win the…No, I didn't win. Why does she think that's so funny? You should see the other guy. Don't worry, I'm okay.

(Oscar Jacobson enters…)

OSCAR JACOBSON: Dinner is ready!

SOPHIE BROUSSE: Oscar, Stephen's wife is on the phone.

OSCAR JACOBSON: He looks distressed. Is everything okay?

SPENCER ASAH: He always looks that way when he talks to Jeanette.

LOIS SMOKEY: Her mom hates him.

STEPHEN MOPOPE: Tell your mother that I don't do anything here but paint. I paint from sun up to sun down. I hardly see the light of day. Tell her someday I will be somebody and then she will understand. No, there are no other women here. Just Lois, and she's my cousin. That was Mrs. Jacobson. Short on meat? How can that be? Oh, your mother is there…well, that explains why you are short on meat. Alright, Jeanette, go ahead and shoot the young bull and butcher it. Yes, the young bull—Leonard. The one with the white spot on its face. No, that's Jethro. Jethro is the old bull—the big one. Leonard is the young one—he is the smaller of the two. I murmur you, too. Goodbye.

(He hangs up.)

OSCAR JACOBSON: You okay, Stephen?
STEPHEN MOPOPE: My wife is out of meat and her mother wants to butcher me.
SOPHIE BROUSSE: Ah, love. It must be hard being apart.
STEPHEN MOPOPE: Jeanette's mother keeps filling her head with suspicion; says I'm running around here with college girls.

(Spencer Asah laughs out loud. Stephen Mopope glares at him…)

SPENCER ASAH: Sorry, uncle. I mean "brother."
STEPHEN MOPOPE: You don't understand what I went through for my wife. If I didn't love her more than art her mother would not be worth the trouble. I proposed three times before she would marry me. She loved me but she knew her family didn't like me. Jeanette's father actually threw me out of the house the first time I asked her to marry me. She is with me despite her family and they never let either of us forget that. They hate everything about me. They hate me for being married once before. They hate me

for dancing. They hate me for going to peyote meetings. They say I am a devil worshipper.

MONROE TSATOKE: We pray to the same creator in the Native American Church as in the Catholic or Methodist or any other Christian church.

STEPHEN MOPOPE: I don't know, but maybe feeding her mother our young bull will hold off the witch hunt, for a little while anyway.

SOPHIE BROUSSE: Speaking of food—dinner is served.

OSCAR JACOBSON: We're having my favorite cowboy dinner—beans and ham hocks.

SPENCER ASAH: Uh oh.

> (The phone rings again. Sophie Brousse answers it...)

SOPHIE BROUSSE: Jacobson residence. The old man? Yes, he's still here. Stephen, your wife is calling again.

STEPHEN MOPOPE: What is this "old man" business? I'm not even 30 years old—I don't think.

SPENCER ASAH: You might be, brother.

LOIS SMOKEY: (TO THE JACOBSONS) He's not sure when he was born.

MONROE TSATOKE: He looks 30.

SPENCER ASAH: Brother, 30 is like 50 in college student years.

STEPHEN MOPOPE: Then respect your elders and keep quiet.

(He takes the phone...)

Jeanette? Yes, the young bull. The one with the white spot on its face—Leonard. No the other one is my registered bull—Jethro. Jethro is very valuable. I paid $1,200 for Jethro. Jeanette...tell me you shot the young bull...Leonard. Does it have a white spot on its face? NO?
SPENCER ASAH: Uh oh.
STEPHEN MOPOPE: Did you shoot Jethro, Jeanette? Stop crying. Yes, I know it is difficult to tell the difference. Well, maybe if you tell your mother she is eating my $1,200 registered bull then she will enjoy it that much more. I'm sure she'll get quite a kick out of it. Stop crying. It's okay, Jeanette. You too. Goodbye.

(He hangs up...)

SPENCER ASAH: Did Jeanette shoot Jethro, brother?

(Stephen Mopope nods in the affirmative...)

SPENCER ASAH: Cheer up, brother. Just think, you still have that young bull to grow up big and fat and then you can eat him too.
STEPHEN MOPOPE: I'm getting too old for this.
OSCAR JACOBSON: Well, we won't' be serving bull tonight, but Sophie's beans pack some powerful protein.

SOPHIE BROUSSE: And dad's cornbread will melt in your mouth.
OSCAR JACOBSON: Let's eat.

(All take places around the table...)

Hopefully this will lift your spirits, Stephen. I have a special announcement. November will mark the inaugural exhibition of new art by our five esteemed Kiowa artist in residence here at the University of Oklahoma.
LOIS SMOKEY: What does that mean, Mr. Jacobson?
OSCAR JACOBSON: It means you will have your first exhibition in November!
LOIS SMOKEY: But we just got here.
OSCAR JACOBSON: I assure you that by November you will have hit an artistic stride that your fellow university students will aspire to for years to come.

(He raises his glass...)

This is an exciting and historic moment, my friends. Here's to the genesis of Native American art.
ALL: A-ho!

# ACT I

## SCENE FIVE

## DOWNSTAGE

(Stephen Mopope paints at an easel. Savoie Lottinville sits in a chair taking notes. As Mopope paints, the image of an eagle dancer emerges on the screen. Simultaneously, Jack Hokeah performs the eagle dance on stage. Tsakoke sings quietly underneath Mopope's dialogue for Hokeah's dance…)

STEPHEN MOPOPE: My name is Stephen Mopope. Mopope means "small deer with spots on its back." Kiowas say Mapop-ee, but other people pronounce it Mopope. My Indian name is Gutkoyday, "Painted Robe." I was born near Red Stone Baptist Mission on the Kiowa Reservation. Like my brother Jack, my grandmother mostly raised me because my mother was very sick. My grandmother and I were very close. When I went to St. Patrick's school, my grandmother camped on the northwest corner of the school campus under a tree. At night, I would sneak over to her tepee and she would give me a little snack of boiled meat, frybread and pudding. That was the highlight of my day. I felt guilty going to school because I felt like I needed to cut wood and do chores for my grandmother at home. But she said, "Do you trust me?" and I said, "Yes." And she said, "Then you go to school at St. Patrick's." So that is what I did.

SAVOIE LOTTINVILLE: How did you get interested in art?

STEPHEN MOPOPE: While growing up, some of the elders saw me drawing designs in the sand. So they decided to teach me how to paint on tanned skins in the old Kiowa way. I am known as a painter here, but among my people I am also known as a dancer and a flute player. This is why I enjoy painting about music as well as dance. Music speaks to me as deeply as dance. When I make a flute, it is made of me as well as of wood. The flute is an extension of me.

SAVOIE LOTTINVILLE: Did you make the flute you are holding in your hand?

STEPHEN MOPOPE: Yes. The flute that I am holding in my hand is made out of cedar, which is a special wood with healing properties. The songs I play on the flute are healing to me and I hope they are to others as well. The flute is also an instrument of courtship. I believe I would not have my wife today had I not played for her during courtship. She liked the way I played.

SAVOIE LOTTINVILLE: Would you share a song on your flute?

STEPHEN MOPOPE: I am always happy to share a song.

(He performs flute song…)

# ACT I

## SCENE SIX

## NATIVE AMERICAN CHURCH

(Silhouettes of the Kiowa men can be
seen by the firelight inside a tepee. Jack
Hokeah sings a Native American church
song. Images of the artists' many
beautiful and powerful "peyote
paintings" are projected on the screen
and perhaps on the tepee throughout the
scene. At the conclusion of the song, the
men sit in silence. Monroe Tsatoke
begins to speak…)

MONROE TSATOKE: I would like to ask for
your prayers, brothers. I have not been well and
I am afraid to go to the white man's doctor for
fear of what he will tell me. Whatever my illness
is, I would like to be treated by our medicine,
not the white man's medicine. My healing will
come through this way—our church way.
ALL: Ha.
JACK HOKEAH: Great Cormorant, messenger
bird who flies inside our tepee, to whom our
prayers may be trusted, you are the only one
who can carry our message to the heart of the
unknown mysteries. Great sun and water bird,
your outstretched wings represent the flight of
the unknown. On your shoulders are the
symbols of Father Peyote. Your blue feathers

represent the sky bird, who is authority in early morning, when the morning song is sung. Our tepee faces east. The beauty of the day in the east becomes apparent. The inspiration rises. It is seen through a veil—an object or a song. The rhythm of beauty begins to spread. The song rises. This rhythm is filling the air, with songs, with prayers, with designs.

ALL: Ha.

MONROE TSATOKE: The man who taught me most about the Cormorant bird was a Comanche, named Quanah Parker. I went into a meeting once and had a vision. I took the herb once and began to understand the time had come for further knowledge about this Cormorant bird. The consciousness awakened. I saw a man to the right. I saw Quanah Parker at first, but then the human form began to go out of existence. In a great tissue of light and sparkling ripples of water came the bird. In the midst of this great moving light was the Cormorant. There was a softness, a coolness in the air. There was a beauty of mists and of rainbows. This great god of birds, this god of waters became apparent. He comes flying and tips the water with his wings. The air fills with birds. They glide and dip and swim. There is a silver light on their feathers. A radiance is around this bird who has authority over all birds of the waters.

ALL: Ha.

STEPHEN MOPOPE: I pray to the unknown mystery which can only be called Light. I pray

constantly to be made humble. Have pity on my crude way of praying. Help me by showing me the great light. Father Peyote, I don't know one little part of you, nor even one little cotton substance of you, but help me to understand. As each bead is a part of your design, help me to know thy will, thy design for me. Make me humble enough to understand this, to do the design in each little particle, in the right way.
ALL: Ha.

MONROE TSATOKE: As the beauty of the light spreads over the sky, I have a vision and it is like a great feather wand. The light glows in the tepee. It is as though a man has been sick and discouraged. He has gone outside the tepee. The splendors of the dawn are coming like great feather rays over the sky in these colors that only nature makes that are the right colors. He looks back to the tepee after seeing this great flower of the dawn and there he sees the divine worshippers. These are silhouetted against the light. They are people from another world, and they are dressed in feathers.
ALL: Ha.

STEPHEN MOPOPE: Thank you, brother. I would like to pray for us as we move toward the first exhibition of our art. May our art always be for the glory of our Creator and for the glory of our people.
ALL: Ha.

(Low lights up outside the tepee…Lois
Smokey and Martha Tsatoke sit by a fire.
Martha Tsatoke holds Peggy…)

LOIS SMOKEY: Would you like me to hold
Peggy, Martha?
MARTHA TSATOKE: That's okay, Lois. I can
handle her just fine by myself. Aren't you going
to take the water in?
LOIS SMOKEY: It's not quiet dawn yet. I will
wait a few more minutes. Did you know that's
how I got my name? Bougetah means "Coming
of the Dawn."
MARTHA TSATOKE: I know that. What I don't
understand is how you decide when to do
woman's work and when to do man's work?
LOIS SMOKEY: I don't understand.
MARTHA TSATOKE: I mean, taking water into
the tepee is a woman's job, but painting is a
man's job.
LOIS SMOKEY: Times are changing, Martha.
Kiowa ways are changing, too. Look at where
we live? Look at how we live? Our ways are so
different now from how they were even ten or
twenty years ago. The whole world is changing.
We have to change with it.
MARTHA TSATOKE: I don't know why we
have to act any way but Kiowa.
LOIS SMOKEY: We have to move forward.
MARTHA TSATOKE: You are either Kiowa or
you are not. And you are either a woman or you
are not. If you are Kiowa then you should act

like a Kiowa. If you are a woman then you should act like a woman.

LOIS SMOKEY: Painting makes me happy.

MARTHA TSATOKE: I am happy to be a Kiowa woman. You should be happy to be a Kiowa woman and you should behave like a Kiowa woman.

LOIS SMOKEY: The dawn is coming. People say the world is darkest just before the dawn. I need to take the water into the tepee now.

(Lois Smokey approaches the tepee with the bucket of water....)

LOIS SMOKEY: Brothers, I am here with the water. Should I come into the tepee now?

(Monroe Tsatoke speaks from inside the tepee...)

MONROE TSATOKE: Yes, it is time, sister.

## ACT I

### SCENE SEVEN

### DOWNSTAGE

(Lois Smokey paints at an easel. Savoie Lottinville sits and takes notes. Smokey's paintings emerge on the screen as she talks with Lottinville. Martha Tsatoke

dances as Monrpe Tsatoke sings under
the dialogue…)

LOIS SMOKEY: My name is Lois Smokey. My
Indian name, Bougetah, translates to "Coming
of the Dawn."
SAVOIE LOTTINVILLE: How did you receive
your name, Lois?
LOIS SMOKEY I received my name when I was
12 years old after I carried water into a tipi just
before dawn. The men inside the tipi sang a
special song and then the man that builds the
fire opened the flap of the tipi and I put the
bucket of water inside by the fire. I received my
name shortly thereafter.
SAVOIE LOTTINVILLE: Can you tell me about
your childhood?
LOIS SMOKEY: I was born in a tent in Old
Town Anadarko. We lived west of Verden, but
my parents wanted to be near a doctor when it
came time for me to be born. So they set up a
camp near the hospital in Anadarko. I went to
grade school at St. Patrick's Mission school in
Anadarko.
SAVOIE LOTTINVILLE: Was going to Catholic
school a good experience for you?
LOIS SMOKEY: I loved St. Pat's. I only wish
they had more grades so I could have stayed
longer.
SAVOIE LOTTINVILLE: How did you get
interested in art?
LOIS SMOKEY: Our field matron, Susie Peters,
got me interested in art. She used to drive us all

to Willie Baze Lane's house for art classes. We had a lot of fun, I remember, drawing on paper with colored chalk.

SAVOIE LOTTINVILLE: Did you graduate from St. Patrick's?

LOIS SMOKEY: I attended Verden High School from 1924 until last year. I played basketball there and also worked on my painting.

SAVOIE LOTTINVILLE: How has your experience been so far here at the University of Oklahoma?

LOIS SMOKEY: I am very honored and happy to be here at school at OU with my Kiowa brothers. It's hard, though. Being a Kiowa woman and painting is very difficult. I don't know. Sometimes I wonder if I am doing the right thing by being here. My mother is here with me. She supports me, but I know she would rather see me at home raising a family, like Martha and Jeanette. She can't wait for me to give her some grandchildren. She is getting older and frail. I worry about her more. Maybe I should be home taking care of her instead of her being here taking care of me. Martha's little Peggy is so cute. I look at her and I wonder when it will be my turn to have a little Peggy. Honestly, I can't wait to have children and a family, instead of just painting them. I don't know...maybe someday.

# ACT I

## SCENE EIGHT

## ART STUDIO

(The artists are finishing getting dressed
in their dance regalia. Oscar Jacobson
addresses the audience...)

OSCAR JACOBSON: The plains tribes, such as
the Kiowa, adorned their tepees with paintings,
usually running in spiral form, the purpose of
which was to proclaim to the world the marital
exploits of the owner. Painted on leather in a
somewhat limited range of pigments, these
pictures had a highly decorative value; they
were full of dash and vigor, full of movement
and carried well the purpose for which they
were intended, having a truly epic character. Of
a similar type were the calendars; painted on
strips of leather or in spiral form on some large
hide, they were intended to record in
chronological sequence the history of the tribe.
They were less decorative than the tepee
paintings, having in some cases attained almost
the status of hieroglyphs in the use of certain
symbols that took the place of the written
language. The recent development in Kiowa
painting is allied to the use of a different
medium—paper instead of leather, water color
and tempera instead of mixed earth pigments
and vegetable dyes. These Kiowa paintings you

see today in their present form follows closely the racial characteristics of Indian art of which it might be said to be the natural evolution. Welcome to the inaugural exhibition of our five Kiowa artists in residence at the University of Oklahoma. Ladies and gentlemen, I give you "The Kiowa Five."

(He solicits applause from the audience...)

These artists are accomplished singers, dancers, and musicians, in addition to being very talented artists. Our young artists will now perform some songs for you from their Kiowa cultural traditions.

(Monroe Tsakoke sings as all dance...They finish...)

LOIS SMOKEY: I would like to take this opportunity to thank the Jacobsons and my Kiowa brothers for the opportunity to be a part of this university art program. I am very honored by my time here and proud of the artwork that we have created. I paint what is important to me—family. My Kiowa people and my elders say family is the most important thing for Kiowa women. That is why I plan to go home now and raise a family.
SOPHIE BROUSSE: You are leaving us, Lois?
LOIS SMOKEY: Yes, Mrs. Jacobson. I know that I have only been here a few months, but I feel

strongly that I have been here long enough. I will miss you the most, I think.

SOPHIE BROUSSE: Merci, Lois. I will miss you too.

OSCAR JACOBSON: I do hope you plan to continue your art, Lois. You have a natural gift.

LOIS SMOKEY: Martha and I plan to join the Mautaum club that Suzie Peters reorganized back home. It is an art program—just a different kind of art. Our Kiowa elder women teach beadwork, quilting, crochet, and other arts.

SOPHIE BROUSSE: I wish you would reconsider, Lois.

LOIS SMOKEY: This is the right thing for me to do. I will miss you all and offer my prayers for you and your work.

> (Lois Smokey puts a shawl on Mrs. Jacobson...)

SOPHIE BROUSSE: Merci, my dear. A-ho. Please stay in touch, Lois.

LOIS SMOKEY: I will.

> (All bid farewell to Lois Smokey with hugs and acknowledgements...)

MONROE TSATOKE: In honor of our sister's announcement, let's send her home with a good song in her heart.

> (All dance...)

# ACT II

## SCENE ONE

### DOWNSTAGE

(Jack Hokeah paints at an easel. Savoie
Lottinville sits and takes notes. Images of
Jack Hokeah's paintings emerge on the
screen as he paints. Spencer Asah sings
under the dialogue...)

JACK HOKEAH: My name is Jack Hokeah. I
was born sometime around 1902. I was
orphaned while I was still young, so my
grandmother raised me before I went off to
school at St. Patrick's. I think I spent more time
at St. Pat's than anywhere else.

SAVOIE LOTTINVILLE: How do you prefer to
express yourself artistically?

JACK HOKEAH: I don't really care much for
conversation. Words can be deceiving, but
music and dance are pure. I work hard at my
art, but dancing is just as important to me.
That's why I primarily paint dancers.

SAVOIE LOTTINVILLE: How does your
spirituality inform your work?

JACK HOKEAH: Some people say that it
appears as if I paint prayer. My grandmother
taught me to pray all the time, so maybe that
comes out in my painting.

SAVOIE LOTTINVILLE: Do you pray when you
paint?

JACK HOKEAH: I pray when I paint, I pray
when I dance, I pray all the time. I pray that our
time here at the university with the Jacobsons
will inspire more Indian artists to paint. A-ho.

## ACT II

### SCENE TWO

### MURAL SITE

(Spencer Asah and Stephen Mopope are
painting on a small scaffolding structure.
Oscar Jacobson makes his way around
the mural offering direction to the artists.
Monroe Tsatoke stands to the side
contemplating the strength of the
scaffolding…)

OSCAR JACOBSON: Gentlemen, mural painting
is much different from painting on a typical
canvas. You must first take into consideration
the size of the space in relation to your subject.
STEPHEN MOPOPE: (PAINTING) I believe I
have determined the scale to be as large as the
wall, Mr. Jacobson.
OSCAR JACOBSON: I must advise that it
typically is best if you begin mural painting by
sketching the figures first, Stephen.
STEPHEN MOPOPE: I am not much of a sketch
artist, Mr. Jacobson. I am first a painter. So I
prefer to paint first.

OSCAR JACOBSON: Painting without sketching is very risky, Stephen. If you make a mistake, then it is a very LARGE mistake in size and therefore very difficult and time-consuming to fix.

STEPHEN MOPOPE: Then I will not make a mistake.

OSCAR JACOBSON: Well, I hope for all of our sakes that you don't. It took a lot of convincing on my part to get permission from President Bizzell for you to paint these murals. When it comes to public art on the university campus, Mr. Bizzell is quite attentive. Frankly, I think it is Mrs. Bizzell who is responsible for making Mr. Bizzell most concerned with campus aesthetics. It makes no difference to me, however, as long as we are able to exercise some artistic license in public spaces. If the university bears the name of our great state of "Oklahoma," a proud name meaning "Red People" in the great Choctaw language, then it seems apropos to me that "Red People" should figure prominently in the university's public art.

SPENCER ASAH: I believe I will sketch my figures first, Mr. Jacobson. I don't like to make mistakes. I think it is mainly because I don't like to clean up my mistakes that I make every effort to avoid making them. In fact, I have started putting porcelain on my easels so that when my paint finds its way off of the paper then it lands on the porcelain, which is very easy to clean. Just one wipe with a wet rag and the paint is gone.

OSCAR JACOBSON: Ingenious, Spencer! Why didn't I think of that? And here I have labored for decades cleaning up paint.

STEPHEN MOPOPE: I wondered what happened to the toilet.

SPENCER ASAH: It still works.

MONROE TSATOKE: I trust the sacrifice of our toilet is worth saving some time cleaning up paint, but what I don't trust is this flimsy scaffolding.

OSCAR JACOBSON: This scaffolding is state of the art, Monroe. It could withstand the weight of 10 men.

MONROE TSATOKE: Sure, 10 white men. But is it sturdy enough to withstand the weight of three Kiowas?

OSCAR JACOBSON: Why, you're as thin as a bird, Monroe. If this scaffolding can hold these two Kiowas then your weight surely will not break it.

MONROE TSATOKE: Perhaps it would be safest if we painted one at a time. I have a family to think of, you know. What if the scaffolding breaks and the fall kills me?

OSCAR JACOBSON: Well, Monroe, just tell me then what is your favorite flower?

(Spencer Asah "doubles up in mirth." A characteristic Mrs. Jacobson wrote of in her memoirs: "He shook all over with laughter that filled his eyes with tears.")

SPENCER ASAH: He means what flowers you want for your funeral, Monroe!

MONROE TSATOKE: I know what he means, Lallo. Then I would say my favorite flower would be the "Indian Paintbrush."

OSCAR JACOBSON: As it should be, my boy.

(Jack Hokeah and Sophie Brousse enter with James Auchiah...)

JACK HOKEAH: My brothers, Mr. Jacobson— James Auchiah has arrived.

ALL: Ha!

OSCAR JACOBSON: Welcome, James!

JAMES AUCHIAH: A-ho, brothers. I am honored to be here.

(All greet each other...)

OSCAR JACOBSON: I trust your trip went smoothly, James.

JACK HOKEAH: All James's trips are smooth, Mr. Jacobson. He has the fanciest car on the rez.

JAMES AUCHIAH: Thank you, brother.

JACK HOKEAH: Be careful you keep your windows rolled down with Lallo, brother. Especially after he eats white man food.

JAMES AUCHIAH: I remember from the school days, brothers.

SPENCER ASAH: Do you remember when we all tried to sneak out that night in Stephen's old Model-T?

JAMES AUCHIAH: Yes, but the joke turned out to be on us.

SPENCER ASAH: Yeah, we all pretended to be tired and went to bed early thinking Jeanette wouldn't be suspicious.

JACK HOKEAH: I think that was our first mistake.

JAMES AUCHIAH: I believe that made her even more suspicious.

STEPHEN MOPOPE: Do you know that I was pretending to snore even as I was putting my clothes on in the bedroom?

SPENCER ASAH: So was I.

MONROE TSATOKE: But there wasn't anyone else in your room, Lallo.

SPENCER ASAH: Oh yeah.

STEPHEN MOPOPE: Jeanette was awake the whole time.

OSCAR JACOBSON: So what were you boys up to besides "no good?"

STEPHEN MOPOPE: We wanted to go to this dance in Medicine Park, but Jeanette didn't want us to go.

SPENCER ASAH: That's because she knew we would be up singing and dancing until sunrise.

SOPHIE BROUSSE: Sounds like trouble to me.

OSCAR JACOBSON: I believe you boys have a bit of mischief in your blood.

STEPHEN MOPOPE: Yes, well so does Jeanette.

SOPHIE BROUSSE: I find myself growing fonder of Jeanette the more I hear about her.

STEPHEN MOPOPE: I think you two would get along very well, Mrs. Jacobson. She speaks French and German, as do I.

SOPHIE BROUSSE: Trés bon.

STEPHEN MOPOPE: Gesundheit.

OSCAR JACOBSON: I presume Jeanette was on to your plan?

SPENCER ASAH: More so than even we were, I think.

JAMES AUCHIAH: We snuck out to Stephen's old Model-T and decided to push it down the hill so the sound of the engine wouldn't wake up Jeanette.

STEPHEN MOPOPE: We pushed it all the way down the hill about a quarter of a mile and then the cursed thing wouldn't start.

JAMES AUCHIAH: It was too far to walk to town so we turned around and started pushing it back up the hill.

JACK HOKEAH: We didn't get back in the house until sun-up.

STEPHEN MOPOPE: Then, wouldn't you know it. We walked in the door to the house and there on the kitchen table was the coil to the engine of my car.

SOPHIE BROUSSE: Doesn't sound like Jeanette was fooled for a minute.

STEPHEN MOPOPE: She had pulled the coil off the car after dinner when she went outside to throw out the dish water.

JACK HOKEAH: I believe she was on to us the whole time.

JAMES AUCHIAH: I believe you are correct, brother.

STEPHEN MOPOPE: Never underestimate the shrewdness of a Kiowa woman.

SOPHIE BROUSSE: Or a French woman, gentlemen. But I am sure any woman would have sniffed out such mischief well in advance.

OSCAR JACOBSON: Just think, if our talented, youngest, and only female member of the group hadn't withdrawn from our program here we would have six Kiowa artists in residence at the university. Alas, you remain five. We are proud and honored to have you join us, James.

JAMES AUCHIAH: I am honored to be among you and these Kiowa gentleman, professor. Painting and drawing has always been an important part of our Kiowa life. In fact, discovering and selecting the most talented men to be the Keepers of the Paint was considered a ceremonial affair to our people. During the Sun Dance encampment, leaders and medicine men of the tribe appointed the painters. They announced the names of the chosen ones throughout the camp circle. Painters commissioned in this way could be either men or women. They commanded respect—their work was sacred to the tribe. My grandmother was chosen to paint baby cradles. She was respected and revered by both men and women.

STEPHEN MOPOPE: I remember when your grandmother gathered all of us children together during the spring one year. She offered a prayer, and then painted each one of us with a yellow circle over our forehead to welcome the summer.

JAMES AUCHIAH: I remember that well.

SPENCER ASAH: I wonder why she painted my cheeks instead of my forehead.

STEPHEN MOPOPE: That was to protect the summer from you, Lallo.

JAMES AUCHIAH: He is joking, of course, Mr. Jacobson. It was also common to paint cheeks. The Keepers of the Paint also painted the legs of the Black-Legging Kiowa Warrior Society black just before battle. This was a sign of bravery in time of victory, and heroism in time of defeat.

ALL: Ha.

OSCAR JACOBSON: Have you painted murals, my boy?

JAMES AUCHIAH: No, sir. But I would very much like to learn.

SOPHIE BROUSSE: This is the other artists' first brush at murals as well as with oil paint.

JACK HOKEAH: Oil is very messy and it takes forever to dry. I prefer watercolors and tempera.

JAMES AUCHIAH: I haven't painted with oil either.

OSCAR JACOBSON: If you can handle yourself in watercolors and tempera then you will be able to manage oil.

SOPHIE BROUSSE: How long have you been painting, James?

JAMES AUCHIAH: I believe that I have painted all my life—as long as I can remember.

JACK HOKEAH: I remember when you were caught painting in class at St. Pat's instead of doing your schoolwork.

JAMES AUCHIAH: Yes, I guess I was inspired because it was near Thanksgiving Day. I was drawing an Indian village with turkeys walking around the tepees. I wanted to take the picture to my mother. But after I was caught painting in class, as punishment, I was required to forfeit my dinner and finish my painting after school. I was glad to do so—I would rather paint than eat.

ALL: A-ho.

STEPHEN MOPOPE: So what news do you have from the moccasin telegraph? What's happening back home?

JAMES AUCHIAH: Stephen, your wife and mother-in-law gave away the most beautiful horse I have ever seen at the dance last weekend.

STEPHEN MOPOPE: What horse?

JAMES AUCHIAH: It was a beautiful horse, brother. Looked strong too—with powerful legs.

STEPHEN MOPOPE: How powerful?

JAMES AUCHIAH: This horse looked as keen as any racehorse, brother.

STEPHEN MOPOPE: (BURIES HIS FACE IN HIS HANDS) Oh no.

JAMES AUCHIAH: That was very generous of you, brother.

SPENCER ASAH: Are you okay, Stephen?

STEPHEN MOPOPE: Oh no.

SPENCER ASAH: Uh oh.

JACK HOKEAH: Did Jeanette give away your racehorse, brother?

(Stephen Mopope nods in the affirmative...)

JACK HOKEAH: (TO JAMES AUCHIAH) Jeanette shot his registered bull last semester.

MONROE TSATOKE: In Jeanette's defense, I certainly don't believe she does these things on purpose.

STEPHEN MOPOPE: My mother-in-law might.

MONROE TSATOKE: I think that it must be difficult for Jeanette being there alone trying to handle these things with her mother constantly reminding her how Stephen is a pagan devil-worshipper.

STEPHEN MOPOPE: (SITS DOWN) I don't think I can paint.

SPENCER ASAH: Well, perhaps our brother Monroe will feel more comfortable on the scaffolding now that it no longer must bear the burden of our brother Stephen.

MONROE TSATOKE: If there is art that needs to be painted above arm's reach then that art belongs to my brothers. For the sake of my wife and my children I will keep my feet firmly planted on the ground.

OSCAR JACOBSON: We will get you up on that scaffolding before long, Monroe. I believe you have tremendous potential as a muralist.

MONROE TSATOKE: I suggest that my brother James here can have any commission of mine that requires that I be elevated beyond the point that the fall from such height could kill me.

JAMES AUCHIAH: I descend from the bravest of all Kiowa warriors. I am not afraid of anything, Mr. Jacobson, except perhaps failure. I would rather die trying than to not try at all.

OSCAR JACOBSON: I respect your determination, James. You, no doubt, have a heredity strain that will make it possible for you to reach the top in the art world. We are honored to have you with us. I am only sorry that we couldn't keep Lois as well. I very much like the sound of our proud group to be known as The Kiowa Six.

SOPHIE BROUSSE: We all understand and appreciate Lois's feminine desire for family and devotion to motherhood.

OSCAR JACOBSON: How is Lois, James?

JAMES AUCHIAH: I am afraid that she doesn't have quite the insights into love as she has for art. She has fallen for a drunkard who is abusive to her.

STEPHEN MOPOPE: He obviously comes from a lower class of Kiowa society. No respectable Kiowa man would ever be abusive to a woman.

JAMES AUCHIAH: He won't allow her to go to church to receive Holy Communion. He even ripped her scapular off of her neck and threw it into the fire.

(All make the sign of the Trinity except
Monroe Tsatoke and Oscar Jacobson…)

MONROE TSATOKE: Is there anything that we
can do for her?

JAMES AUCHIAH: Pray for her. I believe she
will get through this. She has a strong will.

SOPHIE BROUSSE: I am surprised that her
mother would stand for this.

JAMES AUCHIAH: Her mother is getting older
and frail. I think Lois is carrying a heavy cross
these days.

SOPHIE BROUSSE: Mon Dieu. I wish she
would consider coming back.

JAMES AUCHIAH: I believe that it was okay for
Lois to paint here at the university, but I am sure
it was difficult for her to paint outside the
traditional painting, such as my grandmother
did. I believe in Lois's case that tradition is
stronger than ambition.

OSCAR JACOBSON: My natural inclination is to
intervene. Although I earned a fine arts degree,
my first job was as a policeman. In fact, I
patrolled the St. Louis World's Fair and rose to
the rank of sergeant before the king of Sweden
appointed me attaché of the Swedish
commission. Working security for theatres
helped pay my way through Yale. I have
handled more than my fair share of
confrontations. Perhaps I should at least go talk
to the poor couple.

STEPHEN MOPOPE: I too have worked as a
police officer, Mr. Jacobson, following in the

tradition of my relatives that served in the Army Scouts. I even signed up to go to war in 1917, but I got sick and was not able to go.

Nevertheless, as a police officer I patrolled many gatherings and powwows. With all due respect, I believe the Kiowa men will intervene on Lois's behalf if and when it is necessary.

OSCAR JACOBSON: I trust your instincts, Stephen. I didn't realize that you and I had police work in common.

JACK HOKEAH: Stephen is the only dancer that wears a badge.

SPENCER ASAH: That explains why he always wins. The judges are afraid to vote against him.

JAMES AUCHIAH: When he was defeated in a dance competition by a Comanche, this stirred him so deeply that he danced for three days running, capturing all the prizes.

SOPHIE BROUSSE: It is a privilege to see Stephen perform his Eagle dance. It is the dance that he and the other artists love best to portray. Do you paint dancers as well, James?

 JAMES AUCHIAH: I am not a dancer, Mrs. Jacobson. I am a singer. But I enjoy painting dancers as I see them from my seat at the drum. It is a powerful vision to see the dancers moving around me and the other singers. The harder they dance, the harder we sing.

JACK HOKEAH: And the harder they sing, the harder we dance.

MONROE TSATOKE: There are very few dancers that make me sing as hard as our Kiowa brothers here.

324

SPENCER ASAH: Especially when Jack does the windshield wiper.

OSCAR JACOBSON: Your mural has much story left to tell, fellows. Let's get back to work.

(The artists return to work...)

James, the best way to learn to paint a mural is simply to paint a mural. Grab a pencil and let's start with some sketches first. The mural is quite a different artistic process. There are specific mathematic calculations involved in establishing the scale of the work.

STEPHEN MOPOPE: It seems to me that mural painting involves simply making the image larger.

OSCAR JACOBSON: Yes, but...

SOPHIE BROUSSE: He seems to be doing fine without sketches, Oscar. Perhaps you should heed your own advice and allow them to work in their own way.

OSCAR JACOBSON: Touché, ma chéri.

SOPHIE BROUSSE: In spite of their virile quality, there is something in Stephen's work to me that is Rococo.

OSCAR JACOBSON: En garde!

SOPHIE BROUSSE: Allez!

OSCAR JACOBSON: On the contrary, my dear, I think the mural exercise only further proves that these boys' art can neither be dictated nor defined in Western terms and standards.

SOPHIE BROUSSE: Yes, but one can definitively identify his love of swirling lines, of delicate poise, and subtle balances. Perhaps this is due to the Spanish blood which flows in his veins.

STEPHEN MOPOPE: You realize that I am standing right here, don't you? I can hear everything you are saying.

OSCAR JACOBSON: Arrêt, dear. My apologies, Stephen. We tend to get carried away with art criticism. It's our exercise, so to speak.

SOPHIE BROUSSE: We enjoy the jousting to the point of exhaustion.

STEPHEN MOPOPE: Je comprend, Mrs. Jacobson. Mais il est objectivation quand vous parlez de nous comme si nous n'étions pas présents.

SOPHIE BROUSSE: Oui, monsieur. S'il vous plaît pardonnez-nous, Stephen.

STEPHEN MOPOPE: Of course, Mrs. Jacobson. And, it is true. My great grand-mother was a Spanish girl who was captured by the Kiowas. But my work is no more Spanish than James's work is white.

OSCAR JACOBSON: Yes, I have noticed that James uses a lighter skin tone in his paintings.

JAMES AUCHIAH: The skin pigments in my paintings may only be slightly lighter due to color blending.

STEPHEN MOPOPE: Un poquito gringo.

JAMES AUCHIAH: Yes, there may be a drop of blue blood coursing through my veins, but I assure you that I am Kiowa through and through...Amigo.

SOPHIE BROUSSE: I believe your Spanish blood must account for that courteous grande-like manner of yours.

STEPHEN MOPOPE: That might also be my Kiowa-ness, ma-am.

SOPHIE BROUSSE: A Spanish Kiowa. How exotic.

OSCAR JACOBSON: You are such a romantic, Sophie.

SOPHIE BROUSSE: I am French—romance is inherent, as it is for the Spanish.

OSCAR JACOBSON: It appears you have joined quite a romantic studio, James. I know you will bring great pride and leadership along with your innate artistic talents.

JAMES AUCHIAH: Thank you, Mr. Jacobson.

OSCAR JACOBSON: (OBSERVING JAMES AUCHIAH'S WORK) Do all Kiowa men have six fingers, James?

JAMES AUCHIAH: Yes.

OSCAR JACOBSON: Oh…well then…carry on. Don't be too modern, Spencer.

SPENCER ASAH: I know… "Stay flat."

OSCAR JACOBSON: Is that a weasel, Stephen?

STEPHEN MOPOPE: This is a prairie dog, professor. We call him Sha-ton-tay. He is medicine like the ferret.

OSCAR JACOBSON: Interesting. I wouldn't have associated weasels and ferrets with medicine.

STEPHEN MOPOPE: The Cheyenne ornament their war shield with ferret tails so that the enemy bullets will not hit the warriors. The

Comanches also tie ferret tails on their shoulder beads so that the arrows will not hit them.

SPENCER ASAH: I used to tie ferret tails on my leggings to scare away the snakes. They don't like the smell.

JAMES AUCHIAH: It is said that a warrior foretells his own death when he sees his face in ferret blood.

OSCAR JACOBSON: Please only paint animals that are alive, gentlemen.

SOPHIE BROUSSE: (OBSERVING JAMES AUCHIAH'S WORK) James, you possess a color sense that would bewilder the fashion masters of the world. In truth, you are a color dilettante.

JAMES AUCHIAH: Thank you, Mrs. Jacobson. I will tell you a story about color. There were Kiowa twin boys that came from the sun and were the first color mixers. It is said that they spun the first color wheel of the Kiowas, which was laced with rawhide thongs. Each spoke elaborately painted with colored clay. At the same time, Saynday, a mythical being of the Kiowa, discovered paints on our Earth in a riverbed. One day, an approaching herd of horses was guided into a narrow gorge. Kiowas set up scarecrows to attract the animals, and Saynday painted each wooden image like a man, whereupon the Kiowa got their painting materials.

ALL: Ha.

SPENCER ASAH: I have a color story. At one time, the Gods created a horse and painted its body with bright streaks of lightning, using the colors red and blue. It is said that the horse panicked and broke loose from the earthly tribe and went to heaven and became a tornado. The Kiowas refer to this as the "Painted horse." We used to paint the tornado design, like a tree in a whirlwind. But Hitler and the Nazis turned it into a symbol of hatred.

OSCAR JACOBSON: I have observed that the Nazi swastika is an inverted form of your whirlwind design.

SPENCER ASAH: Yes, but still too close for comfort.

STEPHEN MOPOPE: The whirlwind used to be the insignia of the 45th Infantry until Hitler took it. The 45th doesn't even wear an insignia now.

OSCAR JACOBSON: Correct. They are soliciting designs from artists for a new symbol.

SOPHIE BROUSSE: Well, let's hope to heaven that the men of the 45th don't have to wear their new symbol into a war against fascist socialism.

MONROE TSATOKE: Enough talk of war.

OSCAR JACOBSON: Please do lift us out of this sombre subject.

SOPHIE BROUSSE: I have some good news to share. Stephen, your wife called just before I left the house.

SPENCER ASAH: Uh oh.

SOPHIE BROUSSE: She wanted me to tell you…

STEPHEN MOPOPE: No, I don't want to know. No matter what it is, I don't want to know.

SOPHIE BROUSSE: I think you will be happy when I tell you she took some of the money that you earned from art sales and bought a brand new bed for you two.

STEPHEN MOPOPE: What did she do with the old bed?

SOPHIE BROUSSE: She sold it. She said she got $10 for it!

STEPHEN MOPOPE: I think I am going to be sick.

> (Stephen Mopope puts his face in his hands...)

SPENCER ASAH: How much money did you stash in that bed, brother?

> (Stephen Mopope provides the figures using his fingers...)

SPENCER ASAH: SEVEN THOUSAND DOLLARS?

> (Stephen Mopope nods in the affirmative...)

SPENCER ASAH: Well, look on the bright side—at least you have a nice new bed to be sick in.

JAMES AUCHIAH: A $7,000 bed.

SPENCER ASAH: You better get back to painting, brother. You're going to need the money.

STEPHEN MOPOPE: I'm getting too old for this.

JAMES AUCHIAH: Don't worry, brother, we'll have a raffle to raise some money for you.

SPENCER ASAH: Let's have a cake walk.

OSCAR JACOBSON: Perhaps you can sell some work on our tour, Stephen.

STEPHEN MOPOPE: On tour?

SPENCER ASAH: We're going on tour?

OSCAR JACOBSON: Of course. How else would we show the world your art?

SPENCER ASAH: I don't think I'm ready, Mr. Jacobson?

OSCAR JACOBSON: Of course you are ready! The question is, 'is the world ready for Kiowa art?' First stop is the Convention of the American Federation of the Arts in Denver. Then we go from San Francisco to New York, stopping at every major city in between. We catch an ocean liner to Seville, Spain, then Paris, France, and the International Art Congress in Prague, Czechoslovakia.

SPENCER ASAH: Did you say we were taking a boat, Mr. Jacobson?

OSCAR JACOBSON: Well, how else can we get to Europe, my boy?

SPENCER ASAH: I've never taken a boat, Mr. Jacobson.

SOPHIE BROUSSE: Oh, it is a lot of fun. Think of it as an adventure.

SPENCER ASAH: Easy for you to say—all your people came over on boats.

STEPHEN MOPOPE: Mr. Jacobson, if I go away my mother-in-law will give away everything I own.

JAMES AUCHIAH: Look on the bright side, Stephen—you can visit your relatives in Spain.

OSCAR JACOBSON: You should be less afraid of the boats and more concerned about the art critics.

JAMES AUCHIAH: I am not afraid of boats or critics, Mr. Jacobson. When do we leave?

OSCAR JACOBSON: As soon as the semester is finished.

ALL: A-ho.

> (Oscar Jacobson and Sophie Brousse begin to exit. Monroe Tsatoke stops Oscar Jacobson... Sophie Brousse exits...)

MONROE TSATOKE: Could I trouble you for a moment, professor?

OSCAR JACOBSON: Of course, Monroe. Don't worry too much about the trip. We won't be gone very long.

MONROE TSATOKE: It is not the trip I am concerned about, professor.

OSCAR JACOBSON: What seems to be the trouble?

MONROE TSATOKE: I am not feeling well. I haven't felt well for quite a while now. I have been going to church and praying for my health, but it's not helping.

OSCAR JACOBSON: Have you been to the doctor?

MONROE TSATOKE: No, I am afraid he will give me the white man's medicine. I prefer our medicine.

OSCAR JACOBSON: Why don't you go to the university doctor to at least find out what is making you ill. Then you can determine what medicine is best to treat it. If it is a white man's disease then perhaps it is the white man's medicine that is best to treat it.

MONROE TSATOKE: I will go to the university doctor—but only to find out the cause of my illness, not for the treatment of it.

OSCAR JACOBSON: That's a good start, son.

## ACT II

### SCENE THREE

### DOWNSTAGE

(Spencer Asah paints at an easel. Savoie Lottinville sits and takes notes. Spencer's paintings emerge on the screen. Jack Hokeah and Stephen Mopope dance as Monroe Tsatoke and James Auchiah sing under the dialogue...)

SPENCER ASAH: My name is Spencer Asah. I was born around 1905 near Carnegie. My Indian name, Lallo, is translates as "Little Boy." I like to laugh and I like to make people laugh. So I guess that keeps me young at heart.

SAVOIE LOTTINVILLE: Can you talk about your schooling and early training in art?

SPENCER ASAH: Like my sister, Lois, and my brothers, I went to school at St. Patrick's Mission in Anadarko.

SAVOIE LOTTINVILLE: Can you tell me about your family?

SPENCER ASAH: My mother died in childbirth and my father was a Buffalo Medicine Man. The Buffalo Medicine was the Kiowas strongest medicine used for healing warriors wounded in battle. My father took care of the medicine bundle throughout his lifetime. Upon his death, he entrusted it to me saying that someday, in some way, this medicine would give me strength and power. Perhaps this power is painting.

SAVOIE LOTTINVILLE: Can you tell me more about the medicine?

SPENCER ASAH: No, we don't discuss it. I can tell you that a few years ago I served as translator for Chief Yellow Wolf. He revealed the origin of the Buffalo Medicine for Susie Peters when she was our field matron in the Office of Indian Affairs. Ms. Peters was very special to us and that is why we shared this with her. My grandmother takes care of my father's medicine bundle now. Maybe I will take care of it once I finish with school here at the university. I prefer we talk about my art, Mr. Lottinville.

SAVOIE LOTTINVILLE: My pleasure, Mr. Asah. What do you most prefer to paint?

SPENCER ASAH: I am a dancer like my brothers Jack and Stephen. We travel a lot to dances here in Oklahoma and also New Mexico. So I like to paint dancers that I have seen and dances I have performed. Stephen and I wear buffalo headdresses because we are both from the buffalo clan. So you see this headdress in my work, as well as the hoop dance and other dances from around the country. I like to paint very much, but someday I would like to start a dance troupe and travel around dancing and learning new styles of dance. I think that would make me most happy. A-ho.

## ACT II

### SCENE FOUR

### PRAGUE

(Lights up downstage on Sophie Brousse...)

SOPHIE BROUSSE: (TO AUDIENCE) At the International Art congress held in Prague, Czechoslovakia, in the summer of 1928, a group of thirty-five water colors by our young Kiowa artists proved to be the sensation of the exhibit. Heated discussions were caused by them among spectators and critics from throughout the world, for many found it difficult to believe that these water colors could be the work of Indians.

Yet they were precisely that; the work of our talented Kiowa boys from Oklahoma. It was not so long ago that the Kiowa Indians were accounted the fiercest among the plains tribes; even Kit Carson feared them. Several of their old people remember that in their childhood they roamed about hunting buffalo and making bold raids. However, for several decades, the Kiowas have been peacefully settled on their reservation near the Wichita Mountains, where they are trying, with remarkable success, to transform themselves in one generation from nomads and hunters into farmers and husbandmen. It is a fortunate thing that, although the mode of living may change, the spirit of the race is not entirely annihilated. The Kiowas have kept the love of their old rituals; the tribal dances are still held, the songs of old are still sung, the stories of days gone by bring still the same wonder. And although the younger ones now bob their hair, rouge their lips and adopt the latest fads of white fashion, there is still in them the latent love and appreciation of the Indian arts and crafts, patiently developed during the days when Indian life was attuned to the rhythms of the seasons instead of the pursuit of hurried, material progress. For the Indian is still attuned to the soul of nature; for him art is not something to be cultivated but a natural blossoming out, a spontaneous expression of his joy in living, his reverence for the mysteries and wonders of the world, his deep religious instinct and his love for and need of beauty.

(Lights up upstage. A dressing room.
The artists are putting on dance regalia.
Oscar Jacobson is tying his tie and also
getting dressed for the festivities...)

SPENCER ASAH: I've got to admit, Mr.
Jacobson, I didn't think I would enjoy being on
tour. But now I realize that it is just like being on
the powwow trail.

STEPHEN MOPOPE: Except that we don't have
to compete for money. We get paid no matter
what.

ALL: A-ho!

OSCAR JACOBSON: I cannot tell you how
pleased I am with the reception to your work,
gentlemen. I don't think I have to tell you that
American Indian art has never been seen in the
cities in which we have exhibited.

JACK HOKEAH: I don't think Indians have ever
been seen in the cities we've been in.

JAMES AUCHIAH: That was quite the
awkward incident in the cafeteria in Springfield,
MO.

STEPHEN MOPOPE: Ha, brother. I guess it
wasn't enough that we had to enter through the
back door in the kitchen.

SPENCER ASAH: Actually, I didn't mind
entering through the kitchen. It gave me chance
to see what I wanted to eat.

JACK HOKEAH: ...and also what we DID NOT
want to eat.

SPENCER ASAH: Yeah, what is meatloaf anyway? Is it meat or bread?

OSCAR JACOBSON: It's both actually.

STEPHEN MOPOPE: That one white man kept staring at us like we were zoo animals.

JACK HOKEAH: He sure gave the floor a punishment with his face.

SPENCER ASAH: How did that tray end up under his feet anyway?

STEPHEN MOPOPE: He fell like a giant oak tree, didn't he?

OSCAR JACOBSON: I must say how impressed I was that not a one of you even cracked a smile. I could hardly keep from doubling over with laughter.

JAMES AUCHIAH: I don't know which was funnier, that incident or the time Monroe almost got Lallo arrested.

STEPHEN MOPOPE: You were clowning a little more than usual that day in the restaurant, Spencer. I think you were asking for it.

OSCAR JACOBSON: I wondered why you all were hurrying with your meals. But then, as I was paying the bill, I noticed Monroe talking to the cashier and pointing at Spencer.

MONROE TSATOKE: I told her "that man over there needs watching; he steals things."

STEPHEN MOPOPE: I will never forget the look on your face, Lallo, when the cashier stopped you on your way out.

SPENCER ASAH: I still want to know which one of you planted the silverware in my pocket.

The manager threatened to call the police, you know.

MONROE TSATOKE: I think I liked visiting the zoo in St. Louis best of all (SHOWS OSCAR JACOBSON A STYLIZED CHARM OF SILVER HE IS WEARING UNDER HIS BREAST PLATE) This is a cormorant, Mr. Jacobson—our totem. We were honored to see the real one at the zoo. I asked him to stand by us. He is a good totem. I'm glad I know him; we had never seen a live one before.

OSCAR JACOBSON: I am glad to have had the opportunity to meet him as well, Monroe. The cormorant has a powerful presence in so much of your work that I felt as if I knew him already.

MONROE TSTAOKE: I pray you come to know him well, professor.

OSCAR JACOBSON: A-ho, Hunting Horse. Well, are you gentlemen ready?

ALL: Ha.

(Full lights up...)

OSCAR JACOBSON: (TO AUDIENCE) Ladies and gentlemen of the International Art Congress, we are so pleased to be among you, our most esteemed colleagues of the world of art. It has only been three years now since I was introduced to these talented young Kiowa artists by our friend and field matron Suzie Peters. Through their studies at the University of Oklahoma, and with tireless devotion from my assistant, Ms. Edith Mahier, as well as my keenly insightful wife, Sophie Brousse, I am proud to confidently say that American Indian art now stands on firm ground among the fine arts of the world. After several exhibitions throughout the United States, I would like to thank Dr. Royal Farnam, president of the State Norman Art School in Boston, for arranging for the entire collection of the paintings of these artists to be shipped here to Prague. I am profoundly pleased to share with you that a French editor by the name of Szwedzicki plans to publish a limited edition folio of Kiowa Indian art to be released next year in 1929. Thirty-one colored plates illustrate the work of these artists, as well as work by Miss Lois Smokey, our youngest and only female member of the group. The plates will be made by a porchoir process recently perfected in France. These works are without any doubt the most perfect colored reproductions ever made. (…a quick and shameless sales pitch) The volume will sell for thirty-two dollars and I would be happy to take your advance orders after the performance. Ladies and gentlemen, I give you The Kiowa Five.

(The artists, now fully dressed in their regalia, dance…)

# ACT II

## SCENE FIVE

## DOWNSTAGE

(James Auchiah paints at an easel. Savoie
Lottinville sits and takes notes. Spencer
Asah, Stephen Mopope and Jack Hokeah
dance as Monroe Tsatoke sings under the
dialogue.)

JAMES AUCHIAH: My name is James Auchiah.
I was born near Medicine Park, OK, in 1906. I
spent my childhood near Saddle Mountain. I
attended Fort Sill Indian School, St. Patrick's
Mission, and also one year at Cameron State
College before I came here to the University of
Oklahoma. My grandfather was a man named
Satanta. He was the son of Red Tepee, who
stood highest in the Kiowa Medicine Clan.
SAVOIE LOTTINVILLE: Did you learn to paint
from these men in your family?
JAMES AUCHIAH: I believe in my heart that
my painting abilities descend from Red Tepee,
who had the ability to mix natural earth paints
in various shades. He was known to have a
tepee which he kept painted red, as well as
decorated with pictures, and for that reason he
came to be known as "Red Tepee."
SAVOIE LOTTINVILLE: Who was Satanta?
JAMES AUCHIAH: Satanta, my grandfather,
was considered one of the most daring warriors

341

of the Kiowa Tribe and his eloquence in speaking earned him the title "Orator of the Plains." If I can only speak half as well as my grandfather I would be honored. As a member of the Kiowa Tia-Piah Society, Satanta was instrumental in bringing about the signing of the Medicine Lodge treaty of 1867, which was signed by ten Kiowa Chiefs and leaders of the Comanches, Kiowa Apaches, Southern Cheyenne, and Southern Arapaho. The Tia-Piah Society was the body of warriors that governed the tribe. The society is said to have met Lewis and Clark as they passed through Kiowa country.

SAVOIE LOTTINVILLE: What does Tia-Piah mean?

JAMES AUCHIAH: The name Tia-Piah means "Red berry." Long ago, Kiowa warriors fought a fierce defensive battle among bushes of red berries. When they finally drove off their enemies, they honored the plant which had given them concealment by naming their warrior society after it. General Custer once commented that Satanta "could no more resist lifting a scalp or stealing a horse than a child can resist candy." When I was a boy, my father told me how my grandfather acquired an Army bugle somehow and learned the calls of "charge" and "retreat" that the U.S. military used. Satanta blew these signals in battle with the white man, thus throwing the enemy into confusion. It must have been quite a sight. My grandfather is best known for a raid on a wagon

342

train of corn, near Jacksboro, Texas, and the subsequent trial, which included a younger chief named Big Tree. The two Kiowas gained a parole in 1873, but during the Red River War of 1874, soldiers arrested him once again and sent him back to prison alone. He endured the torment of incarceration for four years. But upon learning, in 1878, that he would not be freed, he slashed his wrists and threw himself out of a second story window. Convicts buried him in the prison cemetery beside the walls. After Satanta died, our family was too poor to go to Huntsville to bring him home, so he was left there. It is my personal quest to see that my grandfather is brought home and given a proper burial here among our people. A-ho.

## ACT II

### SCENE SIX

### DANCE GROUNDS

(The full cast is present at a celebration. The artists are in dance regalia...)

MONROE TSATOKE: My Kiowa people, invited guests, and honorees, I thank you for this humble opportunity to speak to you all today. My brothers and sisters and I have travelled great distances with our art. We have sung our songs, and we have danced in cities from coast to coast across the United States. We took a boat across the ocean to Europe and visited many countries where we met many beautiful and kind-hearted people. We travelled as honored artists. We were treated with respect. You can all be proud of my brothers and my sisters here—proud of the way we represented our people—not just Kiowa—ALL Indian people. We come here today to celebrate our return from our travels, and to say thank you to those who made it possible for us to share our art with the world. First, we want to acknowledge Ms. Susie Peters.

(Lois Smokey and Martha Tsatoke place a shawl on Susie Peters...)

MONROE TSATOKE: Ms. Peters, along with Father Al and Sister Olivia, introduced us to art. Without Ms. Peters, we might have never met Professor Jacobson. Ms. Peters believed in us and made us believe in ourselves, and our abilities as artists. She will always stand among us as an honorable woman.
ALL: Ha.
MONROE TSATOKE: Professor Jacobson and Mrs. Jacobson, you have shown us a world that we could have only imagined—a world where we can stand among people of all races, from all parts of our Mother Earth, and stand together on equal ground. Before going across the ocean, we were only Kiowa. But only after a moment of stepping off of that boat onto that European soil,

the home of your ancestors, I realized how it must be for you to live so far from your homelands. Many of us Indian people living in Oklahoma have also travelled great distances, both forced and by treaty, to come to call Oklahoma, "Land of Red People," home. We Kiowas once lived in what is now Canada and in the Black Hills of the northern Plains. We also came a long way to call Oklahoma home. So we are all not so different in this way. We have all made long journeys in our lives to get to where we are today. Over the past years, we have made long journeys together, making tracks side-by-side, walking together on equal ground. While walking these roads in many countries, where people spoke many different languages, I felt more Kiowa than ever before. And in the same moment, I no longer felt like just a Kiowa—I also came to know what means to be an American. Standing in those distance lands, I felt American, maybe for the first time. I was proud to Kiowa, proud to be American, proud to be American Indian. I knew that after that moment I would never be the same.

ALL: Ha.

MONROE TSATOKE: In appreciation of your efforts on our behalf, professor Jacobson, we would like to adopt you into our great Kiowa nation as an honorary Kiowa chief.

> (Lois Smokey and Martha Tsakoke place a shawl on Sophie Brousse and begin to dress Oscar Jacobson in Kiowa regalia...)

MONROE TSATOKE: We adopt you as a war chief, Mr. Jacobson, which is the highest honor among us. You are only the second white man ever to be honored in this way. Your Kiowa name from this point forward is Nah-go-ey, in memory of one of our great warriors of the past. I give you this pipe and this tobacco pouch, which has been adorned with this beautiful porcupine quill by our sister Lois Smokey.

(Oscar Jacobson accepts gifts...)

MONROE TSATOKE: Professor Jacobson, Nah-go-ey, just as you have honored us, we honor you.

> (Monroe Tsatoke and James Auchiah begin to sing and the others dance, including the Jacobsons and Susie Peters...)

## ACT II

### SCENE SEVEN

### JACOBSON HOUSE

(Sophie Brousse works at the desk. Oscar Jacobson enters...)

OSCAR JACOBSON: How is the world of Berber art, my dear?

SOPHIE BROUSSE: Fascinating. At least our trip to Africa won't be remembered only for your calamitous illness. This book will be our memoir of the trip as well as a tribute to Berber art.

OSCAR JACOBSON: Thank goodness for that, too. Considering your book and my collection of African music, I would say the trip was quite successful, despite my illness.

SOPHIE BROUSSE: Do you think the University of Oklahoma Press would oblige that I publish the book under my mother's name, Jeanne d'Ucel? I think I would like the way the name would appear in a typeface. It was designed in 1499 by Francesco Griffo of Bologna.

OSCAR JACOBSON: How could they refuse such a poetic pseudonym? And I gladly carry your surname of Brousse as my middle name, ma chéri.

    (Oscar sits down to read the newspaper...)

SOPHIE BROUSSE: Merci, mon chéri. The wife should not be burdened by carrying her husband's name if the husband does not return the favor in some way or another. I wonder if I am meant to take your Kiowa name as well? Perhaps I should publish under "Jeanne d'Ucel Nah-go-ey."

OSCAR JACOBSON: Quite honestly, my dear, when Monroe presented me with my Kiowa name I thought he said "Now-go-away."

SOPHIE BROUSSE: That would have been an un-adoption ceremony, I am afraid.

OSCAR JACOBSON: Thank goodness the opposite was true. I believe we were outnumbered two-thousand to two.

SOPHIE BROUSSE: That would have given the Death Dance they performed afterward quite a morbid meaning.

OSCAR JACOBSON: (READING FROM THE NEWSPAPER) An oil well has caught fire in Oklahoma City. The gas pressure is so enormous that the flame begins 200 feet above the ground. My goodness…living on top of this black gold is like living on a volcano ready to erupt at any second.

SOPHIE BROUSSE: The well has been burning for days now, Oscar. Haven't you been paying attention to the news?

OSCAR JACOBSON: No. I haven't read the paper in…I don't even remember when.

SOPHIE BROUSSE: Well, you can hear the roar and see the light from here—and we are 16 miles away.

OSCAR JACOBSON: Amazing. Honestly, Sophie, I barely have time to keep up with my teaching schedule. I haven't painted in months. Now I have this WPA project to administer, which I have no time for. But I feel it is my duty—not only to the country, but mostly to the artists. What a great opportunity for our Kiowa artists to receive a federal commission.

SOPHIE BROUSSE: No time can be wasted when you are doing important work.

OSCAR JACOBSON: Sometimes I can't help but long for the old days, Sophie—simpler days. As much as I longed to leave Kansas as a kid, sometimes I miss the old farm in Lindsborg. I miss working as a cowboy, as lonely as it was. I wonder whatever happened to Mustang Jake— that adventurous young Swede that left home when he was teenager and travelled all over the southwest.

SOPHIE BROUSSE: Mustang Jake is right here, Oscar. He had a destiny to fulfill as an artist and a teacher. He has simply grown up to become Professor Oscar Brousse Jacobson.

OSCAR JACOBSON: I never intended to teach, you know. I never even thought Birger Sandzen would allow me to graduate from Bethany College. And how did I repay him—by becoming a policeman. If the Swedish commissioner hadn't hired me as an attaché I think I might still be in law enforcement. There was even a time when I wanted to be a Shakespearean actor. Alas, it was "not to be."

SOPHIE BROUSSE: Don't be silly, Oscar. Just think of how far you have come just since 1915: you built this house; you established the university art department a national reputation in the arts; you nearly single- handedly revolutionized the teaching of art with the "modern" approach of the French painters—

with a little help from an intelligent French wife, of course. And I think John Frank's pottery shows tremendous potential as an artform. No one but you sees pottery as art. You are the only person with the courage and integrity to stand alone in your field and elevate craft to art.

OSCAR JACOBSON: Yes, as Lois says, I am quite a scarecrow.

SOPHIE BROUSSE: You are just tired, dear. Perhaps you should take a vacation. You could paint along the way.

OSCAR JACOBSON: I have been meaning to shuffle off to Buffalo—Buffalo, Oklahoma, that is. Maybe it is all of the touring, or maybe I am just getting older, but I feel as though I have lived a hundred years in one decade. And yet it is the struggle and the romance of it all that gives our lives a richness beyond measure. Oklahoma is a raw, Western land with an intoxicating atmosphere. The lacks and discomforts are compensated by the color, the feeling of stupendous progress, the valiant optimism and the friendliness we have found among Whites and Indians. I tell you, Sophie, I liken this period to the age of chivalry in Europe. Like the knights of old, the cowboys and the Indians are rough, but they have admirable qualities and a high code of honor. They might be unlettered in the accepted meaning of the term, but they have culture of a kind. It seems that the world has finally come to value their epic and romantic tales and songs.

SOPHIE BROUSSE: It is settled then. You need take a break from your crusade, dear. You can't keep running the art school as if you were still the only one there. You have several full-time teachers and assistants now that could manage the load.

OSCAR JACOBSON: This is not a bad idea, Sophie. Shall we go back to Algiers?

SOPHIE BROUSSE: There is no need. My book is finished. Now the world can appreciate Berber art and Kiowa art.

OSCAR JACOBSON: I worry about leaving the artists here alone. There are is no telling what mischief they could get into.

SOPHIE BROUSSE: Oscar, those boys will find mischief with or without you. They will be fine as long as they have Spencer to tease.

OSCAR JACOBSON: He is quite the clown, isn't he? He kept us in stitches on tour. He is funny even when he doesn't mean to be.

SOPHIE BROUSSE: He is a regular roly-poly. It's endearing the way he chuckles through life. This is a merry world for him and he enjoys the good things of life, especially eating. I hope he doesn't gain too much weight to dance.

OSCAR JACOBSON: Oh, when spring comes his nomadic instinct will awaken in him and he will hit the "powwow trail," as they say. He always comes back much thinner.

(Knock at the door...Sophie Brousse answers it. Susie Peters enters...)

SOPHIE BROUSSE: Bonsoir, Susie.

SUSIE PETERS: I need to speak to Mr. Jacobson immediately.

SOPHIE BROUSSE: Certainly. Come in and sit down.

SUSIE PETERS: No, thank you. I prefer to stand.

OSCAR JACOBSON: Is everything alright, Ms. Peters?

SUSIE PETERS: No, everything is not alright, Mr. Jacobson. I have stood idly by watching you falsely take credit for "discovering" the Kiowa artists, for which you received the highest honor in the Kiowa tribe. In my 20 years of service in the Indian community I have never witnessed such an audacious display of vanity. Amidst all of the fanfare, all the newspaper articles about you and your famed "Kiowa Five," those impressionable young boys that you paraded all over the world, never once did you ever acknowledge me and my role in their lives and their careers.

OSCAR JACOBSON: On the contrary, I acknowledged you regularly at our shows.

SUSIE PETERS: I don't desire a gratuitous "thank you," professor. I bought them their first art supplies—with my own money—which could have cost me my job. You recall that I was hired to Anglicize them and teach them how to become White. I was supposed to surpress Indianness and instead I encouraged it. I was well aware of my defiance of government policy when I took them to Chickasha to study art with

Willie Baze Lane. I brought their work to you. And I did it for them—because I cared about them as human beings, not just Indian artists, or "art projects" or "art products," like your silly portfolio. You have very handsomely profited from these Kiowa artists, and I will no longer stand by and let you earn all of the honor and, on top of that, a double salary. I have in my hand a letter to Mr. Bizzell, the President of the university, describing in detail how you have exploited these young artists for both fame and fortune.

OSCAR JACOBSON: I haven't received a cent of commission on the sale of their art, Ms. Peters. I am quite content with my university salary.

SUSIE PETERS: Then where does all of the money go from art sales?

OSCAR JACOBSON: To the artists, of course.

SUSIE PETERS: I don't believe it for a minute, Mr. Jacobson. I also heard that you didn't instruct the students in their art at all. I heard that it was Edith Mahier who instructed the students in class while you were gallivanting around the country giving lectures about how you discovered Indian art.

> (Knock at the door. Sophie Brousse answers it. Jack Hokeah and Monroe Tsotoke enter.)

SOPHIE BROUSSE: Please come in.

OSCAR JACOBSON: Let's ask the students, Ms. Peters. They will tell you the truth.

MONROE TSATOKE: Why are your voices raised? Even Jack heard you from the street.

SOPHIE BROUSSE: Ms. Peters has become the most avid spreader of ugly rumors.

SUSIE PETERS: I am merely sharing what I have been told from the most reliable sources in our community.

MONROE TSATOKE: What rumors?

OSCAR JACOBSON: Ms. Peters has come to believe that I am profiting from the sale of your art.

JACK HOKEAH: This is why I don't like selling my art. Money and art are like oil and water.

OSCAR JACOBSON: Art is not corrupted by money; art, like money, is corrupted by the power of greed.

SOPHIE BROUSSE: On the subject of power, Martha Tsatoke mentioned something to me one day that I thought absurd up until this very moment. She said that you played on superstition, Ms. Peters, by convincing these boys that they owed their "painting power" to you. She said that you told them that if they failed to pay you a commission on their art sales that they would lose their power. At first I thought Martha was slightly ticked in the head, but now I see that it is you who is touched in the head.

OSCAR JACOBSON: Is this true, Monroe?

MONROE TSATOKE: You mean 'is Martha ticked in the head?'

OSCAR JACOBSON: This is no time be funny, Monroe. Does Ms. Peters take a commission on your art sales?

(Monroe Tsatoke remains silent...)

OSCAR JACOBSON: Jack? What is your financial arrangement with Ms. Peters?

(Jack Hokeah remains silent...)

SOPHIE BROUSSE: These boys don't deserve to be put on the spot like this. The question should be posed to Ms. Peters.
SUSIE PETERS: I will not be cornered. After I deliver this letter to President Bizzell I hope that I never again have to tolerate your company.
SOPHIE BROUSSE: See yourself out, Ms. Peters.

(Susie Peters exits...)

OSCAR JACOBSON: Well, gentlemen. I assume you didn't come over to field accusations of exploitation.
MONROE TSATOKE: No, Mr. and Mrs. Jacobson. It is a shame that there must be this mountain between you and Ms. Peters. I can say that the three of you are some of the most important people, Kiowa and non-Kiowa, in our lives.
OSCAR JACOBSON: I'm sorry, too, Monroe. I genuinely enjoyed my first meeting with Ms. Peters.

355

SOPHIE BROUSSE: No love lost on my part for that magpie.

OSCAR JACOBSON: Spoken like a proud French woman.

SOPHIE BROUSSE: Merci, mon chéri.

JACK HOKEAH: You know that I don't care much for conversation, Mr. and Mrs. Jacobson. That is why I have brought my brother Monroe with me to discuss another matter with you.

OSCAR JACOBSON: I understand, Jack. Have a seat.

SOPHIE BROUSSE: I'll make us a nice cup of tea...although I could use a stiff Scotch after that foul duel.

(Sophie exits...The men sit.)

JACK HOKEAH: On a trip to the Inter-tribal Ceremonial Dances in Gallup, New Mexico, I met an elderly woman there, a potter, named Maria Martinez. She invited me to her home at San Ildefonso Pueblo and I visited her and her family there. They were very good to me, professor. They showed me a different way of life; a different way of art; not different in the ways we saw in Europe, but a different Indian way. I wasn't granted the privilege of growing up with my parents, as you know. Ms. Martinez treated me as her son, professor. Only my grandmother has ever treated me in such a way. I really enjoyed my time there and I would very much like to return.

OSCAR JACOBSON: You want to move to New Mexico, Jack?

JACK HOKEAH: I was here in your home the day you spoke to the writer on the telephone.

OSCAR JACOBSON: Lynn Riggs?

JACK HOKEAH: Yes. I met him in Santa Fe during my visit. He said to thank you for your advice. He said that he felt very much at home in Santa Fe and was glad he didn't go to New York instead. I too have the same urge inside of me, professor. I too want to travel and to learn from other people and places. I have been offered a teaching position at the Indian school in Santa Fe. I would like to accept the position, with all due respect to you and Mrs. Jacobson, and my brothers here. I mean no disrespect in my leaving, it is just something that I feel I need to do.

OSCAR JACOBSON: Well, Jack, we have begun the federal commissions with the WPA, as you know. This is a tremendous opportunity for you in public art murals.

JACK HOKEAH: I understand, Mr. Jacobson. But I defer to my brothers here any commission that I might have received. In my brother, Monroe here's case, I defer any commission that does not exceed arm's reach in height, since he is afraid of the scaffolding falling underneath him.

MONROE TSATOKE: Just looking out for my family.

OSCAR JACOBSON: Very well then. How are you set for money, Jack?

JACK HOKEAH: I have about $5,000 saved. I carry it with me in my pipe bag.

OSCAR JACOBSON: Oh my, Jack. That is not a good idea. It is best to save it somewhere safer, or better yet, put it in the bank.

JACK HOKEAH: I don't trust that my money is safe out of my sight.

OSCAR JACOBSON: Well, both of you, Jack and Monroe, take a lesson from Stephen and please don't hide your money in your bed.

MONROE TSATOKE: Martha takes care of my money. I trust her more than I trust myself. I tend to lose things more these days. But I think Jack can manage okay on his own, professor.

JACK HOKEAH: My brothers support me in my decision, professor. Now I have come to ask for your support.

OSCAR JACOBSON: I regret that you will not be working on the murals with us.

JACK HOKEAH: Perhaps I will have an opportunity to paint a mural in Santa Fe.

(Sophie Brousse returns with tea...)

SOPHIE BROUSSE: You're leaving us, Jack?

OSCAR JACOBSON: Yes, darling. Our young painter has found Santa Fe to be quite inspiring, as has our young writer, Lynn Riggs.

SOPHIE BROUSSE: Ç'est magnifique! I think you will find Santa Fe quite an adventure, Jack. It is much better suited for Westerners than, say, New York.

OSCAR JACOBSON: Yes, Santa Fe is not nearly as dense and dangerous as New York, but it is very different from Oklahoma, and especially Kiowa country. But there is a plethora of Indian art to be found there. Santa Fe may be said to be an "Indian New York."

SOPHIE BROUSSE: What a novel concept—an "Indian New York"—although the Santa Fe of today is a far cry from the Santa Fe of even ten years ago. I am so glad we knew the charming city as it was in 1915. Her flavor has been altered, her loveliness has been rubbed off like the fuzz on a peach; her sleepy languor has given way to hurry, noise and gaudy show. Now the Anglos keep to themselves on their side of the river, while the artists and the Spanish-Americans share the delightful concerts and dances on the dusty plaza. Oh, I miss the aroma of burnt piñon and horse manure. Burro Alley was indeed a Burro alley back then, perpetually echoing with the grunts, protests and alarums of the four-footed philosophers. Back then, La Fonda was an old, down-at-heels and rather grim hotel. We spent happy days there and in the surrounding country, drinking in the spirit of the place, re-living its history, loving it all. But that is all changed now. I don't understand why Santa Fe aspires to be cosmopolitan when it is the quaintness of it that is its most enchanting allure.

OSCAR JACOBSON: I couldn't agree more, my dear.

SOPHIE BROUSSE: I can't help but worry about you being there alone, Jack.

JACK HOKEAH: I will not be alone. I will be surrounded by other artists and writers, such as Lynn Riggs. And my God will protect me.

OSCAR JACOBSON: Then God be with you, Jack.

(All bid farewell to Jack Hokeah and head for the door. Monroe Tsakoke stays behind…)

MONROE TSATOKE: Go show them how we dance the windshield wiper, brother.

JACK HOKEAH: A-ho, brother.

(Jack Hokeah exits. Monroe Tsakoke lingers...)

MONROE TSATOKE: Could I trouble you for another moment of your time, Mr. and Mrs. Jacobson?

OSCAR JACOBSON: You aren't going to Santa Fe too, are you, Monroe?

MONROE TSATOKE: No, I am happy to be here near my family. Unfortunately, Jack lost his parents and many of his relatives over the years. Maybe that is why his spirit is of the wondering sort. Maybe he is searching for something.

SOPHIE BROUSSE: Perhaps it is love.

MONROE TSATOKE: Oh, Jack is never short on love. He has had more girlfriends since he has been here at the university than I have had in my entire lifetime. He has always had a charm with women that is magnetic. I suppose it his quietness that makes him somewhat mysterious to women. I am certain that Jack will not suffer from loneliness in Santa Fe. I, on the other hand, am sick with despair.

OSCAR JACOBSON: What's troubling you, son?

MONROE TSATOKE: Martha and Peggy are home on a visit with relatives. I had been looking forward to this time alone in order to have some quiet and to get some work done. My daughter, Peggy, is an angelic tyrant.

SOPHIE BROUSSE: How old is she now, Monroe?

MONROE TSATOKE: She is three.

OSCAR JACOBSON: Yes, that is a tyrannical age.

MONROE TSATOKE: My heart can find no rebuke to scold her even when she is counting coup on my paintings.

SOPHIE BROUSSE: That is adorable. Speaking of adorable, here comes our angelic tyrant.

(Yolande, enters and sits with them…)

MONROE TSATOKE: I save all of the paintings upon which she has "counted coup." They are our "collaborations," as you say, which makes them even more meaningful to me.

OSCAR JACOBSON: Cherish them. I keep all of my daughter's artwork as well. Sometimes I think she may already be a better artist than I am.

MONROE TSATOKE: If I am a good father then I am certain my children will be better than I am in every way. But now that she and Martha are gone, I am so lonesome that I can't work.

SOPHIE BROUSSE: Would you like to stay for dinner, Monroe?

MONROE TSATOKE: Thank you, but I don't have an appetite. I have not been able to eat since they left. I think I would rather be alone.

SOPHIE BROUSSE: That is the opposite of what you need, Monroe. Your girls will be back soon, and when the return, do you want to tell them that you sat alone in sorrow waiting for them to come back? That you couldn't work or even eat without them?

MONROE TSATOKE: That is what I tell them every time they return from a trip.

SOPHIE BROUSSE: You are tragically poetic, Monroe. You remind me a lot of another intensely romantic artist in the room.

OSCAR JACOBSON: My son, I am afraid that you and I are both cursed with hearts the size of these great rolling plains we call home.

SOPHIE BROUSSE: How does Martha cope?

MONROE TSATOKE: She says she feels the same way when she is away from me.

SOPHIE BROUSSE: Your honesty is powerfully poignant, Monroe. Martha and Peggy are lucky to have a man that can express his feelings. It seems to be rare out here on the frontier.

OSCAR JACOBSON: Stay for dinner and then see how you feel afterward.

MONROE TSATOKE: I have no hunger for food, but God has planted a tremendous hungering in my soul for art. I have a burning inside to paint. God surely would never plant a hunger he would not satisfy.

SOPHIE BROUSSE: You sound disproportionately profound today, if I may say. Would you like to try some castor oil? It's said to be a miracle medicine.

MONROE TSATOKE: No, thank you, Mrs. Jacobson. Would it be okay if I played your drum?

OSCAR JACOBSON: Our drum needs to be played, my boy!

SOPHIE BROUSSE: Perhaps you can serenade Yolande, as you do your lovely Martha and Peggy.

(The Jacobsons exit. Monroe Tsatoke goes to drum. Yolande follows him.)

MONROE TSATOKE: As a young man, I loved to listen to the old men sing. In this way, I learned a number of songs that otherwise would have been forgotten. I really enjoy going to powwows to learn new songs. I learned this song just this past weekend.

(Monroe Tsakoke sings. Yolande sits and listens...)

YOLANDE: (POINTS TO MONROE'S HAND) What is that in your hand?

MONROE TSATOKE: It is the tail of a ferret.

YOLANDE: Where is the rest of the ferret?

MONROE TSATOKE: I buried it in the ground.

YOLANDE: Did you kill it?

MONROE TSATOKE: Yes.

YOLANDE: Why?

MONROE TSATOKE: He has medicine for me.

YOLANDE: Oh. Are you sick?

MONROE TSATOKE: Yes.

YOLANDE: I'm sorry. I hope you feel better soon.

MONROE TSATOKE: My wife says as long I have breath there is hope. Would you like for me to sing a song to you that your mother taught me after I first arrived here in Norman?

> (Yolande agrees. Monroe Tsakoke sings Frère Jacques accompanying the song with the drum. Yolande recognizes the song and joins in singing...)

## ACT II

### SCENE EIGHT

### AN EMPTY STAGE

> (Monroe Tsatoke stands behind Martha Tsatoke who is seated in a chair. Monroe Tsatoke brushes her hair. He is there in

spirit...James Auchiah sings a prayer
song under the dialogue.)

MARTHA TSATOKE: My husband's name was
Monroe Tsatoke. He was born in 1904 near
Saddle Mountain. His name, Tsa-To-Kee,
meant...means "Hunting Horse." His father of
the same name was a scout for Custer and
would have been killed along with Custer at the
Battle of Little Big Horn, but he had been given
orders to go further west. The old man has lived
a long life and thankfully he is still with us.
Sadly, he has outlived his son, my husband,
who was taken from us by tuberculosis at the
age of 32. My husband's grandfather, Pea-Lame,
was captured along with his grandmother by
Osages. The Osages gave his grandmother a dull
knife to cut meat to eat. Pea-Lame's mother
taunted the Osages with the knife and shouted,
"I'll kill my son and myself before I will let you
have us as slaves." She then slashed her son's
back with the knife, but the Osages shot her
before she could kill her son or herself. Pea-
Lame bore the scar the rest of his life. The boy
was later traded to the Pawnee and then to the
Wichita's. His name Pea-Lame means "Little
Turtle." He became a warrior and a leader
among the Wichita and also married a Wichita
girl before returning to Kiowa country. Because
of this, Monroe felt he had a kinship with the
Wichita and the Pawnee that he extended to all
tribes and all people. He liked to learn their
songs and sing them for the dancers, like his

brothers Stephen, Jack, and Spencer. I think he would have been very pleased that his final art piece was a "collaboration" with his Kiowa brothers, who finished the mural that he began at the Oklahoma Historical Society. He was just too sick to complete it. He asked me to leave his paint materials to Susie Peters, the field matron. I hung them on the door at her house. Monroe once said that art, music, and family gave his life meaning. He said...

MONROE TSATOKE: Our longing as Indian people for power to achieve, to create, to do great things, so that our people will be better understood, will have a glorious realization in the future.

(Lights up on the full cast... holding bouquets of Indian Paintbrush flowers.)

OSCAR JACOBSON: There was always something in Monroe that was detached and profoundly spiritual—it was as if obscurely knowing that his days here were numbered, he already walked in the company of gods and shared the music of the spheres. This quality is felt in all his works. In company with his fellow Kiowa artists, he ranks as one of the greatest Indian painters of our time.

End.

(The curtain call is performed as a dance.)

(It could be very nice to have living descendants of the artists share "the rest of the story" at the end of the play, if feasible. Otherwise, the actors portraying the artists could share the following additional biographical info with the audience. This ending is optional, and could be included in the written program and/or projected as text on the screen during the final dance of the curtain call.)

Spencer Asah was commissioned murals at the University of Oklahoma, Riverside Indian School, Ft. Sill, Anadarko Federal Building, and the Oklahoma Historical Society Museum in Oklahoma City. He later started a dance troupe, which toured all over the world until his death in 1954.

Jack Hokeah remained in Santa Fe for many years playing semi-professional baseball and teaching art at the Santa Fe Indian school where he did in fact complete a mural project. Although Jack continued to paint, dancing took center stage in his life. He often travelled to Gallup, NM, for the Inter-Tribal Indian Ceremonials, as well as to dances throughout the country until his death in 1969.

James Auchiah continued to paint throughout his life, although not as a career artist. During World War II, while serving in the Coast Guard, stationed in Florida, James discovered and subsequently deciphered pictographs found on the walls of the ancient Costello at Fort Marion where his grandfather, Satanta, had been imprisoned during the Indian wars of the 1860s and 1870s. In 1963, James received permission to reintern the remains of his grandfather, in the cemetery at Ft. Sill. James later became a teacher, an illustrator, and curator of the Ft. Sill museum before he passed away in 1974.

Stephen Mopope could be said to be the most prolific painter of the group. Some of his more notable commissioned murals, include Ft. Sill, The University of Oklahoma, Oklahoma Historical Society Museum, Northeastern State University in Tahlequah, United States Department of the Interior in Washington, D.C., The Federal Building in Muskogee, First National Bank of Anadarko, as well as, the U.S. Post Office in Anadarko and the U.S. Navy Hospital in Carville, LA. He continued to paint, as well as to dance and make flutes throughout his life, before crossing over into the spirit world in 1974, the same year as James.

Lois Smokey remarried twice after leaving her first husband. She went on to have seven children before passing away in 1981. Lois is too often overlooked when the Kiowa Five artists are mentioned; she had an abundance of talent that was never allowed to blossom. Due to its rarity, Lois's art is now the most sought after of all the Kiowa Five artists.

Savoie Lottinville graduated from the University of Oklahoma with an English degree and went on to work as a journalist for the Oklahoma City Times. After three years abroad as a Rhodes Scholar, Savoie returned to Oklahoma with a master's degree from Oxford University. In 1938, he was named director of the University of Oklahoma Press, where he served for some 30 years. Savoie passed away in 1997.

Susie Peters remained in Anadarko for the rest of her 92 years where she helped organize the Anadarko Philomatic Museum, as well the Mautan fine arts club along with Lois Smokey and Martha Tsatoke, which supported and encouraged the arts of Kiowa women. In 1954, Susie was adopted by the Kiowa tribe as a "blood" sister, becoming the only white woman to be given that honor. The Kiowa aptly named Susie Kom-tah-gha, which meant "Good Friend."

An outgrowth of Oscar Jacobson's work after establishing the School of Art was founding the Museum of Art in 1936. His ability and ingenuity resulted in a remarkable collection of Native American, oriental and contemporary art that forms the basis of today's collection in the Fred Jones, Jr. Museum of Art. Jacobson was head of the Museum until 1952. Jacobson left an indelible imprint on The University of Oklahoma, Norman and the World of art. The University of Oklahoma's Visitors Center is located in the original School of Art building, which is now known as Jacobson Hall.